S0-AAZ-352

THE GLENCOE LITERATURE LIBRARY

Things Fall Apart

with Related Readings

Glencoe
McGraw-Hill

New York, New York   Columbus, Ohio   Woodland Hills, California   Peoria, Illinois

Acknowledgments

Grateful acknowledgment is given authors, publishers, photographers, museums, and agents for permission to reprint the following copyrighted material. Every effort has been made to determine copyright owners. In case of any omissions, the Publisher will be pleased to make suitable acknowledgments in future editions.

Things Fall Apart by Chinua Achebe. Copyright © 1959 by Chinua Achebe. Reprinted by arrangement with Heinemann Education, a Division of Reed Educational & Professional Publishing Ltd.

Reprinted with the permission of Scribner, a Division of Simon & Schuster, Inc., from *The Collected Works of W. B. Yeats, Volume 1: The Poems, Revised,* edited by Richard J. Finneran. Copyright © 1924 by The Macmillan Publishing Company, copyright © renewed 1952 by Bertha Georgie Yeats.

"Chinua Achebe: A Storyteller Far From Home" by Somini Sengupta. Copyright © 2001 by the New York Times Co. Reprinted by permission.

From *Facing Mt. Kenya* by Jomo Kenyatta. Used by permission of Alfred A. Knopf, a division of Random House, Inc.

"He Who Has Lost All" by David Diop, translated by Anne Atik. Reprinted by permission of Presence Africaine.

Excerpt from *West with the Night* by Beryl Markham. Copyright © 1942, 1983 by Beryl Markham. Reprinted by permission of North Point Press, a division of Farrar, Straus & Giroux, Inc.

My Children! My Africa! by Athol Fugard. Copyright © 1990 by Athol Fugard. All rights reserved. Originally produced by The Market Theatre in Johannesburg, June 1989. The American premier of this play was produced by the New York Theatre Workshop at the Perry Street Theatre. *Caution:* Professionals and amateurs are hereby warned that My *Children! My Africa!* is subject to a royalty. All rights, including without limitation professional and amateur stage performing, recitation, lecturing, public reading, video or sound recording, all other forms of mechanical or electronic reproduction, and the rights of translation into foreign languages are strictly reserved. Reprinted by arrangement with Theatre Communications Group

Cover Art: *A Tribute to Jacob Lawrence #3,* Elizabeth B. Heuer. Collection of the Artist, Superstock.

NOTE: *This is the story of a man dominated by anger and fear as he finds himself caught in the struggles of tribal life in Nigeria before and during colonialism. Certain situations, language, and descriptions may be offensive to some readers.*

Glencoe/McGraw-Hill

*A Division of The **McGraw·Hill** Companies*

Copyright © 2002 The McGraw-Hill Companies, Inc. All rights reserved. Except as permitted under the United States Copyright Act of 1976, no part of this publication may be reproduced or distributed in any form or by any means, or stored in a database or retrieval system, without prior written permission of the publisher.

Send all inquiries to:
Glencoe/McGraw-Hill
8787 Orion Place
Columbus, OH 43240

ISBN 0-07-828398-1
Printed in the United States of America
3 4 5 6 7 8 9 026 04 03

Contents

Things Fall Apart

Continued

Contents Continued

Related Readings 131

Things Fall Apart

Chinua Achebe

Turning and turning in the widening gyre
The falcon cannot hear the falconer;
Things fall apart; the center cannot hold;
Mere anarchy is loosed upon the world.

—W. B. Yeats, "The Second Coming"

Part One

Chapter One

OKONKWO WAS WELL KNOWN throughout the nine villages and even beyond. His fame rested on solid personal achievements. As a young man of eighteen he had brought honor to his village by throwing Amalinze the Cat. Amalinze was the great wrestler who for seven years was unbeaten, from Umuofia to Mbaino. He was called the Cat because his back would never touch the earth. It was this man that Okonkwo threw in a fight which the old men agreed was one of the fiercest since the founder of their town engaged a spirit of the wild for seven days and seven nights.

The drums beat and the flutes sang and the spectators held their breath. Amalinze was a wily craftsman, but Okonkwo was as slippery as a fish in water. Every nerve and every muscle stood out on their arms, on their backs and their thighs, and one almost heard them stretching to breaking point. In the end Okonkwo threw the Cat.

That was many years ago, twenty years or more, and during this time Okonkwo's fame had grown like a bush-fire in the harmattan. He was tall and huge, and his bushy eyebrows and wide nose gave him a very severe look. He breathed heavily, and it was said that, when he slept, his wives and children in their houses could hear him breathe. When he walked, his heels hardly touched the ground and he seemed to walk on springs, as if he was going to pounce on somebody. And he did pounce on people quite often. He had a slight stammer and whenever he was angry and could not get his words out quickly enough, he would use his fists. He had no patience with unsuccessful men. He had had no patience with his father.

Unoka, for that was his father's name, had died ten years ago. In his day he was lazy and improvident and was quite incapable of thinking about to-morrow. If any money came his way, and it seldom did, he immediately bought gourds of palm-wine, called round his neighbors and made merry. He always said that whenever he saw a dead man's mouth he saw the folly of not eating what one had in one's lifetime. Unoka was, of course, a debtor, and he owed every neighbor some money, from a few cowries to quite substantial amounts.

He was tall but very thin and had a slight stoop. He wore a haggard and mournful look except when he was drinking or playing on his flute. He was very good on his flute, and his happiest moments were the two or three moons after the harvest when the village musicians brought down their instruments, hung above the fireplace. Unoka would play with them, his face beaming with blessedness and peace. Sometimes another village would ask Unoka's band and their dancing *egwugwu* to come and stay with them and teach them their tunes. They would go to such hosts for as long as three or four markets, making music and feasting. Unoka loved the good fare and the good fellowship, and he loved this season of the year, when the rains had stopped and the sun rose every morning with dazzling beauty. And it was not too hot either, because the cold and dry harmattan wind was blowing down from the north. Some years the harmattan was very severe and a dense haze hung on the atmosphere. Old men and children would then sit round log fires, warming their bodies. Unoka loved it all, and he loved the first kites that returned with the dry season, and the children who sang songs of welcome to them. He would remember his own childhood, how he had often wandered around looking for a kite sailing leisurely against the blue sky. As soon as he found one he would sing with his whole being, welcoming it back from its long, long journey, and asking if it had brought home any lengths of cloth.

That was years ago, when he was young. Unoka, the grown-up, was a failure. He was poor and his wife and children had barely enough to eat. People laughed at him because he was a loafer, and they swore never to lend him any more money because he never paid back. But Unoka was such a man that he always succeeded in borrowing more, and piling up his debts.

One day a neighbor called Okoye came in to see him. He was reclining on a mud bed in his hut playing on the flute. He immediately rose and shook hands with Okoye, who then unrolled the goatskin which he carried under his arm, and sat down. Unoka went into an inner room and soon returned with a small wooden disc containing a kola nut, some alligator pepper and a lump of white chalk.

"I have kola," he announced when he sat down, and passed the disc over to his guest.

"Thank you. He who brings kola brings life. But I think you ought to break it," replied Okoye, passing back the disc.

"No, it is for you, I think," and they argued like this for a few moments before Unoka accepted the honor of breaking the kola. Okoye, meanwhile, took the lump of chalk, drew some lines on the floor, and then painted his big toe.

As he broke the kola, Unoka prayed to their ancestors for life and health, and for protection against their enemies. When they had eaten they talked about many things: about the heavy rains which were drowning the yams, about the next ancestral feast and about the impending war with the village of Mbaino. Unoka was never happy when it came to wars. He was in fact a coward and could not bear the sight of blood. And so he changed the subject and talked about music, and his face beamed. He could hear in his mind's ear the blood-stirring and intricate rhythms of the *ekwe* and the *udu* and the *ogene*, and he could hear his own flute weaving in and out of them, decorating them with a colorful and plaintive tune. The total effect was gay and brisk, but if one picked out the flute as it went up and down and then broke up into short snatches, one saw that there was sorrow and grief there.

Okoye was also a musician. He played on the *ogene*. But he was not a failure like Unoka. He had a large barn full of yams and he had three wives. And now he was going to take the Idemili title, the third highest in the land. It was a very expensive ceremony and he was gathering all his resources together. That was in fact the reason why he had come to see Unoka. He cleared his throat and began:

"Thank you for the kola. You may have heard of the title I intend to take shortly."

Having spoken plainly so far, Okoye said the next half a dozen sentences in proverbs. Among the Ibo the art of conversation is regarded very highly, and proverbs are the palm-oil with which words are eaten. Okoye was a great talker and he spoke for a long time, skirting round the subject and then hitting it finally. In short, he was asking Unoka to return the two hundred cowries he had borrowed from him more than two years before. As soon as Unoka understood what his friend was driving at, he burst out laughing. He laughed loud and long and his voice rang out clear as the *ogene*, and tears stood in his eyes. His visitor was amazed, and sat speechless. At the end, Unoka was able to give an answer between fresh outbursts of mirth.

"Look at that wall," he said, pointing at the far wall of his hut, which was rubbed with red earth so that it shone. "Look at those lines of chalk;" and Okoye saw groups of short perpendicular lines drawn in chalk. There were five groups; and the smallest group had ten lines. Unoka had a sense of the dramatic and so he allowed a pause, in which he took a pinch of snuff and sneezed noisily, and then he continued: "Each group there represents a debt to someone, and each stroke is one hundred cowries. You see, I owe that man a thousand cowries. But he has not come to wake me up in the morning for it. I shall pay you, but not today. Our elders say that the sun will shine on those who stand before it shines on those who kneel under them. I shall pay my big debts first." And he took another pinch of snuff, as if that was paying the big debts first. Okoye rolled his goatskin and departed.

When Unoka died he had taken no title at all and he was heavily in debt. Any wonder then that his son Okonkwo was ashamed of him? Fortunately, among these people a man was judged according to his worth and not according to the worth of his father. Okonkwo was clearly cut out for great things. He was still young but he had won fame as the greatest wrestler in the nine villages. He was a wealthy farmer and had two barns full of yams, and had just married his third wife. To crown it all he had taken two titles and had shown incredible prowess in two inter-tribal wars. And so although Okonkwo was still young, he was already one of the greatest men of his time. Age was respected among his people, but achievement was revered. As the elders said, if a child washed his hands he could eat with kings. Okonkwo had clearly washed his hands and so he ate with kings and elders. And that was how he came to look after the doomed lad who was sacrificed to the village of Umuofia by their neighbors to avoid war and bloodshed. The ill-fated lad was called Ikemefuna.

Chapter Two

OKONKWO HAD JUST BLOWN OUT THE PALM-OIL LAMP and stretched himself on his bamboo bed when he heard the *ogene* of the town crier piercing the still night air. G*ome, gome, gome, gome,* boomed the hollow metal. Then the crier gave his message, and at the end of it beat his instrument again. And this was the message. Every man of Umuofia was asked to gather at the market place tomorrow morning. Okonkwo wondered what was amiss, for he knew certainly that something was amiss. He had discerned a clear overtone of tragedy in the crier's voice, and even now he could still hear it as it grew dimmer and dimmer in the distance.

The night was very quiet. It was always quiet except on moonlight nights. Darkness held a vague terror for these people, even the bravest among them. Children were warned not to whistle at night for fear of evil spirits. Dangerous animals became even more sinister and uncanny in the dark. A snake was never called by its name at night, because it would hear. It was called a string. And so on this particular night as the crier's voice was gradually swallowed up in the distance, silence returned to the world, a vibrant silence made more intense by the universal trill of a million million forest insects.

On a moonlight night it would be different. The happy voices of children playing in open fields would then be heard. And perhaps those not so young would be playing in pairs in less open places, and old men and women would remember their youth. As the Ibo say: "When the moon is shining the cripple becomes hungry for a walk."

But this particular night was dark and silent. And in all the nine villages of Umuofia a town crier with his *ogene* asked every man to be present tomorrow morning. Okonkwo on his bamboo bed tried to figure out the nature of the emergency—war with a neighboring clan? That seemed the most likely reason, and he was not afraid of war. He was a man of action, a man of war. Unlike his father he could stand the look of blood. In Umuofia's latest war he was the first to bring home a human head. That was his fifth head; and he was not an old man yet. On great occasions such as the funeral of a village celebrity he drank his palm-wine from his first human head.

In the morning the market place was full. There must have been about ten thousand men there, all talking in low voices. At last Ogbuefi Ezeugo stood up in the midst of them and bellowed four times, "*Umuofia kwenu,*" and on each occasion he faced a different direction and seemed to push the air with a clenched fist. And ten thousand men answered "*Yaa!*" each time. Then there was perfect silence. Ogbuefi Ezeugo was a powerful orator and was always chosen to speak on such occasions. He moved his hand over his white head and stroked his white beard. He then adjusted his cloth, which was passed under his right arm-pit and tied above his left shoulder.

"*Umuofia kwenu*," he bellowed a fifth time, and the crowd yelled in answer. And then suddenly like one possessed he shot out his left hand and pointed in the direction of Mbaino, and said through gleaming white teeth firmly clenched: "Those sons of wild animals have dared to murder a daughter of Umuofia." He threw his head down and gnashed his teeth, and allowed a murmur of suppressed anger to sweep the crowd. When he began again, the anger on his face was gone and in its place a sort of smile hovered, more terrible and more sinister than the anger. And in a clear unemotional voice he told Umuofia how their daughter had gone to market at Mbaino and had been killed. That woman, said Ezeugo, was the wife of Ogbuefi Udo, and he pointed to a man who sat near him with a bowed head. The crowd then shouted with anger and thirst for blood.

Many others spoke, and at the end it was decided to follow the normal course of action. An ultimatum was immediately dispatched to Mbaino asking them to choose between war on the one hand, and on the other the offer of a young man and a virgin as compensation.

Umuofia was feared by all its neighbors. It was powerful in war and in magic, and its priests and medicine men were feared in all the surrounding country. Its most potent war-medicine was as old as the clan itself. Nobody knew how old. But on one point there was general agreement—the active principle in that medicine had been an old woman with one leg. In fact, the medicine itself was called *agadi-nwayi*, or old woman. It had its shrine in the centre of Umuofia, in a cleared spot. And if anybody was so foolhardy as to pass by the shrine after dusk he was sure to see the old woman hopping about.

And so the neighboring clans who naturally knew of these things feared Umuofia, and would not go to war against it without first trying a peaceful settlement. And in fairness to Umuofia it should be recorded that it never went to war unless its case was clear and just and was accepted as such by its Oracle—the Oracle of the Hills and the Caves. And there were indeed occasions when the Oracle had forbidden Umuofia to wage a war. If the clan had disobeyed the Oracle they would surely have been beaten, because their dreaded *agadi-nwayi* would never fight what the Ibo call *a fight of blame*.

But the war that now threatened was a just war. Even the enemy clan knew that. And so when Okonkwo of Umuofia arrived at Mbaino as the proud and imperious emissary of war, he was treated with great honor and respect, and two days later he returned home with a lad of fifteen and a young virgin. The lad's name was Ikemefuna, whose sad story is still told in Umuofia unto this day.

The elders, or *ndichie*, met to hear a report of Okonkwo's mission. At the end they decided, as everybody knew they would, that the girl should go to Ogbuefi Udo to replace his murdered wife. As for the boy, he belonged to the clan as a whole, and there was no hurry to decide his fate. Okonkwo was, therefore, asked on behalf of the clan to look after him in the interim. And so for three years Ikemefuna lived in Okonkwo's household.

Okonkwo ruled his household with a heavy hand. His wives, especially the youngest, lived in perpetual fear of his fiery temper, and so did his little children. Perhaps down in his heart Okonkwo was not a cruel man. But his whole life was dominated by fear, the fear of failure and of weakness. It was deeper and more intimate than the fear of evil and capricious gods and of magic, the fear of the forest, and of the forces of nature, malevolent, red in tooth and claw. Okonkwo's fear was greater than these. It was not external but lay deep within himself. It was the fear of himself, lest he should be found to resemble his father. Even as a little boy he had resented his father's failure and weakness, and even now he still remembered how he had suffered when a playmate had told him that his father was *agbala*. That was how Okonkwo first came to know that *agbala* was not only another name for a woman, it could also mean a man who had taken no title. And so Okonkwo was ruled by one passion—to hate everything that his father Unoka had loved. One of those things was gentleness and another was idleness.

During the planting season Okonkwo worked daily on his farms from cock-crow until the chickens went to roost. He was a very strong man and rarely felt fatigue. But his wives and young children were not as strong, and so they suffered. But they dared not complain openly. Okonkwo's first son, Nwoye, was then twelve years old but was already causing his father great anxiety for his incipient laziness. At any rate, that was how it looked to his father, and he sought to correct him by constant nagging and beating. And so Nwoye was developing into a sad-faced youth.

Okonkwo's prosperity was visible in his household. He had a large compound enclosed by a thick wall of red earth. His own hut, or *obi*, stood immediately behind the only gate in the red walls. Each of his three wives had her own hut, which together formed a half moon behind the *obi*. The barn was built against one end of the red walls, and long stacks of yam stood out prosperously in it. At the opposite end of the compound was a shed for the goats, and each wife built a small attachment to her hut for the hens. Near the barn was a small house, the "medicine house" or shrine where Okonkwo kept the wooden symbols of his personal god and of his ancestral spirits. He worshipped them with sacrifices of kola nut, food and palm-wine, and offered prayers to them on behalf of himself, his three wives and eight children.

So when the daughter of Umuofia was killed in Mbaino, Ikemefuna came into Okonkwo's household. When Okonkwo brought him home that day he called his most senior wife and handed him over to her.

"He belongs to the clan," he told her. "So look after him."

"Is he staying long with us?" she asked.

"Do what you are told, woman," Okonkwo thundered, and stammered. "When did you become one of the *ndichie* of Umuofia?"

And so Nwoye's mother took Ikemefuna to her hut and asked no more questions.

As for the boy himself, he was terribly afraid. He could not understand what was happening to him or what he had done. How could he know that his father had taken a hand in killing a daughter of Umuofia? All he knew was that a few men had arrived at their house, conversing with his father in low tones, and at the end he had been taken out and handed over to a stranger. His mother had wept bitterly, but he had been too surprised to weep. And so the stranger had brought him, and a girl, a long, long way from home, through lonely forest paths. He did not know who the girl was, and he never saw her again.

Chapter Three

OKONKWO DID NOT HAVE THE START IN LIFE which many young men usually had. He did not inherit a barn from his father. There was no barn to inherit. The story was told in Umuofia, of how his father, Unoka, had gone to consult the Oracle of the Hills and the Caves to find out why he always had a miserable harvest.

The Oracle was called Agbala, and people came from far and near to consult it. They came when misfortune dogged their steps or when they had a dispute with their neighbors. They came to discover what the future held for them or to consult the spirits of their departed fathers.

The way into the shrine was a round hole at the side of a hill, just a little bigger than the round opening into a henhouse. Worshippers and those who came to seek knowledge from the god crawled on their belly through the hole and found themselves in a dark, endless space in the presence of Agbala. No one had ever beheld Agbala, except his priestess. But no one who had ever crawled into his awful shrine had come out without the fear of his power. His priestess stood by the sacred fire which she built in the heart of the cave and proclaimed the will of the god. The fire did not burn with a flame. The glowing logs only served to light up vaguely the dark figure of the priestess.

Sometimes a man came to consult the spirit of his dead father or relative. It was said that when such a spirit appeared, the man saw it vaguely in the darkness, but never heard its voice. Some people even said that they had heard the spirits flying and flapping their wings against the roof of the cave.

Many years ago when Okonkwo was still a boy his father, Unoka, had gone to consult Agbala. The priestess in those days was a woman called Chika. She was full of the power of her god, and she was greatly feared. Unoka stood before her and began his story.

"Every year," he said sadly, "before I put any crop in the earth, I sacrifice a cock to Ani, the owner of all land. It is the law of our fathers. I also kill a cock at the shrine of Ifejioku, the god of yams. I clear the bush and set fire to it when it is dry. I sow the yams when the first rain has fallen, and stake them when the young tendrils appear. I weed—"

"Hold your peace!" screamed the priestess, her voice terrible as it echoed through the dark void. "You have offended neither the gods nor your fathers. And when a man is at peace with his gods and his ancestors, his harvest will be good or bad according to the strength of his arm. You, Unoka, are known in all the clan for the weakness of your machete and your hoe. When your neighbors go out with their ax to cut down virgin forests, you sow your yams on exhausted farms that take no labor to clear. They cross seven rivers to make their farms; you stay at home and offer sacrifices to a reluctant soil. Go home and work like a man."

Unoka was an ill-fated man. He had a bad *chi* or personal god, and evil fortune followed him to the grave, or rather to his death, for he had no grave. He died of the swelling which was an abomination to the earth goddess. When a man was afflicted with swelling in the stomach and the limbs he was not allowed to die in the house. He was carried to the Evil Forest and left there to die. There was the story of a very stubborn man who staggered back to his house and had to be carried again to the forest and tied to a tree. The sickness was an abomination to the earth, and so the victim could not be buried in her bowels. He died and rotted away above the earth, and was not given the first or the second burial. Such was Unoka's fate. When they carried him away, he took with him his flute.

With a father like Unoka, Okonkwo did not have the start in life which many young men had. He neither inherited a barn nor a title, nor even a young wife. But in spite of these disadvantages, he had begun even in his father's lifetime to lay the foundations of a prosperous future. It was slow and painful. But he threw himself into it like one possessed. And indeed he was possessed by the fear of his father's contemptible life and shameful death.

There was a wealthy man in Okonkwo's village who had three huge barns, nine wives and thirty children. His name was Nwakibie and he had taken the highest but one title which a man could take in the clan. It was for this man that Okonkwo worked to earn his first seed yams.

He took a pot of palm-wine and a cock to Nwakibie. Two elderly neighbors were sent for, and Nwakibie's two grown-up sons were also present in his *obi*. He presented a kola nut and an alligator pepper, which were passed round for all to see and then returned to him. He broke the nut saying: "We shall all live. We pray for life, children, a good harvest and happiness. You will have what is good for you and I will have what is good for me. Let the kite perch and let the eagle perch too. If one says no to the other, let his wing break."

After the kola nut had been eaten Okonkwo brought his palm-wine from the corner of the hut where it had been placed and stood it in the center of the group. He addressed Nwakibie, calling him "Our father."

"*Nna ayi*," he said. "I have brought you this little kola. As our people say, a man who pays respect to the great paves the way for his own greatness. I have come to pay you my respects and also to ask a favor. But let us drink the wine first."

Everybody thanked Okonkwo and the neighbors brought out their drinking horns from the goatskin bags they carried. Nwakibie brought down his own horn, which was fastened to the rafters. The younger of his sons, who was also the youngest man in the group, moved to the center, raised the pot on his left knee and began to pour out the wine. The first cup went to Okonkwo, who must taste his wine before anyone else. Then the group drank, beginning with the eldest man. When everyone had drunk two or three horns, Nwakibie sent for his wives. Some of them were not at home and only four came in.

"Is Anasi not in?" he asked them. They said she was coming. Anasi was the first wife and the others could not drink before her, and so they stood waiting.

Anasi was a middle-aged woman, tall and strongly built. There was authority in her bearing and she looked every inch the ruler of the women-folk in a large and prosperous family. She wore the anklet of her husband's titles, which the first wife alone could wear.

She walked up to her husband and accepted the horn from him. She then went down on one knee, drank a little and handed back the horn. She rose, called him by his name and went back to her hut. The other wives drank in the same way, in their proper order, and went away.

The men then continued their drinking and talking. Ogbuefi Idigo was talking about the palm-wine tapper, Obiako, who suddenly gave up his trade.

"There must be something behind it," he said, wiping the foam of wine from his mustache with the back of his left hand. "There must be a reason for it. A toad does not run in the daytime for nothing."

"Some people say the Oracle warned him that he would fall off a palm tree and kill himself," said Akukalia.

"Obiako has always been a strange one," said Nwakibie. "I have heard that many years ago, when his father had not been dead very long, he had gone to consult the Oracle. The Oracle said to him, 'Your dead father wants you to sacrifice a goat to him.' Do you know what he told the Oracle? He said, 'Ask my dead father if he ever had a fowl when he was alive.'" Everybody laughed heartily except Okonkwo, who laughed uneasily be-cause, as the saying goes, an old woman is always uneasy when dry bones are mentioned in a proverb. Okonkwo remembered his own father.

At last the young man who was pouring out the wine held up half a horn of the thick, white dregs and said, "What we are eating is finished." "We have seen it," the others replied. "Who will drink the dregs?" he asked. "Whoever has a job in hand," said Idigo, looking at Nwakibie's elder son Igwelo with a malicious twinkle in his eye.

Everybody agreed that Igwelo should drink the dregs. He accepted the half-full horn from his brother and drank it. As Idigo had said, Igwelo had a job in hand because he had married his first wife a month or two before. The thick dregs of palm-wine were supposed to be good for men who were going in to their wives.

After the wine had been drunk Okonkwo laid his difficulties before Nwakibie.

"I have come to you for help," he said. "Perhaps you can already guess what it is. I have cleared a farm but have no yams to sow. I know what it is to ask a man to trust another with his yams, especially these days when young men are afraid of hard work. I am not afraid of work. The lizard that jumped from the high iroko tree to the ground said he would praise himself if no one else did. I began to fend for myself at an age when most people still suck at their mothers' breasts. If you give me some yam seeds I shall not fail you."

Nwakibie cleared his throat. "It pleases me to see a young man like you these days when our youth has gone so soft. Many young men have come to me to ask for yams but I have refused because I knew they would just dump them in the earth and leave them to be choked by weeds. When I say no to them they think I am hard hearted. But it is not so. Eneke the bird says that since men have learned to shoot without missing, he has learned to fly without perching. I have learned to be stingy with my yams. But I can trust you. I know it as I look at you. As our fathers said, you can tell a ripe corn by its look. I shall give you twice four hundred yams. Go ahead and prepare your farm."

Okonkwo thanked him again and again and went home feeling happy. He knew that Nwakibie would not refuse him, but he had not expected he would be so generous. He had not hoped to get more than four hundred seeds. He would now have to make a bigger farm. He hoped to get another four hundred yams from one of his father's friends at Isiuzo.

Share-cropping was a very slow way of building up a barn of one's own. After all the toil one only got a third of the harvest. But for a young man whose father had no yams, there was no other way. And what made it worse in Okonkwo's case was that he had to support his mother and two sisters from his meagre harvest. And supporting his mother also meant supporting his father. She could not be expected to cook and eat while her husband starved. And so at a very early age when he was striving desperately to build a barn through share-cropping Okonkwo was also fending for his father's house. It was like pouring grains of corn into a bag full of holes. His mother and sisters worked hard enough, but they grew women's crops, like coco-yams, beans and cassava. Yam, the king of crops, was a man's crop.

The year that Okonkwo took eight hundred seed-yams from Nwakibie was the worst year in living memory. Nothing happened at its proper time; it was either too early or too late. It seemed as if the world had gone mad. The first rains were late, and, when they came, lasted only a brief moment. The blazing sun returned, more fierce than it had ever been known, and scorched all the green that had appeared with the rains. The earth burned like hot coals and roasted all the yams that had been sown. Like all good farmers, Okonkwo had begun to sow with the first rains. He had sown four hundred seeds when the rains dried up and the heat returned. He watched the sky all day for signs of rain clouds and lay awake all night. In the morning he went back to his farm and saw the withering tendrils. He had tried to protect them from the smoldering earth by making rings of thick sisal leaves around them. But by the end of the day the sisal rings were burned dry and gray. He changed them every day, and prayed that the rain might fall in the night. But the drought continued for eight market weeks and the yams were killed.

Some farmers had not planted their yams yet. They were the lazy easy-going ones who always put off clearing their farms as long as they could. This year they were the wise ones. They sympathized with their neighbors with much shaking of the head, but inwardly they were happy for what they took to be their own foresight.

Okonkwo planted what was left of his seed-yams when the rains finally returned. He had one consolation. The yams he had sown before the drought were his own, the harvest of the previous year. He still had the eight hundred from Nwakibie and the four hundred from his father's friend. So he would make a fresh start.

But the year had gone mad. Rain fell as it had never fallen before. For days and nights together it poured down in violent torrents, and washed away the yam heaps. Trees were uprooted and deep gorges appeared everywhere. Then the rain became less violent. But it went from day to day without a pause. The spell of sunshine which always came in the middle of the wet season did not appear. The yams put on luxuriant green leaves, but every farmer knew that without sunshine the tubers would not grow.

That year the harvest was sad, like a funeral, and many farmers wept as they dug up the miserable and rotting yams. One man tied his cloth to a tree branch and hanged himself.

Okonkwo remembered that tragic year with a cold shiver throughout the rest of his life. It always surprised him when he thought of it later that he did not sink under the load of despair. He knew that he was a fierce fighter, but that year had been enough to break the heart of a lion.

"Since I survived that year," he always said, "I shall survive anything." He put it down to his inflexible will.

His father, Unoka, who was then an ailing man, had said to him during that terrible harvest month: "Do not despair. I know you will not despair. You have a manly and a proud heart. A proud heart can survive a general failure because such a failure does not prick its pride. It is more difficult and more bitter when a man fails *alone*."

Unoka was like that in his last days. His love of talk had grown with age and sickness. It tried Okonkwo's patience beyond words.

Chapter Four

Looking at a king's mouth," said an old man, "one would think he never sucked at his mother's breast." He was talking about Okonkwo, who had risen so suddenly from great poverty and misfortune to be one of the lords of the clan. The old man bore no ill will towards Okonkwo. Indeed he respected him for his industry and success. But he was struck, as most people were, by Okonkwo's brusqueness in dealing with less successful men. Only a week ago a man had contradicted him at a kindred meeting which they held to discuss the next ancestral feast. Without looking at the man Okonkwo had said: "This meeting is for men." The man who had contradicted him had no titles. That was why he had called him a woman. Okonkwo knew how to kill a man's spirit.

Everybody at the kindred meeting took sides with Osugo when Okonkwo called him a woman. The oldest man present said sternly that those whose palm-kernels were cracked for them by a benevolent spirit should not forget to be humble. Okonkwo said he was sorry for what he had said, and the meeting continued.

But it was really not true that Okonkwo's palm-kernels had been cracked for him by a benevolent spirit. He had cracked them himself. Anyone who knew his grim struggle against poverty and misfortune could not say he had been lucky. If ever a man deserved his success, that man was Okonkwo. At an early age he had achieved fame as the greatest wrestler in all the land. That was not luck. At the most one could say that his *chi* or personal god was good. But the Ibo people have a proverb that when a man says yes his *chi* says yes also. Okonkwo said yes very strongly; so his *chi* agreed. And not only his *chi* but his clan too, because it judged a man by the work of his hands. That was why Okonkwo had been chosen by the nine villages to carry a message of war to their enemies unless they agreed to give up a young man and a virgin to atone for the murder of Udo's wife. And such was the deep fear that their enemies had for Umuofia that they treated Okonkwo like a king and brought him a virgin who was given to Udo as wife, and the lad Ikemefuna.

The elders of the clan had decided that Ikemefuna should be in Okonkwo's care for a while. But no one thought it would be as long as three years. They seemed to forget all about him as soon as they had taken the decision.

At first Ikemefuna was very much afraid. Once or twice he tried to run away, but he did not know where to begin. He thought of his mother and his three-year-old sister and wept bitterly. Nwoye's mother was very kind to him and treated him as one of her own children. But all he said was: "When shall I go home?" When Okonkwo heard that he would not eat any food he came into the hut with a big stick in his hand and stood over him while he swallowed his yams, trembling. A few moments later he went behind the hut and began to vomit painfully. Nwoye's mother went to him and placed her hands on his chest and on his back. He was ill for three market weeks, and when he recovered he seemed to have overcome his great fear and sadness.

He was by nature a very lively boy and he gradually became popular in Okonkwo's household, especially with the children. Okonkwo's son, Nwoye, who was two years younger, became quite inseparable from him because he seemed to know everything. He could fashion out flutes from bamboo stems and even from the elephant grass. He knew the names of all the birds and could set clever traps for the little bush rodents. And he knew which trees made the strongest bows.

Even Okonkwo himself became very fond of the boy—inwardly of course. Okonkwo never showed any emotion openly, unless it be the emotion of anger. To show affection was a sign of weakness; the only thing worth demonstrating was strength. He therefore treated Ikemefuna as he treated everybody else—with a heavy hand. But there was no doubt that he liked the boy. Sometimes when he went to big village meetings or communal ancestral feasts he allowed Ikemefuna to accompany him, like a son, carrying his stool and his goat-skin bag. And, indeed, Ikemefuna called him father.

Ikemefuna came to Umuofia at the end of the carefree season between harvest and planting. In fact he recovered from his illness only a few days before the Week of Peace began. And that was also the year Okonkwo broke the peace, and was punished, as was the custom, by Ezeani, the priest of the earth goddess.

Okonkwo was provoked to justifiable anger by his youngest wife, who went to plait her hair at her friend's house and did not return early enough to cook the afternoon meal. Okonkwo did not know at first that she was not at home. After waiting in vain for her dish he went to her hut to see what she was doing. There was nobody in the hut and the fireplace was cold.

"Where is Ojiugo?" he asked his second wife, who came out of her hut to draw water from a gigantic pot in the shade of a small tree in the middle of the compound.

"She has gone to plait her hair."

Okonkwo bit his lips as anger welled up within him.

"Where are her children? Did she take them?" he asked with unusual coolness and restraint.

"They are here," answered his first wife, Nwoye's mother. Okonkwo bent down and looked into her hut. Ojiugo's children were eating with the children of his first wife.

"Did she ask you to feed them before she went?"

"Yes," lied Nwoye's mother, trying to minimize Ojiugo's thoughtlessness.

Okonkwo knew she was not speaking the truth. He walked back to his *obi* to await Ojiugo's return. And when she returned he beat her very heavily. In his anger he had forgotten that it was the Week of Peace. His first two wives ran out in great alarm pleading with him that it was the sacred week. But Okonkwo was not the man to stop beating somebody half-way through, not even for fear of a goddess.

Okonkwo's neighbors heard his wife crying and sent their voices over the compound walls to ask what was the matter. Some of them came over to see for themselves. It was unheard of to beat somebody during the sacred week.

Before it was dusk Ezeani, who was the priest of the earth goddess, Ani, called on Okonkwo in his *obi*. Okonkwo brought out kola nut and placed it before the priest.

"Take away your kola nut. I shall not eat in the house of a man who has no respect for our gods and ancestors."

Okonkwo tried to explain to him what his wife had done, but Ezeani seemed to pay no attention. He held a short staff in his hand which he brought down on the floor to emphasize his points.

"Listen to me," he said when Okonkwo had spoken. "You are not a stranger in Umuofia. You know as well as I do that our forefathers ordained that before we plant any crops in the earth we should observe a week in which a man does not say a harsh word to his neighbor. We live in peace with our fellows to honor our great goddess of the earth without whose blessing our crops will not grow. You have committed a great evil." He brought down his staff heavily on the floor. "Your wife was at fault, but even if you came into your *obi* and found her lover on top of her, you would still have committed a great evil to beat her." His staff came down again. "The evil you have done can ruin the whole clan. The earth goddess whom you have insulted may refuse to give us her increase, and we shall all perish." His tone now changed from anger to command. "You will bring to the shrine of Ani tomorrow one she-goat, one hen, a length of cloth and a hundred cowries." He rose and left the hut.

Okonkwo did as the priest said. He also took with him a pot of palm-wine. Inwardly, he was repentant. But he was not the man to go about telling his neighbors that he was in error. And so people said he had no respect for the gods of the clan. His enemies said his good fortune had gone to his head. They called him the little bird *nza* who so far forgot himself after a heavy meal that he challenged his *chi*.

No work was done during the Week of Peace. People called on their neighbors and drank palm-wine. This year they talked of nothing else but the *nso-ani* which Okonkwo had committed. It was the first time for many years that a man had broken the sacred peace. Even the oldest men could only remember one or two other occasions somewhere in the dim past.

Ogbuefi Ezeudu, who was the oldest man in the village, was telling two other men who came to visit him that the punishment for breaking the Peace of Ani had become very mild in their clan.

"It has not always been so," he said. "My father told me that he had been told that in the past a man who broke the peace was dragged on the ground through the village until he died. But after a while this custom was stopped because it spoiled the peace which it was meant to preserve."

"Somebody told me yesterday," said one of the younger men, "that in some clans it is an abomination for a man to die during the Week of Peace."

"It is indeed true," said Ogbuefi Ezeudu. "They have that custom in Obodoani. If a man dies at this time he is not buried but cast into the Evil Forest. It is a bad custom which these people observe because they lack understanding. They throw away large numbers of men and women without burial. And what is the result? Their clan is full of the evil spirits of these unburied dead, hungry to do harm to the living."

After the Week of Peace every man and his family began to clear the bush to make new farms. The cut bush was left to dry and fire was then set to it. As the smoke rose into the sky kites appeared from different directions and hovered over the burning field in silent valediction. The rainy season was approaching when they would go away until the dry season returned.

Okonkwo spent the next few days preparing his seed-yams. He looked at each yam carefully to see whether it was good for sowing. Sometimes he decided that a yam was too big to be sown as one seed and he split it deftly along its length with his sharp knife. His eldest son, Nwoye, and Ikemefuna helped him by fetching the yams in long baskets from the barn and in counting the prepared seeds in groups of four hundred. Sometimes Okonkwo gave them a few yams each to prepare. But he always found fault with their effort, and he said so with much threatening.

"Do you think you are cutting up yams for cooking?" he asked Nwoye. "If you split another yam of this size, I shall break your jaw. You think you are still a child. I began to own a farm at your age. And you," he said to Ikemefuna, "do you not grow yams where you come from?"

Inwardly Okonkwo knew that the boys were still too young to understand fully the difficult art of preparing seed-yams. But he thought that one could not begin too early. Yam stood for manliness, and he who could feed his family on yams from one harvest to another was a very great man indeed. Okonkwo wanted his son to be a great farmer and a great man. He would stamp out the disquieting signs of laziness which he thought he already saw in him.

"I will not have a son who cannot hold up his head in the gathering of the clan. I would sooner strangle him with my own hands. And if you stand staring at me like that," he swore, "Amadiora will break your head for you!"

Some days later, when the land had been moistened by two or three heavy rains, Okonkwo and his family went to the farm with baskets of seed-yams, their hoes and machetes, and the planting began. They made single mounds of earth in straight lines all over the field and sowed the yams in them.

Yam, the king of crops, was a very exacting king. For three or four moons it demanded hard work and constant attention from cock-crow till the chickens went back to roost. The young tendrils were protected from earth-heat with rings of sisal leaves. As the rains became heavier the women planted maize, melons and beans between the yam mounds. The yams were then staked, first with little sticks and later with tall and big tree branches. The women weeded the farm three times at definite periods in the life of the yams, neither early nor late.

And now the rains had really come, so heavy and persistent that even the village rain-maker no longer claimed to be able to intervene. He could not stop the rain now, just as he would not attempt to start it in the heart of the dry season, without serious danger to his own health. The personal dynamism required to counter the forces of these extremes of weather would be far too great for the human frame.

And so nature was not interfered with in the middle of the rainy season. Sometimes it poured down in such thick sheets of water that earth and sky seemed merged in one gray wetness. It was then uncertain whether the low rumbling of Amadiora's thunder came from above or below. At such times, in each of the countless thatched huts of Umuofia, children sat around their mother's cooking fire telling stories, or with their father in his *obi* warming themselves from a log fire, roasting and eating maize. It was a brief resting period between the exacting and arduous planting season and the equally exacting but light-hearted month of harvests.

Ikemefuna had begun to feel like a member of Okonkwo's family. He still thought about his mother and his three-year-old sister, and he had moments of sadness and depression. But he and Nwoye had become so deeply attached to each other that such moments became less frequent and less poignant. Ikemefuna had an endless stock of folk tales. Even those which Nwoye knew already were told with a new freshness and the local flavor of a different clan. Nwoye remembered this period very vividly till the end of his life. He even remembered how he had laughed when Ikemefuna told him that the proper name for a corn cob with only a few scattered grains was *eze-agadi-nwayi*, or the teeth of an old woman. Nwoye's mind had gone immediately to Nwayieke, who lived near the udala tree. She had about three teeth and was always smoking her pipe.

Gradually the rains became lighter and less frequent, and earth and sky once again became separate. The rain fell in thin, slanting showers through sunshine and quiet breeze. Children no longer stayed indoors but ran about singing:

> *"The rain is falling, the sun is shining,*
> *Alone Nnadi is cooking and eating."*

Nwoye always wondered who Nnadi was and why he should live all by himself, cooking and eating. In the end he decided that Nnadi must live in that land of Ikemefuna's favorite story where the ant holds his court in splendor and the sands dance forever.

Chapter Five

THE FEAST OF THE NEW YAM was approaching and Umuofia was in a festival mood. It was an occasion for giving thanks to Ani, the earth goddess and the source of all fertility. Ani played a greater part in the life of the people than any other deity. She was the ultimate judge of morality and conduct. And what was more, she was in close communion with the departed fathers of the clan whose bodies had been committed to earth.

The Feast of the New Yam was held every year before the harvest began, to honor the earth goddess and the ancestral spirits of the clan. New yams could not be eaten until some had first been offered to these powers. Men and women, young and old, looked forward to the New Yam Festival because it began the season of plenty—the new year. On the last night before the festival, yams of the old year were all disposed of by those who still had them. The new year must begin with tasty, fresh yams and not the shriveled and fibrous crop of the previous year. All cooking pots, calabashes and wooden bowls were thoroughly washed, especially the wooden mortar in which yam was pounded. Yam foo-foo and vegetable soup was the chief food in the celebration. So much of it was cooked that, no matter how heavily the family ate or how many friends and relatives they invited from neighboring villages, there was always a large quantity of food left over at the end of the day. The story was always told of a wealthy man who set before his guests a mound of foo-foo so high that those who sat on one side could not see what was happening on the other, and it was not until late in the evening that one of them saw for the first time his in-law who had arrived during the course of the meal and had fallen to on the opposite side. It was only then that they exchanged greetings and shook hands over what was left of the food.

The New Yam Festival was thus an occasion for joy throughout Umuofia. And every man whose arm was strong, as the Ibo people say, was expected to invite large numbers of guests from far and wide. Okonkwo always asked his wives' relations, and since he now had three wives his guests would make a fairly big crowd.

But somehow Okonkwo could never become as enthusiastic over feasts as most people. He was a good eater and he could drink one or two fairly big gourds of palm-wine. But he was always uncomfortable sitting around for days waiting for a feast or getting over it. He would be very much happier working on his farm.

The festival was now only three days away. Okonkwo's wives had scrubbed the walls and the huts with red earth until they reflected light. They had then drawn patterns on them in white, yellow and dark green. They then set about painting themselves with cam wood and drawing beautiful black patterns on their stomachs and on their backs. The children were also decorated, especially their hair, which was shaved in beautiful patterns. The three women talked excitedly about the relations who had been invited, and the children reveled in the thought of being spoiled by these visitors from the motherland. Ikemefuna was equally excited. The New Yam Festival seemed to him to be a much bigger event here than in his own village, a place which was already becoming remote and vague in his imagination.

And then the storm burst. Okonkwo, who had been walking about aimlessly in his compound in suppressed anger, suddenly found an outlet.

"Who killed this banana tree?" he asked.

A hush fell on the compound immediately.

"Who killed this tree? Or are you all deaf and dumb?"

As a matter of fact the tree was very much alive. Okonkwo's second wife had merely cut a few leaves off it to wrap some food, and she said so. Without further argument Okonkwo gave her a sound beating and left her and her only daughter weeping. Neither of the other wives dared to interfere beyond an occasional and tentative, "It is enough, Okonkwo," pleaded from a reasonable distance.

His anger thus satisfied, Okonkwo decided to go out hunting. He had an old rusty gun made by a clever blacksmith who had come to live in Umuofia long ago. But although Okonkwo was a great man whose prowess was universally acknowledged, he was not a hunter. In fact he had not killed a rat with his gun. And so when he called Ikemefuna to fetch his gun, the wife who had just been beaten murmured something about guns that never shot. Unfortunately for her, Okonkwo heard it and ran madly into his room for the loaded gun, ran out again and aimed at her as she clambered over the dwarf wall of the barn. He pressed the trigger and there was a loud report accompanied by the wail of his wives and children. He threw down the gun and jumped into the barn, and there lay the woman, very much shaken and frightened but quite unhurt. He heaved a heavy sigh and went away with the gun.

In spite of this incident the New Yam Festival was celebrated with great joy in Okonkwo's household. Early that morning as he offered a sacrifice of new yam and palm-oil to his ancestors he asked them to protect him, his children and their mothers in the new year.

As the day wore on his in-laws arrived from three surrounding villages, and each party brought with them a huge pot of palm-wine. And there was eating and drinking till night, when Okonkwo's in-laws began to leave for their homes.

The second day of the new year was the day of the great wrestling match between Okonkwo's village and their neighbors. It was difficult to say which the people enjoyed more—the feasting and fellowship of the first day or the wrestling contest of the second. But there was one woman who had no doubt whatever in her mind. She was Okonkwo's second wife, Ekwefi, whom he nearly shot. There was no festival in all the seasons of the year which gave her as much pleasure as the wrestling match. Many years ago when she was the village beauty Okonkwo had won her heart by throwing the Cat in the greatest contest within living memory. She did not marry him then because he was too poor to pay her bride-price. But a few years later she ran away from her husband and came to live with Okonkwo. All this happened many years ago. Now Ekwefi was a woman of forty-five who had suffered a great deal in her time. But her love of wrestling contests was still as strong as it was thirty years ago.

It was not yet noon on the second day of the New Yam Festival. Ekwefi and her only daughter, Ezinma, sat near the fireplace waiting for the water in the pot to boil. The fowl Ekwefi had just killed was in the wooden mortar. The water began to boil, and in one deft movement she lifted the pot from the fire and poured the boiling water over the fowl. She put back the empty pot on the circular pad in the corner, and looked at her palms, which were black with soot. Ezinma was always surprised that her mother could lift a pot from the fire with her bare hands.

"Ekwefi," she said, "is it true that when people are grown up, fire does not burn them?" Ezinma, unlike most children, called her mother by her name.

"Yes," replied Ekwefi, too busy to argue. Her daughter was only ten years old but she was wiser than her years.

"But Nwoye's mother dropped her pot of hot soup the other day and it broke on the floor."

Ekwefi turned the hen over in the mortar and began to pluck the feathers.

"Ekwefi," said Ezinma, who had joined in plucking the feathers, "my eyelid is twitching."

"It means you are going to cry," said her mother.

"No," Ezinma said, "it is this eyelid, the top one."

"That means you will see something."

"What will I see?" she asked.

"How can I know?" Ekwefi wanted her to work it out herself.

"Oho," said Ezinma at last. "I know what it is—the wrestling match."

At last the hen was plucked clean. Ekwefi tried to pull out the horny beak but it was too hard. She turned round on her low stool and put the beak in the fire for a few moments. She pulled again and it came off.

"Ekwefi!" a voice called from one of the other huts. It was Nwoye's mother, Okonkwo's first wife.

"Is that me?" Ekwefi called back. That was the way people answered calls from outside. They never answered yes for fear it might be an evil spirit calling.

"Will you give Ezinma some fire to bring to me?" Her own children and Ikemefuna had gone to the stream.

Ekwefi put a few live coals into a piece of broken pot and Ezinma carried it across the clean swept compound to Nwoye's mother.

"Thank you, Nma," she said. She was peeling new yams, and in a basket beside her were green vegetables and beans.

"Let me make the fire for you," Ezinma offered.

"Thank you, Ezigbo," she said. She often called her Ezigbo, which means "the good one."

Ezinma went outside and brought some sticks from a huge bundle of firewood. She broke them into little pieces across the sole of her foot and began to build a fire, blowing it with her breath.

"You will blow your eyes out," said Nwoye's mother, looking up from the yams she was peeling. "Use the fan." She stood up and pulled out the fan which was fastened into one of the rafters. As soon as she got up, the troublesome nannygoat, which had been dutifully eating yam peelings, dug her teeth into the real thing, scooped out two mouthfuls and fled from the hut to chew the cud in the goats' shed. Nwoye's mother swore at her and settled down again to her peeling. Ezinma's fire was now sending up thick clouds of smoke. She went on fanning it until it burst into flames. Nwoye's mother thanked her and she went back to her mother's hut.

Just then the distant beating of drums began to reach them. It came from the direction of the *ilo*, the village playground. Every village had its own *ilo* which was as old as the village itself and where all the great ceremonies and dances took place. The drums beat the unmistakable wrestling dance—quick, light and gay, and it came floating on the wind.

Okonkwo cleared his throat and moved his feet to the beat of the drums. It filled him with fire as it had always done from his youth. He trembled with the desire to conquer and subdue. It was like the desire for women.

"We shall be late for the wrestling," said Ezinma to her mother.

"They will not begin until the sun goes down."

"But they are beating the drums."

"Yes. The drums begin at noon but the wrestling waits until the sun begins to sink. Go and see if your father has brought out yams for the afternoon."

"He has. Nwoye's mother is already cooking."

"Go and bring our own, then. We must cook quickly or we shall be late for the wrestling."

Ezinma ran in the direction of the barn and brought back two yams from the dwarf wall.

Ekwefi peeled the yams quickly. The troublesome nannygoat sniffed about, eating the peelings. She cut the yams into small pieces and began to prepare a pottage, using some of the chicken.

At that moment they heard someone crying just outside their compound. It was very much like Obiageli, Nwoye's sister.

"Is that not Obiageli weeping?" Ekwefi called across the yard to Nwoye's mother.

"Yes," she replied. "She must have broken her waterpot."

The weeping was now quite close and soon the children filed in, carrying on their heads various sizes of pots suitable to their years. Ikemefuna came first with the biggest pot, closely followed by Nwoye and his two younger brothers. Obiageli brought up the rear, her face streaming with tears. In her hand was the cloth pad on which the pot should have rested on her head.

"What happened?" her mother asked, and Obiageli told her mournful story. Her mother consoled her and promised to buy her another pot.

Nwoye's younger brothers were about to tell their mother the true story of the accident when Ikemefuna looked at them sternly and they held their peace. The fact was that Obiageli had been making *inyanga* with her pot. She had balanced it on her head, folded her arms in front of her and began to sway her waist like a grown-up young lady. When the pot fell down and broke she burst out laughing. She only began to weep when they got near the iroko tree outside their compound.

The drums were still beating, persistent and unchanging. Their sound was no longer a separate thing from the living village. It was like the pulsation of its heart. It throbbed in the air, in the sunshine, and even in the trees, and filled the village with excitement.

Ekwefi ladled her husband's share of the pottage into a bowl and covered it. Ezinma took it to him in his *obi*.

Okonkwo was sitting on a goatskin already eating his first wife's meal. Obiageli, who had brought it from her mother's hut, sat on the floor waiting for him to finish. Ezinma placed her mother's dish before him and sat with Obiageli.

"Sit like a woman!" Okonkwo shouted at her. Ezinma brought her two legs together and stretched them in front of her.

"Father, will you go to see the wrestling?" Ezinma asked after a suitable interval.

"Yes," he answered. "Will you go?"

"Yes." And after a pause she said: "Can I bring your chair for you?"

"No, that is a boy's job." Okonkwo was specially fond of Ezinma. She looked very much like her mother, who was once the village beauty. But his fondness only showed on very rare occasions.

"Obiageli broke her pot today," Ezinma said.

"Yes, she has told me about it," Okonkwo said between mouthfuls.

"Father," said Obiageli, "people should not talk when they are eating or pepper may go down the wrong way."

"That is very true. Do you hear that, Ezinma? You are older than Obiageli but she has more sense."

He uncovered his second wife's dish and began to eat from it. Obiageli took the first dish and returned to her mother's hut. And then Nkechi came in, bringing the third dish. Nkechi was the daughter of Okonkwo's third wife.

In the distance the drums continued to beat.

Chapter Six

THE WHOLE VILLAGE TURNED OUT on the *ilo*, men, women and children. They stood round in a huge circle leaving the center of the playground free. The elders and grandees of the village sat on their own stools brought there by their young sons or slaves. Okonkwo was among them. All others stood except those who came early enough to secure places on the few stands which had been built by placing smooth logs on forked pillars.

The wrestlers were not there yet and the drummers held the field. They too sat just in front of the huge circle of spectators, facing the elders. Behind them was the big and ancient silk-cotton tree which was sacred. Spirits of good children lived in that tree waiting to be born. On ordinary days young women who desired children came to sit under its shade.

There were seven drums and they were arranged according to their sizes in a long wooden basket. Three men beat them with sticks, working feverishly from one drum to another. They were possessed by the spirit of the drums.

The young men who kept order on these occasions dashed about, consulting among themselves and with the leaders of the two wrestling teams, who were still outside the circle, behind the crowd. Once in a while two young men carrying palm fronds ran round the circle and kept the crowd back by beating the ground in front of them or, if they were stubborn, their legs and feet.

At last the two teams danced into the circle and the crowd roared and clapped. The drums rose to a frenzy. The people surged forward. The young men who kept order flew around, waving their palm fronds. Old men nodded to the beat of the drums and remembered the days when they wrestled to its intoxicating rhythm.

The contest began with boys of fifteen or sixteen. There were only three such boys in each team. They were not the real wrestlers; they merely set the scene. Within a short time the first two bouts were over. But the third created a big sensation even among the elders who did not usually show their excitement so openly. It was as quick as the other two, perhaps even quicker. But very few people had ever seen that kind of wrestling before. As soon as the two boys closed in, one of them did something which no one could describe because it had been as quick as a flash. And the other boy was flat on his back. The crowd roared and clapped and for a while drowned the frenzied drums. Okonkwo sprang to his feet and quickly sat down again. Three young men from the victorious boy's team ran forward, carried him shoulder high and danced through the cheering crowd. Everybody soon knew who the boy was. His name was Maduka, the son of Obierika.

The drummers stopped for a brief rest before the real matches. Their bodies shone with sweat, and they took up fans and began to fan themselves. They also drank water from small pots and ate kola nuts. They became ordinary human beings again, talking and laughing among themselves and with others who stood near them. The air, which had been stretched taut with excitement, relaxed again. It was as if water had been poured on the tightened skin of a drum. Many people looked around, perhaps for the first time, and saw those who stood or sat next to them.

"I did not know it was you," Ekwefi said to the woman who had stood shoulder to shoulder with her since the beginning of the matches.

"I do not blame you," said the woman. "I have never seen such a large crowd of people. Is it true that Okonkwo nearly killed you with his gun?"

"It is true indeed, my dear friend. I cannot yet find a mouth with which to tell the story."

"Your *chi* is very much awake, my friend. And how is my daughter, Ezinma?"

"She has been very well for some time now. Perhaps she has come to stay."

"I think she has. How old is she now?"

"She is about ten years old."

"I think she will stay. They usually stay if they do not die before the age of six."

"I pray she stays," said Ekwefi with a heavy sigh.

The woman with whom she talked was called Chielo. She was the priestess of Agbala, the Oracle of the Hills and the Caves. In ordinary life Chielo was a widow with two children. She was very friendly with Ekwefi and they shared a common shed in the market. She was particularly fond of Ekwefi's only daughter, Ezinma, whom she called "my daughter." Quite often she bought beancakes and gave Ekwefi some to take home to Ezinma. Anyone seeing Chielo in ordinary life would hardly believe she was the same person who prophesied when the spirit of Agbala was upon her.

The drummers took up their sticks and the air shivered and grew tense like a tightened bow.

The two teams were ranged facing each other across the clear space. A young man from one team danced across the center to the other side and pointed at whomever he wanted to fight. They danced back to the center together and then closed in.

There were twelve men on each side and the challenge went from one side to the other. Two judges walked around the wrestlers and when they thought they were equally matched, stopped them. Five matches ended in this way. But the really exciting moments were when a man was thrown. The huge voice of the crowd then rose to the sky and in every direction. It was even heard in the surrounding villages.

The last match was between the leaders of the teams. They were among the best wrestlers in all the nine villages. The crowd wondered who would throw the other this year. Some said Okafo was the better man; others said he was not the equal of Ikezue. Last year neither of them had thrown the other even though the judges had allowed the contest to go on longer than was the custom. They had the same style and one saw the other's plans beforehand. It might happen again this year.

Dusk was already approaching when their contest began. The drums went mad and the crowds also. They surged forward as the two young men danced into the circle. The palm fronds were helpless in keeping them back.

Ikezue held out his right hand. Okafo seized it, and they closed in. It was a fierce contest. Ikezue strove to dig in his right heel behind Okafo so as to pitch him backwards in the clever *ege* style. But the one knew what the other was thinking. The crowd had surrounded and swallowed up the drummers, whose frantic rhythm was no longer a mere disembodied sound but the very heartbeat of the people.

The wrestlers were now almost still in each other's grip. The muscles on their arms and their thighs and on their backs stood out and twitched. It looked like an equal match. The two judges were already moving forward to separate them when Ikezue, now desperate, went down quickly on one knee in an attempt to fling his man backwards over his head. It was a sad miscalculation. Quick as the lightning of Amadiora, Okafo raised his right leg and swung it over his rival's head. The crowd burst into a thunderous roar. Okafo was swept off his feet by his supporters and carried home shoulder high. They sang his praise and the young women clapped their hands:

> "Who will wrestle for our village?
>   Okafo will wrestle for our village.
> Has he thrown a hundred men?
>   He has thrown four hundred men.
> Has he thrown a hundred Cats?
>   He has thrown four hundred Cats.
> Then send him word to fight for us."

Chapter Seven

FOR THREE YEARS Ikemefuna lived in Okonkwo's household and the elders of Umuofia seemed to have forgotten about him. He grew rapidly like a yam tendril in the rainy season, and was full of the sap of life. He had become wholly absorbed into his new family. He was like an elder brother to Nwoye, and from the very first seemed to have kindled a new fire in the younger boy. He made him feel grown-up; and they no longer spent the evenings in mother's hut while she cooked, but now sat with Okonkwo in his *obi*, or watched him as he tapped his palm tree for the evening wine. Nothing pleased Nwoye now more than to be sent for by his mother or another of his father's wives to do one of those difficult and masculine tasks in the home, like splitting wood, or pounding food. On receiving such a message through a younger brother or sister, Nwoye would feign annoyance and grumble aloud about women and their troubles.

Okonkwo was inwardly pleased at his son's development, and he knew it was due to Ikemefuna. He wanted Nwoye to grow into a tough young man capable of ruling his father's household when he was dead and gone to join the ancestors. He wanted him to be a prosperous man, having enough in his barn to feed the ancestors with regular sacrifices. And so he was always happy when he heard him grumbling about women. That showed that in time he would be able to control his women-folk. No matter how prosperous a man was, if he was unable to rule his women and his children (and especially his women) he was not really a man. He was like the man in the song who had ten and one wives and not enough soup for his foo-foo.

So Okonkwo encouraged the boys to sit with him in his *obi*, and he told them stories of the land—masculine stories of violence and bloodshed. Nwoye knew that it was right to be masculine and to be violent, but somehow he still preferred the stories that his mother used to tell, and which she no doubt still told to her younger children—stories of the tortoise and his wily ways, and of the bird *eneke-nti-oba* who challenged the whole world to a wrestling contest and was finally thrown by the cat. He remembered the story she often told of the quarrel between Earth and Sky long ago, and how Sky withheld rain for seven years, until crops withered and the dead could not be buried because the hoes broke on the stony Earth. At last Vulture was sent to plead with Sky, and to soften his heart with a song of the suffering of the sons of men. Whenever Nwoye's mother sang this song he felt carried away to the distant scene in the sky where Vulture, Earth's emissary, sang for mercy. At last Sky was moved to pity, and he gave to Vulture rain wrapped in leaves of coco-yam. But as he flew home his long talon pierced the leaves and the rain fell as it had never fallen before. And so heavily did it rain on Vulture that he did not return to deliver his message but flew to a distant land, from where he had espied a fire. And when he got there he found it was a man making a sacrifice. He warmed himself in the fire and ate the entrails.

That was the kind of story that Nwoye loved. But he now knew that they were for foolish women and children, and he knew that his father wanted him to be a man. And so he feigned that he no longer cared for women's stories. And when he did this he saw that his father was pleased, and no longer rebuked him or beat him. So Nwoye and Ikemefuna would listen to Okonkwo's stories about tribal wars, or how, years ago, he had stalked his victim, overpowered him and obtained his first human head. And as he told them of the past they sat in darkness or the dim glow of logs, waiting for the women to finish their cooking. When they finished, each brought her bowl of foo-foo and bowl of soup to her husband. An oil lamp was lit and Okonkwo tasted from each bowl, and then passed two shares to Nwoye and Ikemefuna.

In this way the moons and the seasons passed. And then the locusts came. It had not happened for many a long year. The elders said locusts came once in a generation, reappeared every year for seven years and then disappeared for another lifetime. They went back to their caves in a distant land, where they were guarded by a race of stunted men. And then after another lifetime these men opened the caves again and the locusts came to Umuofia.

They came in the cold harmattan season after the harvests had been gathered, and ate up all the wild grass in the fields.

Okonkwo and the two boys were working on the red outer walls of the compound. This was one of the lighter tasks of the after-harvest season. A new cover of thick palm branches and palm leaves was set on the walls to protect them from the next rainy season. Okonkwo worked on the outside of the wall and the boys worked from within. There were little holes from one side to the other in the upper levels of the wall, and through these Okonkwo passed the rope, or *tie-tie*, to the boys and they passed it round the wooden stays and then back to him; and in this way the cover was strengthened on the wall.

The women had gone to the bush to collect firewood, and the little children to visit their playmates in the neighboring compounds. The harmattan was in the air and seemed to distill a hazy feeling of sleep on the world. Okonkwo and the boys worked in complete silence, which was only broken when a new palm frond was lifted on to the wall or when a busy hen moved dry leaves about in her ceaseless search for food.

And then quite suddenly a shadow fell on the world, and the sun seemed hidden behind a thick cloud. Okonkwo looked up from his work and wondered if it was going to rain at such an unlikely time of the year. But almost immediately a shout of joy broke out in all directions, and Umuofia, which had dozed in the noon-day haze, broke into life and activity.

"Locusts are descending," was joyfully chanted everywhere, and men, women and children left their work or their play and ran into the open to see the unfamiliar sight. The locusts had not come for many, many years, and only the old people had seen them before.

At first, a fairly small swarm came. They were the harbingers sent to survey the land. And then appeared on the horizon a slowly-moving mass like a boundless sheet of black cloud drifting towards Umuofia. Soon it covered half the sky, and the solid mass was now broken by tiny eyes of light like shining star dust. It was a tremendous sight, full of power and beauty.

Everyone was now about, talking excitedly and praying that the locusts should camp in Umuofia for the night. For although locusts had not visited Umuofia for many years, everybody knew by instinct that they were very good to eat. And at last the locusts did descend. They settled on every tree and on every blade of grass; they settled on the roofs and covered the bare ground. Mighty tree branches broke away under them, and the whole country became the brown-earth color of the vast, hungry swarm.

Many people went out with baskets trying to catch them, but the elders counseled patience till nightfall. And they were right. The locusts settled in the bushes for the night and their wings became wet with dew. Then all Umuofia turned out in spite of the cold harmattan, and everyone filled his bags and pots with locusts. The next morning they were roasted in clay pots and then spread in the sun until they became dry and brittle. And for many days this rare food was eaten with solid palm-oil.

Okonkwo sat in his *obi* crunching happily with Ikemefuna and Nwoye, and drinking palm-wine copiously, when Ogbuefi Ezeudu came in. Ezeudu was the oldest man in this quarter of Umuofia. He had been a great and fearless warrior in his time, and was now accorded great respect in all the clan. He refused to join in the meal, and asked Okonkwo to have a word with him outside. And so they walked out together, the old man supporting himself with his stick. When they were out of earshot, he said to Okonkwo:

"That boy calls you father. Do not bear a hand in his death." Okonkwo was surprised, and was about to say something when the old man continued:

"Yes, Umuofia has decided to kill him. The Oracle of the Hills and the

Caves has pronounced it. They will take him outside Umuofia as is the custom, and kill him there. But I want you to have nothing to do with it. He calls you his father."

The next day a group of elders from all the nine villages of Umuofia came to Okonkwo's house early in the morning, and before they began to speak in low tones Nwoye and Ikemefuna were sent out. They did not stay very long, but when they went away Okonkwo sat still for a very long time supporting his chin in his palms. Later in the day he called Ikemefuna and told him that he was to be taken home the next day. Nwoye overheard it and burst into tears, whereupon his father beat him heavily. As for Ikemefuna, he was at a loss. His own home had gradually become very faint and distant. He still missed his mother and his sister and would be very glad to see them. But somehow he knew he was not going to see them. He remembered once when men had talked in low tones with his father; and it seemed now as if it was happening all over again.

Later, Nwoye went to his mother's hut and told her that Ikemefuna was going home. She immediately dropped her pestle with which she was grinding pepper, folded her arms across her breast and sighed, "Poor child."

The next day, the men returned with a pot of wine. They were all fully dressed as if they were going to a big clan meeting or to pay a visit to a neighboring village. They passed their cloths under the right arm-pit, and hung their goatskin bags and sheathed machetes over their left shoulders. Okonkwo got ready quickly and the party set out with Ikemefuna carrying the pot of wine. A deathly silence descended on Okonkwo's compound. Even the very little children seemed to know. Throughout that day Nwoye sat in his mother's hut and tears stood in his eyes.

At the beginning of their journey the men of Umuofia talked and laughed about the locusts, about their women, and about some effeminate men who had refused to come with them. But as they drew near to the outskirts of Umuofia silence fell upon them too.

The sun rose slowly to the center of the sky, and the dry sandy footway began to throw up the heat that lay buried in it. Some birds chirruped in the forests around. The men trod dry leaves on the sand. All else was silent. Then from the distance came the faint beating of the *ekwe*. It rose and faded with the wind—a peaceful dance from a distant clan.

"It is an *ozo* dance," the men said among themselves. But no one was sure where it was coming from. Some said Ezimili, others Abame or Aninta. They argued for a short while and fell into silence again, and the elusive dance rose and fell with the wind. Somewhere a man was taking one of the titles of his clan, with music and dancing and a great feast.

The footway had now become a narrow line in the heart of the forest. The short trees and sparse undergrowth which surrounded the men's village began to give way to giant trees and climbers which perhaps had stood from the beginning of things, untouched by the ax and the bush-fire. The sun breaking through their leaves and branches threw a pattern of light and shade on the sandy footway.

Ikemefuna heard a whisper close behind him and turned round sharply. The man who had whispered now called out aloud, urging the others to hurry up.

"We still have a long way to go," he said. Then he and another man went before Ikemefuna and set a faster pace.

Thus the men of Umuofia pursued their way, armed with sheathed machetes, and Ikemefuna, carrying a pot of palm-wine on his head, walked in their midst. Although he had felt uneasy at first, he was not afraid now. Okonkwo walked behind him. He could hardly imagine that Okonkwo was not his real father. He had never been fond of his real father, and at the end of three years he had become very distant indeed. But his mother and his three-year-old sister . . . of course she would not be three now, but six. Would he recognize her now? She must have grown quite big. How his mother would weep for joy, and thank Okonkwo for having looked after him so well and for bringing him back. She would want to hear everything that had happened to him in all these years. Could he remember them all? He would tell her about Nwoye and his mother, and about the locusts . . . Then quite suddenly a thought came upon him. His mother might be dead. He tried in vain to force the thought out of his mind. Then he tried to settle the matter the way he used to settle such matters when he was a little boy. He still remembered the song:

> *Eze elina, elina!*
> > *Sala*
> *Eze ilikwa ya*
> *Ikwaba akwa oligholi*
> *Ebe Danda nechi eze*
> *Ebe Uzuzu nete egwu*
> > *Sala*

He sang it in his mind, and walked to its beat. If the song ended on his right foot, his mother was alive. If it ended on his left, she was dead. No, not dead, but ill. It ended on the right. She was alive and well. He sang the song again, and it ended on the left. But the second time did not count. The first voice gets to Chukwu, or God's house. That was a favorite saying of children. Ikemefuna felt like a child once more. It must be the thought of going home to his mother.

One of the men behind him cleared his throat. Ikemefuna looked back, and the man growled at him to go on and not stand looking back. The way he said it sent cold fear down Ikemefuna's back. His hands trembled vaguely on the black pot he carried. Why had Okonkwo withdrawn to the rear? Ikemefuna felt his legs melting under him. And he was afraid to look back.

As the man who had cleared his throat drew up and raised his machete. Okonkwo looked away. He heard the blow. The pot fell and broke in the sand. He heard Ikemefuna cry, "My father, they have killed me!" as he ran towards him. Dazed with fear, Okonkwo drew his machete and cut him down. He was afraid of being thought weak.

As soon as his father walked in, that night, Nwoye knew that Ikemefuna had been killed, and something seemed to give way inside him, like the snapping of a tightened bow. He did not cry. He just hung limp. He had had the same kind of feeling not long ago, during the last harvest season. Every child loved the harvest season. Those who were big enough to carry even a few yams in a tiny basket went with grown-ups to the farm. And if they could not help in digging up the yams, they could gather firewood together for roasting the ones that would be eaten there on the farm. This roasted yam soaked in red palm-oil and eaten in the open farm was sweeter than any meal at home. It was after such a day at the farm during the last harvest that Nwoye had felt for the first time a snapping inside him like the one he now felt. They were returning home with baskets of yams from a distant farm across the stream when they heard the voice of an infant crying in the thick forest. A sudden hush had fallen on the women, who had been talking, and they had quickened their steps. Nwoye had heard that twins were put in earthenware pots and thrown away in the forest, but he had never yet come across them. A vague chill had descended on him and his head had seemed to swell, like a solitary walker at night who passes an evil spirit on the way. Then something had given way inside him. It descended on him again, this feeling, when his father walked in, that night after killing Ikemefuna.

Chapter Eight

OKONKWO DID NOT TASTE ANY FOOD for two days after the death of Ikemefuna. He drank palm-wine from morning till night, and his eyes were red and fierce like the eyes of a rat when it was caught by the tail and dashed against the floor. He called his son, Nwoye, to sit with him in his *obi*. But the boy was afraid of him and slipped out of the hut as soon as he noticed him dozing.

He did not sleep at night. He tried not to think about Ikemefuna, but the more he tried the more he thought about him. Once he got up from bed and walked about his compound. But he was so weak that his legs could hardly carry him. He felt like a drunken giant walking with the limbs of a mosquito. Now and then a cold shiver descended on his head and spread down his body.

On the third day he asked his second wife, Ekwefi, to roast plantains for him. She prepared it the way he liked—with slices of oil-bean and fish.

"You have not eaten for two days," said his daughter Ezinma when she brought the food to him. "So you must finish this." She sat down and stretched her legs in front of her. Okonkwo ate the food absent-mindedly. 'She should have been a boy,' he thought as he looked at his ten-year-old daughter. He passed her a piece of fish.

"Go and bring me some cold water," he said. Ezinma rushed out of the hut, chewing the fish, and soon returned with a bowl of cool water from the earthen pot in her mother's hut.

Okonkwo took the bowl from her and gulped the water down. He ate a few more pieces of plantain and pushed the dish aside.

"Bring me my bag," he asked, and Ezinma brought his goatskin bag from the far end of the hut. He searched in it for his snuff-bottle. It was a deep bag and took almost the whole length of his arm. It contained other things apart from his snuff-bottle. There was a drinking horn in it, and also a drinking gourd, and they knocked against each other as he searched. When he brought out the snuff-bottle he tapped it a few times against his knee-cap before taking out some snuff on the palm of his left hand. Then he remembered that he had not taken out his snuff-spoon. He searched his bag again and brought out a small, flat, ivory spoon, with which he carried the brown snuff to his nostrils.

Ezinma took the dish in one hand and the empty water bowl in the other and went back to her mother's hut. "She should have been a boy," Okonkwo said to himself again. His mind went back to Ikemefuna and he shivered. If only he could find some work to do he would be able to forget. But it was the season of rest between the harvest and the next planting season. The only work that men did at this time was covering the walls of their compound with new palm fronds. And Okonkwo had already done that. He had finished it on the very day the locusts came, when he had worked on one side of the wall and Ikemefuna and Nwoye on the other.

"When did you become a shivering old woman," Okonkwo asked himself, "you, who are known in all the nine villages for your valor in war? How can a man who has killed five men in battle fall to pieces because he has added a boy to their number? Okonkwo, you have become a woman indeed."

He sprang to his feet, hung his goatskin bag on his shoulder and went to visit his friend, Obierika.

Obierika was sitting outside under the shade of an orange tree making thatches from leaves of the raffia-palm. He exchanged greetings with Okonkwo and led the way into his *obi*.

"I was coming over to see you as soon as I finished that thatch," he said, rubbing off the grains of sand that clung to his thighs.

"Is it well?" Okonkwo asked.

"Yes," replied Obierika. "My daughter's suitor is coming today and I hope we will clinch the matter of the bride-price. I want you to be there."

Just then Obierika's son, Maduka, came into the *obi* from outside, greeted Okonkwo and turned towards the compound.

"Come and shake hands with me," Okonkwo said to the lad. "Your wrestling the other day gave me much happiness." The boy smiled, shook hands with Okonkwo and went into the compound.

"He will do great things," Okonkwo said. "If I had a son like him I should be happy. I am worried about Nwoye. A bowl of pounded yams can throw him in a wrestling match. His two younger brothers are more promising. But I can tell you, Obierika, that my children do not resemble me. Where are the young suckers that will grow when the old banana tree dies? If Ezinma had been a boy I would have been happier. She has the right spirit."

"You worry yourself for nothing," said Obierika. "The children are still very young."

"Nwoye is old enough to impregnate a woman. At his age I was already fending for myself. No, my friend, he is not too young. A chick that will grow into a cock can be spotted the very day it hatches. I have done my best to make Nwoye grow into a man, but there is too much of his mother in him."

"Too much of his grandfather," Obierika thought, but he did not say it. The same thought also came to Okonkwo's mind. But he had long learned how to lay that ghost. Whenever the thought of his father's weakness and failure troubled him he expelled it by thinking about his own strength and success. And so he did now. His mind went to his latest show of manliness.

"I cannot understand why you refused to come with us to kill that boy," he asked Obierika.

"Because I did not want to," Obierika replied sharply. "I had something better to do."

"You sound as if you question the authority and the decision of the Oracle, who said he should die."

"I do not. Why should I? But the Oracle did not ask me to carry out its decision."

"But someone had to do it. If we were all afraid of blood, it would not be done. And what do you think the Oracle would do then?"

"You know very well, Okonkwo, that I am not afraid of blood; and if anyone tells you that I am, he is telling a lie. And let me tell you one thing, my friend. If I were you I would have stayed at home. What you have done will not please the Earth. It is the kind of action for which the goddess wipes out whole families."

"The Earth cannot punish me for obeying her messenger," Okonkwo said. "A child's fingers are not scalded by a piece of hot yam which its mother puts into its palm."

"That is true," Obierika agreed. "But if the Oracle said that my son should be killed I would neither dispute it nor be the one to do it."

They would have gone on arguing had Ofoedu not come in just then. It was clear from his twinkling eyes that he had important news. But it would be impolite to rush him. Obierika offered him a lobe of the kola nut he had broken with Okonkwo. Ofoedu ate slowly and talked about the locusts. When he finished his kola nut he said:

"The things that happen these days are very strange."

"What has happened?" asked Okonkwo.

"Do you know Ogbuefi Ndulue?" Ofoedu asked.

"Ogbuefi Ndulue of Ire village," Okonkwo and Obierika said together.

"He died this morning," said Ofoedu.

"That is not strange. He was the oldest man in Ire," said Obierika.

"You are right," Ofoedu agreed. "But you ought to ask why the drum has not beaten to tell Umuofia of his death."

"Why?" asked Obierika and Okonkwo together.

"That is the strange part of it. You know his first wife who walks with a stick?"

"Yes. She is called Ozoemena."

"That is so," said Ofoedu. "Ozoemena was, as you know, too old to attend Ndulue during his illness. His younger wives did that. When he died this morning, one of these women went to Ozoemena's hut and told her. She rose from her mat, took her stick and walked over to the *obi*. She knelt on her knees and hands at the threshold and called her husband, who was laid on a mat. 'Ogbuefi Ndulue,' she called, three times, and went back to her hut. When the youngest wife went to call her again to be present at the washing of the body, she found her lying on the mat, dead."

"That is very strange indeed," said Okonkwo. "They will put off Ndulue's funeral until his wife has been buried."

"That is why the drum has not been beaten to tell Umuofia."

"It was always said that Ndulue and Ozoemena had one mind," said Obierika. "I remember when I was a young boy there was a song about them. He could not do anything without telling her."

"I did not know that," said Okonkwo. "I thought he was a strong man in his youth."

"He was indeed," said Ofoedu.

Okonkwo shook his head doubtfully.

"He led Umuofia to war in those days," said Obierika.

Okonkwo was beginning to feel like his old self again. All that he required was something to occupy his mind. If he had killed Ikemefuna during the busy planting season or harvesting it would not have been so bad; his mind would have been centered on his work. Okonkwo was not a man of thought but of action. But in absence of work, talking was the next best.

Soon after Ofoedu left, Okonkwo took up his goatskin bag to go.

"I must go home to tap my palm trees for the afternoon," he said.

"Who taps your tall trees for you?" asked Obierika.

"Umezulike," replied Okonkwo.

"Sometimes I wish I had not taken the *ozo* title," said Obierika. "It wounds my heart to see these young men killing palm trees in the name of tapping."

"It is so indeed," Okonkwo agreed. "But the law of the land must be obeyed."

"I don't know how we got that law," said Obierika. "In many other clans a man of title is not forbidden to climb the palm tree. Here we say he cannot climb the tall tree but he can tap the short ones standing on the ground. It is like Dimaragana, who would not lend his knife for cutting up dogmeat because the dog was taboo to him, but offered to use his teeth."

"I think it is good that our clan holds the *ozo* title in high esteem," said Okonkwo. "In those other clans you speak of, *ozo* is so low that every beggar takes it."

"I was only speaking in jest," said Obierika. "In Abame and Aninta the title is worth less than two cowries. Every man wears the thread of title on his ankle, and does not lose it even if he steals."

"They have indeed soiled the name of *ozo*," said Okonkwo as he rose to go.

"It will not be very long now before my in-laws come," said Obierika.

"I shall return very soon," said Okonkwo, looking at the position of the sun.

There were seven men in Obierika's hut when Okonkwo returned. The suitor was a young man of about twenty-five, and with him were his father and uncle. On Obierika's side were his two elder brothers and Maduka, his sixteen-year-old son.

"Ask Akueke's mother to send us some kola nuts," said Obierika to his son. Maduka vanished into the compound like lightning. The conversation at once centered on him, and everybody agreed that he was as sharp as a razor.

"I sometimes think he is too sharp," said Obierika, somewhat indulgently. "He hardly ever walks. He is always in a hurry. If you are sending him on an errand he flies away before he has heard half of the message."

"You were very much like that yourself," said his eldest brother. "As our people say, 'When mother-cow is chewing grass its young ones watch its mouth.' Maduka has been watching your mouth."

As he was speaking the boy returned, followed by Akueke, his half-sister, carrying a wooden dish with three kola nuts and alligator pepper. She gave the dish to her father's eldest brother and then shook hands, very shyly, with her suitor and his relatives. She was about sixteen and just ripe for marriage. Her suitor and his relatives surveyed her young body with expert eyes as if to assure themselves that she was beautiful and ripe.

She wore a coiffure which was done up into a crest in the middle of the head. Cam wood was rubbed lightly into her skin, and all over her body were black patterns drawn with *uli*. She wore a black necklace which hung down in three coils just above her full, succulent breasts. On her arms were red and yellow bangles, and on her waist four or five rows of *jigida*, or waist beads.

When she had shaken hands, or rather held out her hand to be shaken, she returned to her mother's hut to help with the cooking.

"Remove your *jigida* first," her mother warned as she moved near the fireplace to bring the pestle resting against the wall. "Every day I tell you that *jigida* and fire are not friends. But you will never hear. You grew your ears for decoration, not for hearing. One of these days your *jigida* will catch fire on your waist, and then you will know."

Akueke moved to the other end of the hut and began to remove i waist beads. It had to be done slowly and carefully, taking each string separately, else it would break and the thousand tiny rings would have to be strung together again. She rubbed each string downwards with her palm, until it passed the buttocks and slipped down to the floor around her feet.

The men in the *obi* had already begun to drink the palm-wine which Akueke's suitor had brought. It was a very good wine and powerful, for in spite of the palm fruit hung across the mouth of the pot to restrain the lively liquor, white foam rose and spilled over.

"That wine is the work of a good tapper," said Okonkwo.

The young suitor, whose name was Ibe, smiled broadly and said to his father: "Do you hear that?" He then said to the others: "He will never admit that I am a good tapper."

"He tapped three of my best palm trees to death," said his father, Ukegbu.

"That was about five years ago," said Ibe, who had begun to pour out the wine, "before I learned how to tap." He filled the first horn and gave to his father. Then he poured out for the others. Okonkwo brought out his big horn from the goatskin bag, blew into it to remove any dust that might be there and gave it to Ibe to fill.

As the men drank, they talked about everything except the thing for which they had gathered. It was only after the pot had been emptied that the suitor's father cleared his voice and announced the object of their visit.

Obierika then presented to him a small bundle of short broomsticks. Ukegbu counted them.

"They are thirty?" he asked.

Obierika nodded in agreement.

"We are at last getting somewhere," Ukegbu said, and then turning to his brother and his son he said: "Let us go out and whisper together." The three rose and went outside. When they returned Ukegbu handed the bundle of sticks back to Obierika. He counted them; instead of thirty there were now only fifteen. He passed them over to his eldest brother, Machi, who also counted them and said:

"We had not thought to go below thirty. But as the dog said, 'If I fall down for you and you fall down for me, it is play'. Marriage should be a play and not a fight; so we are falling down again." He then added ten sticks to the fifteen and gave the bundle to Ukegbu.

In this way Akueke's bride-price was finally settled at twenty bags of cowries. It was already dusk when the two parties came to this agreement.

"Go and tell Akueke's mother that we have finished," Obierika said to his son, Maduka. Almost immediately the women came in with a big bowl of foo-foo. Obierika's second wife followed with a pot of soup, and Maduka brought in a pot of palm-wine.

As the men ate and drank palm-wine they talked about the customs of their neighbors.

"It was only this morning," said Obierika, "that Okonkwo and I were talking about Abame and Aninta, where titled men climb trees and pound foo-foo for their wives."

"All their customs are upside-down. They do not decide bride-price as we do, with sticks. They haggle and bargain as if they were buying a goat or a cow in the market."

"That is very bad," said Obierika's eldest brother. "But what is good in one place is bad in another place. In Umunso they do not bargain at all, not even with broomsticks. The suitor just goes on bringing bags of cowries until his in-laws tell him to stop. It is a bad custom because it always leads to a quarrel."

"The world is large," said Okonkwo. "I have even heard that in some tribes a man's children belong to his wife and her family."

"That cannot be," said Machi. "You might as well say that the woman lies on top of the man when they are making the children."

"It is like the story of white men who, they say, are white like this piece of chalk," said Obierika. He held up a piece of chalk, which every man kept in his *obi* and with which his guests drew lines on the floor before they ate kola nuts. "And these white men, they say, have no toes."

"And have you ever seen them?" asked Machi.

"Have you?" asked Obierika.

"One of them passes here frequently," said Machi. "His name is Amadi."

Those who knew Amadi laughed. He was a leper, and the polite name for leprosy was "the white skin."

Chapter Nine

FOR THE FIRST TIME IN THREE NIGHTS, Okonkwo slept. He woke up once in the middle of the night and his mind went back to the past three days without making him feel uneasy. He began to wonder why he had felt uneasy at all. It was like a man wondering in broad daylight why a dream had appeared so terrible to him at night. He stretched himself and scratched his thigh where a mosquito had bitten him as he slept. Another one was wailing near his right ear. He slapped the ear and hoped he had killed it. Why do they always go for one's ears? When he was a child his mother had told him a story about it. But it was as silly as all women's stories. Mosquito, she had said, had asked Ear to marry him, whereupon Ear fell on the floor in uncontrollable laughter. "How much longer do you think you will live?" she asked. "You are already a skeleton." Mosquito went away humiliated, and any time he passed her way he told Ear that he was still alive.

Okonkwo turned on his side and went back to sleep. He was roused in the morning by someone banging on his door.

"Who is that?" he growled. He knew it must be Ekwefi. Of his three wives Ekwefi was the only one who would have the audacity to bang on his door.

"Ezinma is dying," came her voice, and all the tragedy and sorrow of her life were packed in those words.

Okonkwo sprang from his bed, pushed back the bolt on his door and ran into Ekwefi's hut.

Ezinma lay shivering on a mat beside a huge fire that her mother had kept burning all night.

"It is *iba*," said Okonkwo as he took his machete and went into the bush to collect the leaves and grasses and barks of trees that went into making the medicine for *iba*.

Ekwefi knelt beside the sick child, occasionally feeling with her palm the wet, burning forehead.

Ezinma was an only child and the center of her mother's world. Very often it was Ezinma who decided what food her mother should prepare. Ekwefi even gave her such delicacies as eggs, which children were rarely allowed to eat because such food tempted them to steal. One day as Ezinma was eating an egg Okonkwo had come in unexpectedly from his hut. He was greatly shocked and swore to beat Ekwefi if she dared to give the child eggs

again. But it was impossible to refuse Ezinma anything. After her father's re-
buke she developed an even keener appetite for eggs. And she enjoyed
above all the secrecy in which she now ate them. Her mother always took
her into their bedroom and shut the door.

Ezinma did not call her mother *Nne* like all children. She called her by
her name, Ekwefi, as her father and other grown-up people did. The relationship between them was not only that of mother and child. There was
something in it like the companionship of equals, which was strengthened
by such little conspiracies as eating eggs in the bedroom.

Ekwefi had suffered a good deal in her life. She had borne ten children
and nine of them had died in infancy, usually before the age of three. As she
buried one child after another her sorrow gave way to despair and then to
grim resignation. The birth of her children, which should be a woman's
crowning glory, became for Ekwefi mere physical agony devoid of promise.
The naming ceremony after seven market weeks became an empty ritual.
Her deepening despair found expression in the names she gave her children.
One of them was a pathetic cry, Onwumbiko—"Death, I implore you." But
Death took no notice; Onwumbiko died in his fifteenth month. The next
child was a girl, Ozoemena—"May it not happen again." She died in her
eleventh month, and two others after her. Ekwefi then became defiant and
called her next child Onwuma—"Death may please himself." And he did.

After the death of Ekwefi's second child, Okonkwo had gone to a medicine man, who was also a diviner of the Afa Oracle, to inquire what was
amiss. This man told him that the child was an *ogbanje*, one of those wicked
children who, when they died, entered their mothers' wombs to be born
again.

"When your wife becomes pregnant again," he said, "let her not sleep in
her hut. Let her go and stay with her people. In that way she will elude her
wicked tormentor and break its evil cycle of birth and death."

Ekwefi did as she was asked. As soon as she became pregnant she went
to live with her old mother in another village. It was there that her third
child was born and circumcised on the eighth day. She did not return to
Okonkwo's compound until three days before the naming ceremony. The
child was called Onwumbiko.

Onwumbiko was not given proper burial when he died. Okonkwo had
called in another medicine man who was famous in the clan for his great
knowledge about *ogbanje* children. His name was Okagbue Uyanwa.
Okagbue was a very striking figure, tall, with a full beard and a bald head.
He was light in complexion and his eyes were red and fiery. He always
gnashed his teeth as he listened to those who came to consult him. He
asked Okonkwo a few questions about the dead child. All the neighbors and
relations who had come to mourn gathered round them.

"On what market-day was it born?" he asked.

"*Oye*," replied Okonkwo.

"And it died this morning?"

Okonkwo said yes, and only then realized for the first time that
had died on the same market-day as it had been born. The neighbors and relations also saw the coincidence and said among themselves that it was very
significant.

"Where do you sleep with your wife, in your *obi* or in her own hut?"
asked the medicine man.

"In her hut."

"In future call her into your *obi*."

The medicine man then ordered that there should be no mourning for
the dead child. He brought out a sharp razor from the goatskin bag slung
from his left shoulder and began to mutilate the child. Then he took it away
to bury in the Evil Forest, holding it by the ankle and dragging it on the
ground behind him. After such treatment it would think twice before coming again, unless it was one of the stubborn ones who returned, carrying the
stamp of their mutilation—a missing finger or perhaps a dark line where the
medicine man's razor had cut them.

By the time Onwumbiko died Ekwefi had become a very bitter woman.
Her husband's first wife had already had three sons, all strong and healthy.
When she had borne her third son in succession, Okonkwo had slaughtered
a goat for her, as was the custom. Ekwefi had nothing but good wishes for
her. But she had grown so bitter about her own *chi* that she could not rejoice
with others over their good fortune. And so, on the day that Nwoye's
mother celebrated the birth of her three sons with feasting and music,
Ekwefi was the only person in the happy company who went about with a
cloud on her brow. Her husband's wife took this for malevolence, as hus-
bands' wives were wont to. How could she know that Ekwefi's bitterness did
not flow outwards to others but inwards into her own soul; that she did not
blame others for their good fortune but her own evil *chi* who denied her any?

At last Ezinma was born, and although ailing she seemed determined to
live. At first Ekwefi accepted her, as she had accepted others—with listless
resignation. But when she lived on to her fourth, fifth and sixth years, love
returned once more to her mother, and, with love, anxiety. She determined
to nurse her child to health, and she put all her being into it. She was re-
warded by occasional spells of health during which Ezinma bubbled with energy like fresh palm-wine. At such times she seemed beyond danger. But all
of a sudden she would go down again. Everybody knew she was an *ogbanje*.
These sudden bouts of sickness and health were typical of her kind. But she
had lived so long that perhaps she had decided to stay. Some of them did become tired of their evil rounds of birth and death, or took pity on their

.nothers, and stayed. Ekwefi believed deep inside her that Ezinma had come to stay. She believed because it was that faith alone that gave her own life any kind of meaning. And this faith had been strengthened when a year or so ago a medicine man had dug up Ezinma's *iyi-uwa*. Everyone knew then that she would live because her bond with the world of *ogbanje* had been broken. Ekwefi was reassured. But such was her anxiety for her daughter that she could not rid herself completely of her fear. And although she believed that the *iyi-uwa* which had been dug up was genuine, she could not ignore the fact that some really evil children sometimes misled people into digging up a specious one.

But Ezinma's *iyi-uwa* had looked real enough. It was a smooth pebble wrapped in a dirty rag. The man who dug it up was the same Okagbue who was famous in all the clan for his knowledge in these matters. Ezinma had not wanted to cooperate with him at first. But that was only to be expected. No *ogbanje* would yield her secrets easily, and most of them never did because they died too young—before they could be asked questions.

"Where did you bury your *iyi-uwa?*" Okagbue had asked Ezinma. She was nine then and was just recovering from a serious illness.

"What is *iyi-uwa?*" she asked in return.

"You know what it is. You buried it in the ground somewhere so that you can die and return again to torment your mother."

Ezinma looked at her mother, whose eyes, sad and pleading, were fixed on her.

"Answer the question at once," roared Okonkwo, who stood beside her. All the family were there and some of the neighbors too.

"Leave her to me," the medicine man told Okonkwo in a cool, confident voice. He turned again to Ezinma. "Where did you bury your *iyi-uwa?*"

"Where they bury children," she replied, and the quiet spectators murmured among themselves.

"Come along then and show me the spot," said the medicine man.

The crowd set out with Ezinma leading the way and Okagbue following closely behind her. Okonkwo came next and Ekwefi followed him. When she came to the main road, Ezinma turned left as if she was going to the stream.

"But you said it was where they bury children?" asked the medicine man.

"No," said Ezinma, whose feeling of importance was manifest in her sprightly walk. She sometimes broke into a run and stopped again suddenly. The crowd followed her silently. Women and children returning from the stream with pots of water on their heads wondered what was happening until they saw Okagbue and guessed that it must be something to do with *ogbanje*. And they all knew Ekwefi and her daughter very well.

When she got to the big udala tree Ezinma turned left into the bush, and the crowd followed her. Because of her size she made her way through trees and creepers more quickly than her followers. The bush was alive with the tread of feet on dry leaves and sticks and the moving aside of tree branches. Ezinma went deeper and deeper and the crowd went with her. Then she suddenly turned round and began to walk back to the road. Everybody stood to let her pass and then filed after her.

"If you bring us all this way for nothing I shall beat sense into you," Okonkwo threatened.

"I have told you to let her alone. I know how to deal with them," said Okagbue.

Ezinma led the way back to the road, looked left and right and turned right. And so they arrived home again.

"Where did you bury your *iyi-uwa?*" asked Okagbue when Ezinma finally stopped outside her father's *obi*. Okagbue's voice was unchanged. It was quiet and confident.

"It is near that orange tree," Ezinma said.

"And why did you not say so, you wicked daughter of Akalogoli?" Okonkwo swore furiously. The medicine man ignored him.

"Come and show me the exact spot," he said quietly to Ezinma.

"It is here," she said when they got to the tree.

"Point at the spot with your finger," said Okagbue.

"It is here," said Ezinma touching the ground with her finger. Okonkwo stood by, rumbling like thunder in the rainy season.

"Bring me a hoe," said Okagbue.

When Ekwefi brought the hoe, he had already put aside his goatskin bag and his big cloth and was in his underwear, a long and thin strip of cloth wound round the waist like a belt and then passed between the legs to be fastened to the belt behind. He immediately set to work digging a pit where Ezinma had indicated. The neighbors sat around watching the pit becoming deeper and deeper. The dark top soil soon gave way to the bright red earth with which women scrubbed the floors and walls of huts. Okagbue worked tirelessly and in silence, his back shining with perspiration. Okonkwo stood by the pit. He asked Okagbue to come up and rest while he took a hand. But Okagbue said he was not tired yet.

Ekwefi went into her hut to cook yams. Her husband had brought out more yams than usual because the medicine man had to be fed. Ezinma went with her and helped in preparing the vegetables.

"There is too much green vegetable," she said.

"Don't you see the pot is full of yams?" Ekwefi asked. "And you know how leaves become smaller after cooking."

"Yes," said Ezinma, "that was why the snake-lizard killed his mother."

"Very true," said Ekwefi.

He gave his mother seven baskets of vegetables to cook and in the end e were only three. And so he killed her," said Ezinma.

"That is not the end of the story."

"Oho," said Ezinma. "I remember now. He brought another seven baskets and cooked them himself. And there were again only three. So he killed himself too."

Outside the *obi* Okagbue and Okonkwo were digging the pit to find where Ezinma had buried her *iyi-uwa*. Neighbors sat around, watching. The pit was now so deep that they no longer saw the digger. They only saw the red earth he threw up mounting higher and higher. Okonkwo's son, Nwoye, stood near the edge of the pit because he wanted to take in all that happened.

Okagbue had again taken over the digging from Okonkwo. He worked, as usual, in silence. The neighbors and Okonkwo's wives were now talking. The children had lost interest and were playing.

Suddenly Okagbue sprang to the surface with the agility of a leopard.

"It is very near now," he said. "I have felt it."

There was immediate excitement and those who were sitting jumped to their feet.

"Call your wife and child," he said to Okonkwo. But Ekwefi and Ezinma had heard the noise and run out to see what it was.

Okagbue went back into the pit, which was now surrounded by spectators. After a few more hoe-fuls of earth he struck the *iyi-uwa*. He raised it carefully with the hoe and threw it to the surface. Some women ran away in fear when it was thrown. But they soon returned and everyone was gazing at the rag from a reasonable distance. Okagbue emerged and without saying a word or even looking at the spectators he went to his goatskin bag, took out two leaves and began to chew them. When he had swallowed them, he took up the rag with his left hand and began to untie it. And then the smooth, shiny pebble fell out. He picked it up.

"Is this yours?" he asked Ezinma.

"Yes," she replied. All the women shouted with joy because Ekwefi's troubles were at last ended.

All this had happened more than a year ago and Ezinma had not been ill since. And then suddenly she had begun to shiver in the night. Ekwefi brought her to the fireplace, spread her mat on the floor and built a fire. But she had got worse and worse. As she knelt by her, feeling with her palm the wet, burning forehead, she prayed a thousand times. Although her husband's wives were saying that it was nothing more than *iba*, she did not hear them.

Okonkwo returned from the bush carrying on his left shoulder a large bundle of grasses and leaves, roots and barks of medicinal trees and shrubs. He went into Ekwefi's hut, put down his load and sat down.

"Get me a pot," he said, "and leave the child alone."

Ekwefi went to bring the pot and Okonkwo selected the best from his bundle, in their due proportions, and cut them up. He put them in the pot and Ekwefi poured in some water.

"Is that enough?" she asked when she had poured in about half of the water in the bowl.

"A little more . . . I said *a little*. Are you deaf?" Okonkwo roared at her.

She set the pot on the fire and Okonkwo took up his machete to return to his *obi*.

"You must watch the pot carefully," he said as he went, "and don't allow it to boil over. If it does its power will be gone." He went away to his hut and Ekwefi began to tend the medicine pot almost as if it was itself a sick child. Her eyes went constantly from Ezinma to the boiling pot and back to Ezinma.

Okonkwo returned when he felt the medicine had cooked long enough. He looked it over and said it was done.

"Bring me a low stool for Ezinma," he said, "and a thick mat."

He took down the pot from the fire and placed it in front of the stool. He then roused Ezinma and placed her on the stool, astride the steaming pot. The thick mat was thrown over both. Ezinma struggled to escape from the choking and overpowering steam, but she was held down. She started to cry.

When the mat was at last removed she was drenched in perspiration. Ekwefi mopped her with a piece of cloth and she lay down on a dry mat and was soon asleep.

Chapter Ten

LARGE CROWDS BEGAN TO GATHER on the village *ilo* as soon as the edge had worn off the sun's heat and it was no longer painful on the body. Most communal ceremonies took place at that time of the day, so that even when it was said that a ceremony would begin "after the midday meal" everyone understood that it would begin a long time later, when the sun's heat had softened.

It was clear from the way the crowd stood or sat that the ceremony was for men. There were many women, but they looked on from the fringe like outsiders. The titled men and elders sat on their stools waiting for the trials to begin. In front of them was a row of stools on which nobody sat. There were nine of them. Two little groups of people stood at a respectable distance beyond the stools. They faced the elders. There were three men in one group and three men and one woman in the other. The woman was Mgbafo and the three men with her were her brothers. In the other group were her husband, Uzowulu, and his relatives. Mgbafo and her brothers were as still as statues into whose faces the artist has molded defiance. Uzowulu and his relatives, on the other hand, were whispering together. It looked like whispering, but they were really talking at the top of their voices. Everybody in the crowd was talking. It was like the market. From a distance the noise was a deep rumble carried by the wind.

An iron gong sounded, setting up a wave of expectation in the crowd. Everyone looked in the direction of the *egwugwu* house. *Gome, gome, gome, gome* went the gong, and a powerful flute blew a high-pitched blast. Then came the voices of the *egwugwu*, guttural and awesome. The wave struck the women and children and there was a backward stampede. But it was momentary. They were already far enough where they stood and there was room for running away if any of the *egwugwu* should go towards them.

The drum sounded again and the flute blew. The *egwugwu* house was now a pandemonium of quavering voices: *Aru oyim de de de dei!* filled the air as the spirits of the ancestors, just emerged from the earth, greeted themselves in their esoteric language. The *egwugwu* house into which they emerged faced the forest, away from the crowd, who saw only its back with the many-colored patterns and drawings done by specially chosen women at regular intervals. These women never saw the inside of the hut. No woman ever did. They scrubbed and painted the outside walls under the supervision of men. If they imagined what was inside, they kept their imagination to themselves. No woman ever asked questions about the most powerful and the most secret cult in the clan.

Aru oyim de de de dei! flew around the dark, closed hut like tongues of fire. The ancestral spirits of the clan were abroad. The metal gong beat continuously now and the flute, shrill and powerful, floated on the chaos.

And then the *egwugwu* appeared. The women and children sent up a great shout and took to their heels. It was instinctive. A woman fled as soon as an *egwugwu* came in sight. And when, as on that day, nine of the greatest masked spirits in the clan came out together it was a terrifying spectacle. Even Mgbafo took to her heels and had to be restrained by her brothers.

Each of the nine *egwugwu* represented a village of the clan. Their leader was called Evil Forest. Smoke poured out of his head.

The nine villages of Umuofia had grown out of the nine sons of the first father of the clan. Evil Forest represented the village of Umueru, or the children of Eru, who was the eldest of the nine sons.

"*Umuofia kwenu!*" shouted the leading *egwugwu*, pushing the air with his raffia arms. The elders of the clan replied, "*Yaa!*"

"*Umuofia kwenu!*"

"*Yaa!*"

"*Umuofia kwenu!*"

"*Yaa!*"

Evil Forest then thrust the pointed end of his rattling staff into the earth. And it began to shake and rattle, like something agitating with a metallic life. He took the first of the empty stools and the eight other *egwugwu* began to sit in order of seniority after him.

Okonkwo's wives, and perhaps other women as well, might have noticed that the second *egwugwu* had the springy walk of Okonkwo. And they might also have noticed that Okonkwo was not among the titled men and elders who sat behind the row of *egwugwu*. But if they thought these things they kept them within themselves. The *egwugwu* with the springy walk was one of the dead fathers of the clan. He looked terrible with the smoked raffia body, a huge wooden face painted white except for the round hollow eyes and the charred teeth that were as big as a man's fingers. On his head were two powerful horns.

When all the *egwugwu* had sat down and the sound of the many tiny bells and rattles on their bodies had subsided, Evil Forest addressed the two groups of people facing them.

"Uzowulu's body, I salute you," he said. Spirits always addressed humans as "bodies." Uzowulu bent down and touched the earth with his right hand as a sign of submission.

"Our father, my hand has touched the ground," he said.

"Uzowulu's body, do you know me?" asked the spirit.

"How can I know you, father? You are beyond our knowledge."

Evil Forest then turned to the other group and addressed the eldest of the three brothers.

"The body of Odukwe, I greet you," he said, and Odukwe bent down and touched the earth. The hearing then began.

Uzowulu stepped forward and presented his case.

"That woman standing there is my wife, Mgbafo. I married her with my money and my yams. I do not owe my in-laws anything. I owe them no yams. I owe them no coco-yams. One morning three of them came to my house, beat me up and took my wife and children away. This happened in the rainy season. I have waited in vain for my wife to return. At last I went to my in-laws and said to them, 'You have taken back your sister. I did not send her away. You yourselves took her. The law of the clan is that you should return her bride-price.' But my wife's brothers said they had nothing to tell me. So I have brought the matter to the fathers of the clan. My case is finished. I salute you."

"Your words are good," said the leader of the *egwugwu*. "Let us hear Odukwe. His words may also be good."

Odukwe was short and thickset. He stepped forward, saluted the spirits and began his story.

"My in-law has told you that we went to his house, beat him up and took our sister and her children away. All that is true. He told you that he came to take back her bride-price and we refused to give it him. That also is true. My in-law, Uzowulu, is a beast. My sister lived with him for nine years. During those years no single day passed in the sky without his beating the woman. We have tried to settle their quarrels time without number and on each occasion Uzowulu was guilty—"

"It is a lie!" Uzowulu shouted.

"Two years ago," continued Odukwe, "when she was pregnant, he beat her until she miscarried."

"It is a lie. She miscarried after she had gone to sleep with her lover."

"Uzowulu's body, I salute you," said Evil Forest, silencing him. "What kind of lover sleeps with a pregnant woman?" There was a loud murmur of approbation from the crowd. Odukwe continued:

"Last year when my sister was recovering from an illness, he beat her again so that if the neighbors had not gone in to save her she would have been killed. We heard of it, and did as you have been told. The law of Umuofia is that if a woman runs away from her husband her bride-price is returned. But in this case she ran away to save her life. Her two children belong to Uzowulu. We do not dispute it, but they are too young to leave their mother. If, in the other hand, Uzowulu should recover from his madness and come in the proper way to beg his wife to return she will do so on the understanding that if he ever beats her again we shall cut off his genitals for him."

The crowd roared with laughter. Evil Forest rose to his feet and order was immediately restored. A steady cloud of smoke rose from his head. He sat down again and called two witnesses. They were both Uzowulu's neighbors, and they agreed about the beating. Evil Forest then stood up, pulled out his staff and thrust it into the earth again. He ran a few steps in the direction of the women; they all fled in terror, only to return to their places almost immediately. The nine *egwugwu* then went away to consult together in their house. They were silent for a long time. Then the metal gong sounded and the flute was blown. The *egwugwu* had emerged once again from their underground home. They saluted one another and then reappeared on the *ilo*.

"*Umuofia kwenu!*" roared Evil Forest, facing the elders and grandees of the clan.

"*Yaa!*" replied the thunderous crowd; then silence descended from the sky and swallowed the noise.

Evil Forest began to speak and all the while he spoke everyone was silent. The eight other *egwugwu* were as still as statues.

"We have heard both sides of the case," said Evil Forest. "Our duty is not to blame this man or to praise that, but to settle the dispute." He turned to Uzowulu's group and allowed a short pause.

"Uzowulu's body, I salute you," he said.

"Our father, my hand has touched the ground," replied Uzowulu, touching the earth.

"Uzowulu's body, do you know me?"

"How can I know you, father? You are beyond our knowledge," Uzowulu replied.

"I am Evil Forest. I kill a man on the day that his life is sweetest to him."

"That is true," replied Uzowulu.

"Go to your in-laws with a pot of wine and beg your wife to return to you. It is not bravery when a man fights with a woman." He turned to Odukwe, and allowed a brief pause.

"Odukwe's body, I greet you," he said.

"My hand is on the ground," replied Odukwe.

"Do you know me?"

"No man can know you," replied Odukwe.

"I am Evil Forest, I am Dry-meat-that-fills-the-mouth, I am Fire-that-burns-without-faggots. If your in-law brings wine to you, let your sister go with him. I salute you." He pulled his staff from the hard earth and thrust it back.

"*Umuofia kwenu!*" he roared, and the crowd answered.

"I don't know why such a trifle should come before the *egwugwu*," said one elder to another.

"Don't you know what kind of man Uzowulu is? He will not listen to any other decision," replied the other.

As they spoke two other groups of people had replaced the first before the *egwugwu*, and a great land case began.

Chapter Eleven

THE NIGHT WAS IMPENETRABLY DARK. The moon had been rising later and later every night until now it was seen only at dawn. And whenever the moon forsook evening and rose at cock-crow the nights were as black as charcoal.

Ezinma and her mother sat on a mat on the floor after their supper of yam foo-foo and bitter-leaf soup. A palm-oil lamp gave out yellowish light. Without it, it would have been impossible to eat; one could not have known where one's mouth was in the darkness of that night. There was an oil lamp in all the four huts on Okonkwo's compound, and each hut seen from the others looked like a soft eye of yellow half-light set in the solid massiveness of night.

The world was silent except for the shrill cry of insects, which was part of the night, and the sound of wooden mortar and pestle as Nwayieke pounded her foo-foo. Nwayieke lived four compounds away, and she was notorious for her late cooking. Every woman in the neighborhood knew the sound of Nwayieke's mortar and pestle. It was also part of the night.

Okonkwo had eaten from his wives' dishes and was now reclining with his back against the wall. He searched his bag and brought out his snuff-bottle. He turned it on to his left palm, but nothing came out. He hit the bottle against his knee to shake up the tobacco. That was always the trouble with Okeke's snuff. It very quickly went damp, and there was too much saltpeter in it. Okonkwo had not bought snuff from him for a long time. Idigo was the man who knew how to grind good snuff. But he had recently fallen ill.

Low voices, broken now and again by singing, reached Okonkwo from his wives' huts as each woman and her children told folk stories. Ekwefi and her daughter, Ezinma, sat on a mat on the floor. It was Ekwefi's turn to tell a story.

"Once upon a time," she began, "all the birds were invited to a feast in the sky. They were very happy and began to prepare themselves for the great day. They painted their bodies with red cam wood and drew beautiful patterns on them with *uli*.

"Tortoise saw all these preparations and soon discovered what it all meant. Nothing that happened in the world of the animals ever escaped his notice; he was full of cunning. As soon as he heard of the great feast in the sky his throat began to itch at the very thought. There was a famine in those days and Tortoise had not eaten a good meal for two moons. His body rattled like a piece of dry stick in his empty shell. So he began to plan how he would go to the sky."

"But he had no wings," said Ezinma.

"Be patient," replied her mother. "That is the story. Tortoise had no wings, but he went to the birds and asked to be allowed to go with them.

" 'We know you too well,' said the birds when they had heard him. 'You are full of cunning and you are ungrateful. If we allow you to come with us you will soon begin your mischief.'

" 'You do not know me,' said Tortoise. 'I am a changed man. I have learned that a man who makes trouble for others is also making it for himself.'

"Tortoise had a sweet tongue, and within a short time all the birds agreed that he was a changed man, and they each gave him a feather, with which he made two wings.

"At last the great day came and Tortoise was the first to arrive at the meeting place. When all the birds had gathered together, they set off in a body. Tortoise was very happy and voluble as he flew among the birds, and he was soon chosen as the man to speak for the party because he was a great orator.

" 'There is one important thing which we must not forget,' he said as they flew on their way. 'When people are invited to a great feast like this, they take new names for the occasion. Our hosts in the sky will expect us to honor this age-old custom.'

"None of the birds had heard of this custom but they knew that Tortoise, in spite of his failings in other directions, was a widely-traveled man who knew the customs of different peoples. And so they each took a new name. When they had all taken, Tortoise also took one. He was to be called *All of you*.

"At last the party arrived in the sky and their hosts were very happy to see them. Tortoise stood up in his many-colored plumage and thanked them for their invitation. His speech was so eloquent that all the birds were glad they had brought him, and nodded their heads in approval of all he said. Their hosts took him as the king of the birds, especially as he looked somewhat different from the others.

"After kola nuts had been presented and eaten, the people of the sky set before their guests the most delectable dishes Tortoise had ever seen or dreamed of. The soup was brought out hot from the fire and in the very pot in which it had been cooked. It was full of meat and fish. Tortoise began to sniff aloud. There was pounded yam and also yam pottage cooked with palm-oil and fresh fish. There were also pots of palm-wine. When everything had been set before the guests, one of the people of the sky came forward and tasted a little from each pot. He then invited the birds to eat. But Tortoise jumped to his feet and asked: 'For whom have you prepared this feast?'

" 'For all of you,' replied the man.

"Tortoise turned to the birds and said: 'You remember that my name is *All of you*. The custom here is to serve the spokesman first and the others later. They will serve you when I have eaten.'

"He began to eat and the birds grumbled angrily. The people of the sky thought it must be their custom to leave all the food for their king. And so Tortoise ate the best part of the food and then drank two pots of palm-wine, so that he was full of food and drink and his body filled out in his shell.

"The birds gathered round to eat what was left and to peck at the bones he had thrown all about the floor. Some of them were too angry to eat. They chose to fly home on an empty stomach. But before they left each took back the feather he had lent to Tortoise. And there he stood in his hard shell full of food and wine but without any wings to fly home. He asked the birds to take a message for his wife, but they all refused. In the end Parrot, who had felt more angry than the others, suddenly changed his mind and agreed to take the message.

" 'Tell my wife,' said Tortoise, 'to bring out all the soft things in my house and cover the compound with them so that I can jump down from the sky without very great danger.'

"Parrot promised to deliver the message, and then flew away. But when he reached Tortoise's house he told his wife to bring out all the hard things in the house. And so she brought out her husband's hoes, machetes, spears, guns and even his cannon. Tortoise looked down from the sky and saw his wife bringing things out, but it was too far to see what they were. When all seemed ready he let himself go. He fell and fell and fell until he began to fear that he would never stop falling. And then like the sound of his cannon he crashed on the compound."

"Did he die?" asked Ezinma.

"No," replied Ekwefi. "His shell broke into pieces. But there was a great medicine man in the neighborhood. Tortoise's wife sent for him and he gathered all the bits of shell and stuck them together. That is why Tortoise's shell is not smooth."

"There is no song in the story," Ezinma pointed out.

"No," said Ekwefi. "I shall think of another one with a song. But it is your turn now."

"Once upon a time," Ezinma began, "Tortoise and Cat went to wrestle against Yams—no, that is not the beginning. Once upon a time there was a great famine in the land of animals. Everybody was lean except Cat, who was fat and whose body shone as if oil was rubbed on it . . . ”

She broke off because at that very moment a loud and high-pitched voice broke the outer silence of the night. It was Chielo, the priestess of Agbala, prophesying. There was nothing new in that. Once in a while Chielo was possessed by the spirit of her god and she began to prophesy. But tonight she was addressing her prophecy and greetings to Okonkwo, and so everyone in his family listened. The folk stories stopped.

“*Agbala do-o-o-o! Agbala ekeneo-o-o-o,*” came the voice like a sharp knife cutting through the night. “*Okonkwo! Agbala ekene gio-o-o-o! Agbala cholu ifu ada ya Ezinmao-o-o-o!*”

At the mention of Ezinma’s name Ekwefi jerked her head sharply like an animal that had sniffed death in the air. Her heart jumped painfully within her.

The priestess had now reached Okonkwo’s compound and was talking with him outside his hut. She was saying again and again that Agbala wanted to see his daughter, Ezinma. Okonkwo pleaded with her to come back in the morning because Ezinma was now asleep. But Chielo ignored what he was trying to say and went on shouting that Agbala wanted to see his daughter. Her voice was as clear as metal, and Okonkwo’s women and children heard from their huts all that she said. Okonkwo was still pleading that the girl had been ill of late and was asleep. Ekwefi quickly took her to their bedroom and placed her on their high bamboo bed.

The priestess screamed. “Beware, Okonkwo!” she warned. “Beware of exchanging words with Agbala. Does a man speak when a god speaks? Beware!”

She walked through Okonkwo’s hut into the circular compound and went straight toward Ekwefi’s hut. Okonkwo came after her.

“Ekwefi,” she called, “Agbala greets you. Where is my daughter, Ezinma? Agbala wants to see her.”

Ekwefi came out from her hut carrying her oil lamp in her left hand. There was a light wind blowing, so she cupped her right hand to shelter the flame. Nwoye’s mother, also carrying an oil lamp, emerged from her hut. The children stood in the darkness outside their hut watching the strange event. Okonkwo’s youngest wife also came out and joined the others.

“Where does Agbala want to see her?” Ekwefi asked.

“Where else but in his house in the hills and the caves?” replied the priestess.

“I will come with you, too,” Ekwefi said firmly.

“*Tufia-a!*” the priestess cursed, her voice cracking like the angry bark of thunder in the dry season. “How dare you, woman, to go before the mighty

Agbala of your own accord? Beware, woman, lest he strike you in his anger. Bring me my daugher."

Ekwefi went into her hut and came out again with Ezinma.

"Come, my daughter," said the priestess. "I shall carry you on my back. A baby on its mother's back does not know that the way is long."

Ezinma began to cry. She was used to Chielo calling her "my daughter." But it was a different Chielo she now saw in the yellow half-light.

"Don't cry, my daughter," said the priestess, "lest Agbala be angry with you."

"Don't cry," said Ekwefi, "she will bring you back very soon. I shall give you some fish to eat." She went into the hut again and brought down the smoke-black basket in which she kept her dried fish and other ingredients for cooking soup. She broke a piece in two and gave it to Ezinma, who clung to her.

"Don't be afraid," said Ekwefi, stroking her head, which was shaved in places, leaving a regular pattern of hair. They went outside again. The priestess bent down on one knee and Ezinma climbed on her back, her left palm closed on her fish and her eyes gleaming with tears.

"*Agbala do-o-o-o! Agbala ekeneo-o-o-o!* . . ." Chielo began once again to chant greetings to her god. She turned round sharply and walked through Okonkwo's hut, bending very low at the eaves. Ezinma was crying loudly now, calling on her mother. The two voices disappeared into the thick darkness.

A strange and sudden weakness descended on Ekwefi as she stood gazing in the direction of the voices like a hen whose only chick has been carried away by a kite. Ezinma's voice soon faded away and only Chielo was heard moving farther and farther into the distance.

"Why do you stand there as though she had been kidnapped?" asked Okonkwo as he went back to his hut.

"She will bring her back soon," Nwoye's mother said.

But Ekwefi did not hear these consolations. She stood for a while, and then, all of a sudden, made up her mind. She hurried through Okonkwo's hut and went outside. "Where are you going?" he asked.

"I am following Chielo," she replied and disappeared in the darkness. Okonkwo cleared his throat, and brought out his snuff-bottle from the goatskin bag by his side.

The priestess' voice was already growing faint in the distance. Ekwefi hurried to the main footpath and turned left in the direction of the voice. Her eyes were useless to her in the darkness. But she picked her way easily on the sandy footpath hedged on either side by branches and damp leaves. She began to run, holding her breasts with her hands to stop them flapping noisily against her body. She hit her left foot against an outcropped root, and terror seized her. It was an ill omen. She ran faster. But Chielo's voice was still a long way away. Had she been running too? How could she go so fast with Ezinma on her back? Although the night was cool, Ekwefi was beginning to feel hot from her running. She continually ran into the luxuriant weeds and creepers that walled in the path. Once she tripped up and fell. Only then did she realize, with a start, that Chielo had stopped her chanting. Her heart beat violently and she stood still. Then Chielo's renewed outburst came from only a few paces ahead. But Ekwefi could not see her. She shut her eyes for a while and opened them again in an effort to see. But it was useless. She could not see beyond her nose.

There were no stars in the sky because there was a raincloud. Fireflies went about with their tiny green lamps, which only made the darkness more profound. Between Chielo's outbursts the night was alive with the shrill tremor of forest insects woven into the darkness.

"*Agbala do-o-o-o!* . . . *Agbala ekeneo-o-o-o!* . . ." Ekwefi trudged behind, neither getting too near nor keeping too far back. She thought they must be going towards the sacred cave. Now that she walked slowly she had time to think. What would she do when they got to the cave? She would not dare to enter. She would wait at the mouth, all alone in that fearful place. She thought of all the terrors of the night. She remembered that night, long ago, when she had seen *Ogbu-agali-odu,* one of those evil essences loosed upon the world by the potent "medicines" which the tribe had made in the distant past against its enemies but had now forgotten how to control. Ekwefi had been returning from the stream with her mother on a dark night like this when they saw its glow as it flew in their direction. They had thrown down their waterpots and lain by the roadside expecting the sinister light to descend on them and kill them. That was the only time Ekwefi ever saw *Ogbu-agali-odu.* But although it had happened so long ago, her blood still ran cold whenever she remembered that night.

The priestess' voice came at longer intervals now, but its vigor was undiminished. The air was cool and damp with dew. Ezinma sneezed. Ekwefi muttered, "Life to you." At the same time the priestess also said, "Life to you, my daughter." Ezinma's voice from the darkness warmed her mother's heart. She trudged slowly along.

And then the priestess screamed. "Somebody is walking behind me!" she said. "Whether you are spirit or man, may Agbala shave your head with a blunt razor! May he twist your neck until you see your heels!"

Ekwefi stood rooted to the spot. One mind said to her: "Woman, go home before Agbala does you harm." But she could not. She stood until Chielo had increased the distance between them and she began to follow again. She had already walked so long that she began to feel a slight numbness in the limbs and in the head. Then it occurred to her that they could not have been heading for the cave. They must have bypassed it long ago; they must be going towards Umuachi, the farthest village in the clan. Chielo's voice now came after long intervals.

It seemed to Ekwefi that the night had become a little lighter. The cloud had lifted and a few stars were out. The moon must be preparing to rise, its sullenness over. When the moon rose late in the night, people said it was refusing food, as a sullen husband refuses his wife's food when they have quarrelled.

"*Agbala do-o-o-o! Umuachi! Agbala ekene unuo-o-o!*" It was just as Ekwefi had thought. The priestess was now saluting the village of Umuachi. It was unbelievable, the distance they had covered. As they emerged into the open village from the narrow forest track the darkness was softened and it became possible to see the vague shape of trees. Ekwefi screwed her eyes up in an effort to see her daughter and the priestess, but whenever she thought she saw their shape it immediately dissolved like a melting lump of darkness. She walked numbly along.

Chielo's voice was now rising continuously, as when she first set out. Ekwefi had a feeling of spacious openness, and she guessed they must be on the village *ilo*, or playground. And she realized too with something like a jerk that Chielo was no longer moving forward. She was, in fact, returning. Ekwefi quickly moved away from her line of retreat. Chielo passed by, and they began to go back the way they had come.

It was a long and weary journey and Ekwefi felt like a sleepwalker most of the way. The moon was definitely rising, and although it had not yet appeared on the sky its light had already melted down the darkness. Ekwefi could now discern the figure of the priestess and her burden. She slowed down her pace so as to increase the distance between them. She was afraid of what might happen if Chielo suddenly turned round and saw her.

She had prayed for the moon to rise. But now she found the half-light of the incipient moon more terrifying than darkness. The world was now peopled with vague, fantastic figures that dissolved under her steady gaze and then formed again in new shapes. At one stage Ekwefi was so afraid that she nearly called out to Chielo for companionship and human sympathy. What she had seen was the shape of a man climbing a palm tree, his head pointing to the earth and his legs skywards. But at that very moment Chielo's voice rose again in her possessed chanting, and Ekwefi recoiled, because there was no humanity there. It was not the same Chielo who sat with her in the market and sometimes bought beancakes for Ezinma, whom she called her daughter. It was a different woman—the priestess of Agbala, the Oracle of the Hills and Caves. Ekwefi trudged along between two fears. The sound of her benumbed steps seemed to come from some other person walking behind her. Her arms were folded across her bare breasts. Dew fell heavily and the air was cold. She could no longer think, not even about the terrors of night. She just jogged along in a half-sleep, only waking to full life when Chielo sang.

At last they took a turning and began to head for the caves. From then on, Chielo never ceased in her chanting. She greeted her god in a multitude of names—the owner of the future, the messenger of earth, the god who cut a man down when his life was sweetest to him. Ekwefi was also awakened and her benumbed fears revived.

The moon was now up and she could see Chielo and Ezinma clearly. How a woman could carry a child of that size so easily and for so long was a miracle. But Ekwefi was not thinking about that. Chielo was not a woman that night.

"*Agbala do-o-o-o! Agbala ekeneo-o-o-o! Chi negbu madu ubosi ndu ya nato ya uto daluo-o-o! . . .*"

Ekwefi could already see the hills looming in the moonlight. They formed a circular ring with a break at one point through which the foot-track led to the center of the circle.

As soon as the priestess stepped into this ring of hills her voice was not only doubled in strength but was thrown back on all sides. It was indeed the shrine of a great god. Ekwefi picked her way carefully and quietly. She was already beginning to doubt the wisdom of her coming. Nothing would happen to Ezinma, she thought. And if anything happened to her could she stop it? She would not dare to enter the underground caves. Her coming was quite useless, she thought.

As these things went through her mind she did not realize how close they were to the cave mouth. And so when the priestess with Ezinma on her back disappeared through a hole hardly big enough to pass a hen, Ekwefi broke into a run as though to stop them. As she stood gazing at the circular darkness which had swallowed them, tears gushed from her eyes, and she swore within her that if she heard Ezinma cry she would rush into the cave to defend her against all the gods in the world. She would die with her.

Having sworn that oath, she sat down on a stony ledge and waited. Her fear had vanished. She could hear the priestess' voice, all its metal taken out of it by the vast emptiness of the cave. She buried her face in her lap and waited.

She did not know how long she waited. It must have been a very long time. Her back was turned on the footpath that led out of the hills. She must have heard a noise behind her and turned round sharply. A man stood there with a machete in his hand. Ekwefi uttered a scream and sprang to her feet.

"Don't be foolish," said Okonkwo's voice. "I thought you were going into the shrine with Chielo," he mocked.

Ekwefi did not answer. Tears of gratitude filled her eyes. She kn daughter was safe.

"Go home and sleep," said Okonkwo. "I shall wait here."

"I shall wait too. It is almost dawn. The first cock has crowed."

As they stood there together, Ekwefi's mind went back to the days when they were young. She had married Anene because Okonkwo was too poor then to marry. Two years after her marriage to Anene she could bear it no longer and she ran away to Okonkwo. It had been early in the morning. The moon was shining. She was going to the stream to fetch water. Okonkwo's house was on the way to the stream. She went in and knocked at his door and he came out. Even in those days he was not a man of many words. He just carried her into his bed and in the darkness began to feel around her waist for the loose end of her cloth.

Chapter Twelve

ON THE FOLLOWING MORNING the entire neighborhood wore a festive air because Okonkwo's friend, Obierika, was celebrating his daughter's *uri*. It was the day on which her suitor (having already paid the greater part of her bride-price) would bring palm-wine not only to her parents and immediate relatives but to the wide and extensive group of kinsmen called *umunna*. Everybody had been invited—men, women and children. But it was really a woman's ceremony and the central figures were the bride and her mother.

As soon as day broke, breakfast was hastily eaten and women and children began to gather at Obierika's compound to help the bride's mother in her difficult but happy task of cooking for a whole village.

Okonkwo's family was astir like any other family in the neighborhood. Nwoye's mother and Okonkwo's youngest wife were ready to set out for Obierika's compound with all their children. Nwoye's mother carried a basket of coco-yams, a cake of salt and smoked fish which she would present to Obierika's wife. Okonkwo's youngest wife, Ojiugo, also had a basket of plantains and coco-yams and a small pot of palm-oil. Their children carried pots of water.

Ekwefi was tired and sleepy from the exhausting experiences of the previous night. It was not very long since they had returned. The priestess, with Ezinma sleeping on her back, had crawled out of the shrine on her belly like a snake. She had not as much as looked at Okonkwo and Ekwefi or shown any surprise at finding them at the mouth of the cave. She looked straight ahead of her and walked back to the village. Okonkwo and his wife followed at a respectful distance. They thought the priestess might be going to her house, but she went to Okonkwo's compound, passed through his *obi* and into Ekwefi's hut and walked into her bedroom. She placed Ezinma carefully on the bed and went away without saying a word to anybody.

Ezinma was still sleeping when everyone else was astir, and Ekwefi asked Nwoye's mother and Ojiugo to explain to Obierika's wife that she would be late. She had got ready her basket of coco-yams and fish, but she must wait for Ezinma to wake.

"You need some sleep yourself," said Nwoye's mother. "You look very tired."

As they spoke Ezinma emerged from the hut, rubbing her eyes and stretching her spare frame. She saw the other children with their water-pots and remembered that they were going to fetch water for Obierika's wife. She went back to the hut and brought her pot.

"Have you slept enough?" asked her mother.

"Yes," she replied. "Let us go."

"Not before you have had your breakfast," said Ekwefi. And she went into her hut to warm the vegetable soup she had cooked last night.

"We shall be going," said Nwoye's mother. "I will tell Obierika's wife that you are coming later." And so they all went to help Obierika's wife—Nwoye's mother with her four children and Ojiugo with her two.

As they trooped through Okonkwo's *obi* he asked: "Who will prepare my afternoon meal?"

"I shall return to do it," said Ojiugo.

Okonkwo was also feeling tired, and sleepy, for although nobody else knew it, he had not slept at all last night. He had felt very anxious but did not show it. When Ekwefi had followed the priestess, he had allowed what he regarded as a reasonable and manly interval to pass and then gone with his machete to the shrine, where he thought they must be. It was only when he had got there that it had occurred to him that the priestess might have chosen to go round the villages first. Okonkwo had returned home and sat waiting. When he thought he had waited long enough he again returned to the shrine. But the Hills and the Caves were as silent as death. It was only on his fourth trip that he had found Ekwefi, and by then he had become gravely worried.

Obierika's compound was as busy as an anthill. Temporary cooking tripods were erected on every available space by bringing together three blocks of sun-dried earth and making a fire in their midst. Cooking pots went up and down the tripods, and foo-foo was pounded in a hundred wooden mortars. Some of the women cooked the yams and the cassava, and others prepared vegetable soup. Young men pounded the foo-foo or split firewood. The children made endless trips to the stream.

Three young men helped Obierika to slaughter the two goats with which the soup was made. They were very fat goats, but the fattest of all was tethered to a peg near the wall of the compound. It was as big as a small cow. Obierika had sent one of his relatives all the way to Umuike to buy that goat. It was the one he would present alive to his in-laws.

"The market of Umuike is a wonderful place," said the young man who had been sent by Obierika to buy the giant goat. "There are so many people on it that if you threw up a grain of sand it would not find a way to fall to earth again."

"It is the result of a great medicine," said Obierika. "The people of Umuike wanted their market to grow and swallow up the markets of their neighbors. So they made a powerful medicine. Every market day, before the first cock-crow, this medicine stands on the market ground in the shape of an old woman with a fan. With this magic fan she beckons to the market all the neighboring clans. She beckons in front of her and behind her, to her right and to her left."

"And so everybody comes," said another man, "honest men and thieves. They can steal your cloth from off your waist in that market."

"Yes," said Obierika. "I warned Nwankwo to keep a sharp eye and a sharp ear. There was once a man who went to sell a goat. He led it on a thick rope which he tied round his wrist. But as he walked through the market he realized that people were pointing at him as they do to a madman. He could not understand it until he looked back and saw that what he led at the end of the tether was not a goat but a heavy log of wood."

"Do you think a thief can do that kind of thing single-handed?" asked Nwankwo.

"No," said Obierika. "They use medicine."

When they had cut the goats' throats and collected the blood in a bowl, they held them over an open fire to burn off the hair, and the smell of burning hair blended with the smell of cooking. Then they washed them and cut them up for the women who prepared the soup.

All this anthill activity was going smoothly when a sudden interruption came. It was a cry in the distance: *Oji odu achu ijiji-o-o!* (*The one that uses its tail to drive flies away!*) Every woman immediately abandoned whatever she was doing and rushed out in the direction of the cry.

"We cannot all rush out like that, leaving what we are cooking to burn in the fire," shouted Chielo, the priestess. "Three or four of us should stay behind."

"It is true," said another woman. "We will allow three or four women to stay behind."

Five women stayed behind to look after the cooking-pots, and all the rest rushed away to see the cow that had been let loose. When they saw it they drove it back to its owner, who at once paid the heavy fine which the village imposed on anyone whose cow was let loose on his neighbors' crops. When the women had exacted the penalty they checked among themselves to see if any woman had failed to come out when the cry had been raised.

"Where is Mgbogo?" asked one of them.

"She is ill in bed," said Mgbogo's next-door neighbor. "She has *iba*."

"The only other person is Udenkwo," said another woman, "and her child is not twenty-eight days yet."

Those women whom Obierika's wife had not asked to help her with the cooking returned to their homes, and the rest went back, in a body, to Obierika's compound.

"Whose cow was it?" asked the women who had been allowed to stay behind.

"It was my husband's," said Ezelagbo. "One of the young children had opened the gate of the cow-shed."

Early in the afternoon the first two pots of palm-wine arrived from Obierika's in-laws. They were duly presented to the women, who drank a cup or two each, to help them in their cooking. Some of it also went to the bride and her attendant maidens, who were putting the last delicate touches of razor to her coiffure and cam wood on her smooth skin.

When the heat of the sun began to soften, Obierika's son, Maduka, took a long broom and swept the ground in front of his father's *obi*. And as if they had been waiting for that, Obierika's relatives and friends began to arrive, every man with his goatskin bag hung on one shoulder and a rolled goatskin mat under his arm. Some of them were accompanied by their sons bearing carved wooden stools. Okonkwo was one of them. They sat in a half-circle and began to talk of many things. It would not be long before the suitors came.

Okonkwo brought out his snuff-bottle and offered it to Ogbuefi Ezenwa, who sat next to him. Ezenwa took it, tapped it on his kneecap, rubbed his left palm on his body to dry it before tipping a little snuff into it. His actions were deliberate, and he spoke as he performed them:

"I hope our in-laws will bring many pots of wine. Although they come from a village that is known for being closefisted, they ought to know that Akueke is the bride for a king."

"They dare not bring fewer than thirty pots," said Okonkwo. "I shall tell them my mind if they do."

At that moment Obierika's son, Maduka, led out the giant goat from the inner compound, for his father's relatives to see. They all admired it and said that that was the way things should be done. The goat was then led back to the inner compound.

Very soon after, the in-laws began to arrive. Young men and boys in single file, each carrying a pot of wine, came first. Obierika's relatives counted the pots as they came. Twenty, twenty-five. There was a long break, and the hosts looked at each other as if to say, "I told you." Then more pots came. Thirty, thirty-five, forty, forty-five. The hosts nodded in approval and seemed to say, "Now they are behaving like men." Altogether there were fifty pots of wine. After the pot-bearers came Ibe, the suitor, and the elders of his family. They sat in a half-moon, thus completing a circle with their hosts. The pots of wine stood in their midst. Then the bride, her mother and half a dozen other women and girls emerged from the inner compound, and went round the circle shaking hands with all. The bride's mother led the way, followed by the bride and the other women. The married women wore their best cloths and the girls wore red and black waistbeads and anklets of brass.

When the women retired, Obierika presented kola nuts to his in-laws. His eldest brother broke the first one. "Life to all of us," he said as he broke it. "And let there be friendship between your family and ours."

The crowd answered: *"Ee-e-e!"*

"We are giving you our daughter today. She will be a good wife to you. She will bear you nine sons like the mother of our town."

"Ee-e-e!"

The oldest man in the camp of the visitors replied: "It will be good for you and it will be good for us."

"Ee-e-e!"

"This is not the first time my people have come to marry your daughter. My mother was one of you."

"Ee-e-e!"

"And this will not be the last, because you understand us and we understand you. You are a great family."

"Ee-e-e!"

"Prosperous men and great warriors." He looked in the direction of Okonkwo. "Your daughter will bear us sons like you."

"Ee-e-e!"

The kola was eaten and the drinking of palm-wine began. Groups of four or five men sat round with a pot in their midst. As the evening wore on, food was presented to the guests. There were huge bowls of foo-foo and steaming pots of soup. There were also pots of yam pottage. It was a great feast.

As night fell, burning torches were set on wooden tripods and the young men raised a song. The elders sat in a big circle and the singers went round singing each man's praise as they came before him. They had something to say for every man. Some were great farmers, some were orators who spoke for the clan; Okonkwo was the greatest wrestler and warrior alive. When they had gone round the circle they settled down in the center, and girls came from the inner compound to dance. At first the bride was not among them. But when she finally appeared holding a cock in her right hand, a

loud cheer rose from the crowd. All the other dancers made w
presented the cock to the musicians and began to dance. Her l
rattled as she danced and her body gleamed with cam wood in
low light. The musicians with their wood, clay and metal instru
from song to song. And they were all gay. They sang the latest s
village:

"If I hold her hand
     She says, 'Don't touch!'
If I hold her foot
     She says, 'Don't touch!'
But when I hold her waist beads
     She pretends not to know."

The night was already far spent when the guests rose to go, taking their
bride home to spend seven market weeks with her suitor's family. They sang
songs as they went, and on their way they paid short courtesy visits to
prominent men like Okonkwo, before they finally left for their village.
Okonkwo made a present of two cocks to them.

Chapter Thirteen

GO-DI-DI-GO-GO-DI-GO. DI-GO-GO-DI-GO. It was the *ekwe* talking to the clan. One of the things every man learned was the language of the hollowed-out wooden instrument. Diim! Diim! Diim! boomed the cannon at intervals.

The first cock had not crowed, and Umuofia was still swallowed up in sleep and silence when the *ekwe* began to talk, and the cannon shattered the silence. Men stirred on their bamboo beds and listened anxiously. Somebody was dead. The cannon seemed to rend the sky. Di-go-go-di-go-di-di-go-go floated in the message-laden night air. The faint and distant wailing of women settled like a sediment of sorrow on the earth. Now and again a full-chested lamentation rose above the wailing whenever a man came into the place of death. He raised his voice once or twice in manly sorrow and then sat down with the other men listening to the endless wailing of the women and the esoteric language of the *ekwe*. Now and again the cannon boomed. The wailing of the women would not be heard beyond the village, but the *ekwe* carried the news to all the nine villages and even beyond. It began by naming the clan: *Umuofia obodo dike,* "the land of the brave." *Umuofia obodo dike! Umuofia obodo dike!* It said this over and over again, and as it dwelt on it, anxiety mounted in every heart that heaved on a bamboo bed that night. Then it went nearer and named the village: "*Iguedo of the yellow grinding-stone!*" It was Okonkwo's village. Again and again Iguedo was called and men waited breathlessly in all the nine villages. At last the man was named and people sighed "E-u-u, Ezeudu is dead." A cold shiver ran down Okonkwo's back as he remembered the last time the old man had visited him. "That boy calls you father," he had said. "Bear no hand in his death."

Ezeudu was a great man, and so all the clan was at his funeral. The ancient drums of death beat, guns and cannon were fired, and men dashed about in frenzy, cutting down every tree or animal they saw, jumping over walls and dancing on the roof. It was a warrior's funeral, and from morning till night warriors came and went in their age groups. They all wore smoked raffia skirts and their bodies were painted with chalk and charcoal. Now and again an ancestral spirit or *egwugwu* appeared from the underworld, speaking in a tremulous, unearthly voice and completely covered in raffia. Some of them were very violent, and there had been a mad rush for shelter earlier in the day when one appeared with a sharp machete and was only prevented from doing serious harm by two men who restrained him with the help of a strong rope tied round his waist. Sometimes he turned round and chased those men, and they ran for their lives. But they always returned to the long rope he trailed behind. He sang, in a terrifying voice, that Ekwensu, or Evil Spirit, had entered his eye.

But the most dreaded of all was yet to come. He was always alone and was shaped like a coffin. A sickly odor hung in the air wherever he went, and flies went with him. Even the greatest medicine men took shelter when he was near. Many years ago another *egwugwu* had dared to stand his ground before him and had been transfixed to the spot for two days. This one had only one hand and it carried a basket full of water.

But some of the *egwugwu* were quite harmless. One of them was so old and infirm that he leaned heavily on a stick. He walked unsteadily to the place where the corpse was laid, gazed at it a while and went away again—to the underworld.

The land of the living was not far removed from the domain of the ancestors. There was coming and going between them, especially at festivals and also when an old man died, because an old man was very close to the ancestors. A man's life from birth to death was a series of transition rites which brought him nearer and nearer to his ancestors.

Ezeudu had been the oldest man in his village, and at his death there were only three men in the whole clan who were older, and four or five others in his own age group. Whenever one of these ancient men appeared in the crowd to dance unsteadily the funeral steps of the tribe, younger men gave way and the tumult subsided.

It was a great funeral, such as befitted a noble warrior. As the evening drew near, the shouting and the firing of guns, the beating of drums and the brandishing and clanging of machetes increased.

Ezeudu had taken three titles in his life. It was a rare achievement. There were only four titles in the clan, and only one or two men in any generation ever achieved the fourth and highest. When they did, they became the lords of the land. Because he had taken titles, Ezeudu was to be buried after dark with only a glowing brand to light the sacred ceremony.

But before this quiet and final rite, the tumult increased tenfold. Drums beat violently and men leaped up and down in frenzy. Guns were fired on all sides and sparks flew out as machetes clanged together in warriors' salutes. The air was full of dust and the smell of gunpowder. It was then that the one-handed spirit came, carrying a basket full of water. People made way for him on all sides and the noise subsided. Even the smell of gunpowder was swallowed in the sickly smell that now filled the air. He danced a few steps to the funeral drums and then went to see the corpse.

"Ezeudu!" he called in his guttural voice. "If you had been poor in your last life I would have asked you to be rich when you come again. But you were rich. If you had been a coward, I would have asked you to bring courage. But you were a fearless warrior. If you had died young, I would have asked you to get life. But you lived long. So I shall ask you to come again the way you came before. If your death was the death of nature, go in peace. But if a man caused it, do not allow him a moment's rest." He danced a few more steps and went away.

The drums and the dancing began again and reached fever-heat. Darkness was around the corner, and the burial was near. Guns fired the last salute and the cannon rent the sky. And then from the center of the delirious fury came a cry of agony and shouts of horror. It was as if a spell had been cast. All was silent. In the center of the crowd a boy lay in a pool of blood. It was the dead man's sixteen-year-old son, who with his brothers and half-brothers had been dancing the traditional farewell to their father. Okonkwo's gun had exploded and a piece of iron had pierced the boy's heart.

The confusion that followed was without parallel in the tradition of Umuofia. Violent deaths were frequent, but nothing like this had ever happened.

The only course open to Okonkwo was to flee from the clan. It was a crime against the earth goddess to kill a clansman, and a man who committed it must flee from the land. The crime was of two kinds, male and female. Okonkwo had committed the female, because it had been inadvertent. He could return to the clan after seven years.

That night he collected his most valuable belongings into head-loads. His wives wept bitterly and their children wept with them without knowing why. Obierika and half a dozen other friends came to help and to console him. They each made nine or ten trips carrying Okonkwo's yams to store in Obierika's barn. And before the cock crowed Okonkwo and his family were fleeing to his motherland. It was a little village called Mbanta, just beyond the borders of Mbaino.

As soon as the day broke, a large crowd of men from Ezeudu's quarter stormed Okonkwo's compound, dressed in garbs of war. They set fire to his houses, demolished his red walls, killed his animals and destroyed his barn. It was the justice of the earth goddess, and they were merely her messengers. They had no hatred in their hearts against Okonkwo. His greatest friend,

Obierika, was among them. They were merely cleansing the land which Okonkwo had polluted with the blood of a clansman.

Obierika was a man who thought about things. When the will of the goddess had been done, he sat down in his *obi* and mourned his friend's calamity. Why should a man suffer so grievously for an offense he had committed inadvertently? But although he thought for a long time he found no answer. He was merely led into greater complexities. He remembered his wife's twin children, whom he had thrown away. What crime had they committed? The Earth had decreed that they were an offense on the land and must be destroyed. And if the clan did not exact punishment for an offense against the great goddess, her wrath was loosed on all the land and not just on the offender. As the elders said, if one finger brought oil it soiled the others.

Part Two

Part Two

Chapter
Fourteen

Okonkwo was well received by his mother's kinsmen in Mbanta. The old man who received him was his mother's younger brother, who was now the eldest surviving member of that family. His name was Uchendu, and it was he who had received Okonkwo's mother twenty and ten years before when she had been brought home from Umuofia to be buried with her people. Okonkwo was only a boy then and Uchendu still remembered him crying the traditional farewell: "Mother, mother, mother is going."

That was many years ago. Today Okonkwo was not bringing his mother home to be buried with her people. He was taking his family of three wives and their children to seek refuge in his motherland. As soon as Uchendu saw him with his sad and weary company he guessed what had happened, and asked no questions. It was not until the following day that Okonkwo told him the full story. The old man listened silently to the end and then said with some relief: "It is a female *ochu*." And he arranged the requisite rites and sacrifices.

Okonkwo was given a plot of ground on which to build his compound, and two or three pieces of land on which to farm during the coming planting season. With the help of his mother's kinsmen he built himself an *obi* and three huts for his wives. He then installed his personal god and the symbols of his departed fathers. Each of Uchendu's fine sons contributed three hundred seed-yams to enable their cousin to plant a farm, for as soon as the first rain came farming would begin.

At last the rain came. It was sudden and tremendous. For two or three moons the sun had been gathering strength till it seemed to breathe a breath of fire on the earth. All the grass had long been scorched brown, and the sands felt like live coals to the feet. Evergreen trees wore a dusty coat of brown. The birds were silenced in the forests, and the world lay panting under the live, vibrating heat. And then came the clap of thunder. It was an angry, metallic and thirsty clap, unlike the deep and liquid rumbling of the rainy season. A mighty wind arose and filled the air with dust. Palm trees swayed as the wind combed their leaves into flying crests like strange and fantastic coiffure.

hen the rain finally came, it was in large, solid drops of frozen water which the people called "the nuts of the water of heaven." They were hard and painful on the body as they fell, yet young people ran about happily picking up the cold nuts and throwing them into their mouths to melt.

The earth quickly came to life and the birds in the forests fluttered around and chirped merrily. A vague scent of life and green vegetation was diffused in the air. As the rain began to fall more soberly and in smaller liquid drops, children sought for shelter, and all were happy, refreshed and thankful.

Okonkwo and his family worked very hard to plant a new farm. But it was like beginning life anew without the vigor and enthusiasm of youth, like learning to become left-handed in old age. Work no longer had for him the pleasure it used to have, and when there was no work to do he sat in a silent half-sleep.

His life had been ruled by a great passion—to become one of the lords of the clan. That had been his life-spring. And he had all but achieved it. Then everything had been broken. He had been cast out of his clan like a fish onto a dry, sandy beach, panting. Clearly his personal god or *chi* was not made for great things. A man could not rise beyond the destiny of his *chi*. The saying of the elders was not true—that if a man said yea his *chi* also affirmed. Here was a man whose *chi* said nay despite his own affirmation.

The old man, Uchendu, saw clearly that Okonkwo had yielded to despair and he was greatly troubled. He would speak to him after the *isa-ifi* ceremony.

The youngest of Uchendu's five sons, Amikwu, was marrying a new wife. The bride-price had been paid and all but the last ceremony had been performed. Amikwu and his people had taken palm-wine to the bride's kinsmen about two moons before Okonkwo's arrival in Mbanta. And so it was time for the final ceremony of confession.

The daughters of the family were all there, some of them having come a long way from their homes in distant villages. Uchendu's eldest daughter had come from Obodo, nearly half a day's journey away. The daughters of Uchendu's brothers were also there. It was a full gathering of *umuada*, in the same way as they would meet if a death occurred in the family. There were twenty-two of them.

They sat in a big circle on the ground and the bride sat in the center with a hen in her right hand. Uchendu sat by her, holding the ancestral staff of the family. All the other men stood outside the circle, watching. Their wives watched also. It was evening and the sun was setting.

Uchendu's eldest daughter, Njide, asked the questions.

"Remember that if you do not answer truthfully you will suffer or even die at childbirth," she began. "How many men have lain with you since my brother first expressed the desire to marry you?"

"None," she answered simply.

"Answer truthfully," urged the other women.

"None?" asked Njide.

"None," she answered.

"Swear on this staff of my fathers," said Uchendu.

"I swear," said the bride.

Uchendu took the hen from her, slit its throat with a sharp knife and allowed some of the blood to fall on his ancestral staff.

From that day Amikwu took the young bride to his hut and she became his wife. The daughters of the family did not return to their homes immediately but spent two or three days with their kinsmen.

On the second day Uchendu called together his sons and daughters and his nephew, Okonkwo. The men brought their goatskin mats, with which they sat on the floor, and the women sat on a sisal mat spread on a raised bank of earth. Uchendu pulled gently at his gray beard and gnashed his teeth. Then he began to speak, quietly and deliberately, picking his words with great care:

"It is Okonkwo that I primarily wish to speak to," he began. "But I want all of you to note what I am going to say. I am an old man and you are all children. I know more about the world than any of you. If there is any one among you who thinks he knows more let him speak up." He paused, but no one spoke.

"Why is Okonkwo with us today? This is not his clan. We are only his mother's kinsmen. He does not belong here. He is an exile, condemned for seven years to live in a strange land. And so he is bowed with grief. But there is just one question I would like to ask him. Can you tell me, Okonkwo, why it is that one of the commonest names we give our children is Nneka, or "Mother is Supreme?" We all know that a man is the head of the family and his wives do his bidding. A child belongs to its father and his family and not to its mother and her family. A man belongs to his fatherland and not to his motherland. And yet we say Nneka—'Mother is Supreme.' Why is that?"

There was silence. "I want Okonkwo to answer me," said Uchendu.

"I do not know the answer," Okonkwo replied.

"You do not know the answer? So you see that you are a child. You have many wives and many children—more children than I have. You are a great man in your clan. But you are still a child, my child. Listen to me and I shall tell you. But there is one more question I shall ask you. Why is it that when a woman dies she is taken home to be buried with her own kinsmen? She is

with her husband's kinsmen. Why is that? Your mother was
ome to me and buried with my people. Why was that?"
kwo shook his head.

oes not know that either," said Uchendu, "and yet he is full of sorrow because he has come to live in his motherland for a few years." He
laughed a mirthless laughter, and turned to his sons and daughters. "What
about you? Can you answer my question?"

They all shook their heads.

"Then listen to me," he said and cleared his throat. "It's true that a child
belongs to its father. But when a father beats his child, it seeks sympathy in
its mother's hut. A man belongs to his fatherland when things are good and
life is sweet. But when there is sorrow and bitterness he finds refuge in his
motherland. Your mother is there to protect you. She is buried there. And
that is why we say that mother is supreme. Is it right that you, Okonkwo,
should bring to your mother a heavy face and refuse to be comforted? Be
careful or you may displease the dead. Your duty is to comfort your wives
and children and take them back to your fatherland after seven years. But if
you allow sorrow to weigh you down and kill you, they will all die in exile."
He paused for a long while. "These are now your kinsmen." He waved at his
sons and daughters. "You think you are the greatest sufferer in the world? Do
you know that men are sometimes banished for life? Do you know that men
sometimes lose all their yams and even their children? I had six wives once.
I have none now except that young girl who knows not her right from her
left. Do you know how many children I have buried—children I begot in
my youth and strength? Twenty-two. I did not hang myself, and I am still
alive. If you think you are the greatest sufferer in the world ask my daughter,
Akueni, how many twins she has borne and thrown away. Have you not
heard the song they sing when a woman dies?

" 'For whom is it well, for whom is it well?
There is no one for whom it is well.'

"I have no more to say to you."

Chapter Fifteen

It was in the second year of Okonkwo's exile that his friend, Obierika, came to visit him. He brought with him two young men, each of them carrying a heavy bag on his head. Okonkwo helped them put down their loads. It was clear that the bags were full of cowries.

Okonkwo was very happy to receive his friend. His wives and children were very happy too, and so were his cousins and their wives when he sent for them and told them who his guest was.

"You must take him to salute our father," said one of the cousins.

"Yes," replied Okonkwo. "We are going directly." But before they went he whispered something to his first wife. She nodded, and soon the children were chasing one of their cocks.

Uchendu had been told by one of his grandchildren that three strangers had come to Okonkwo's house. He was therefore waiting to receive them. He held out his hands to them when they came into his *obi*, and after they had shaken hands he asked Okonkwo who they were.

"This is Obierika, my great friend. I have already spoken to you about him."

"Yes," said the old man, turning to Obierika. "My son has told me about you, and I am happy you have come to see us. I knew your father, Iweka. He was a great man. He had many friends here and came to see them quite often. Those were good days when a man had friends in distant clans. Your generation does not know that. You stay at home, afraid of your next-door neighbor. Even a man's motherland is strange to him nowadays." He looked at Okonkwo. "I am an old man and I like to talk. That is all I am good for now." He got up painfully, went into an inner room and came back with a kola nut.

"Who are the young men with you?" he asked as he sat down again on his goatskin. Okonkwo told him.

"Ah," he said. "Welcome, my sons." He presented the kola nut to them, and when they had seen it and thanked him, he broke it and they ate.

"Go into that room," he said to Okonkwo, pointing with his finger. "You will find a pot of wine there."

Okonkwo brought the wine and they began to drink. It was a day old, and very strong.

"Yes," said Uchendu after a long silence. "People traveled more in those days. There is not a single clan in these parts that I do not know very well. Aninta, Umuazu, Ikeocha, Elumelu, Abame—I know them all."

"Have you heard," asked Obierika, "that Abame is no more?"

"How is that?" asked Uchendu and Okonkwo together.

"Abame has been wiped out," said Obierika. "It is a strange and terrible story. If I had not seen the few survivors with my own eyes and heard their story with my own ears, I would not have believed. Was it not on an Eke day that they fled into Umuofia?" he asked his two companions, and they nodded their heads.

"Three moons ago," said Obierika, "on an Eke market day a little band of fugitives came into our town. Most of them were sons of our land whose mothers had been buried with us. But there were some too who came because they had friends in our town, and others who could think of nowhere else open to escape. And so they fled into Umuofia with a woeful story." He drank his palm-wine, and Okonkwo filled his horn again. He continued:

"During the last planting season a white man had appeared in their clan."

"An albino," suggested Okonkwo.

"He was not an albino. He was quite different." He sipped his wine. "And he was riding an iron horse. The first people who saw him ran away, but he stood beckoning to them. In the end the fearless ones went near and even touched him. The elders consulted their Oracle and it told them that the strange man would break their clan and spread destruction among them." Obierika again drank a little of his wine. "And so they killed the white man and tied his iron horse to their sacred tree because it looked as if it would run away to call the man's friends. I forgot to tell you another thing which the Oracle said. It said that other white men were on their way. They were locusts, it said, and that first man was their harbinger sent to explore the terrain. And so they killed him."

"What did the white man say before they killed him?" asked Uchendu.

"He said nothing," answered one of Obierika's companions.

"He said something, only they did not understand him," said Obierika. "He seemed to speak through his nose."

"One of the men told me," said Obierika's other companion, "that he repeated over and over again a word that resembled Mbaino. Perhaps he had been going to Mbaino and had lost his way."

"Anyway," resumed Obierika, "they killed him and tied up his iron horse. This was before the planting season began. For a long time nothing happened. The rains had come and yams had been sown. The iron horse was still tied to the sacred silk-cotton tree. And then one morning three white men led by a band of ordinary men like us came to the clan. They saw the iron horse and went away again. Most of the men and women of Abame had gone to their farms. Only a few of them saw these white men and their followers. For many market weeks nothing else happened. They have a big market in Abame on every other Afo day and, as you know, the whole clan gathers there. That was the day it happened. The three white men and a very large number of other men surrounded the market. They must have used a powerful medicine to make themselves invisible until the market was full. And they began to shoot. Everybody was killed, except the old and the sick who were at home and a handful of men and women whose *chi* were wide awake and brought them out of that market." He paused.

"Their clan is now completely empty. Even the sacred fish in their mysterious lake have fled and the lake has turned the color of blood. A great evil has come upon their land as the Oracle had warned."

There was a long silence. Uchendu ground his teeth together audibly. Then he burst out:

"Never kill a man who says nothing. Those men of Abame were fools. What did they know about the man?" He ground his teeth again and told a story to illustrate his point. "Mother Kite once sent her daughter to bring food. She went, and brought back a duckling. 'You have done very well,' said Mother Kite to her daughter, 'but tell me, what did the mother of this duckling say when you swooped and carried its child away?' 'It said nothing,' replied the young kite. 'It just walked away.' 'You must return the duckling,' said Mother Kite. 'There is something ominous behind the silence.' And so Daughter Kite returned the duckling and took a chick instead. 'What did the mother of this chick do?' asked the old kite. 'It cried and raved and cursed at me,' said the young kite. 'Then we can eat the chick,' said her mother. 'There is nothing to fear from someone who shouts.' Those men of Abame were fools."

"They were fools," said Okonkwo after a pause. "They had been warned that danger was ahead. They should have armed themselves with their guns and their machetes even when they went to market."

"They have paid for their foolishness," said Obierika. "But I am greatly afraid. We have heard stories about white men who made the powerful guns and the strong drinks and took slaves away across the seas, but no one thought the stories were true."

"There is no story that is not true," said Uchendu. "The world has no end, and what is good among one people is an abomination with others. We have albinos among us. Do you not think that they came to our clan by mistake, that they have strayed from their way to a land where everybody is like them?"

Okonkwo's first wife soon finished her cooking and set before their guests a big meal of pounded yams and bitter-leaf soup. Okonkwo's son, Nwoye, brought in a pot of sweet wine tapped from the raffia palm.

"You are a big man now," Obierika said to Nwoye. "Your friend Anene asked me to greet you."

"Is he well?" asked Nwoye.

"We are all well," said Obierika.

Ezinma brought them a bowl of water with which to wash their hands. After that they began to eat and to drink the wine.

"When did you set out from home?" asked Okonkwo.

"We had meant to set out from my house before cock-crow," said Obierika. "But Nweke did not appear until it was quite light. Never make an early morning appointment with a man who has just married a new wife." They all laughed.

"Has Nweke married a wife?" asked Okonkwo.

"He has married Okadigbo's second daughter," said Obierika.

"That is very good," said Okonkwo. "I do not blame you for not hearing the cock crow."

When they had eaten, Obierika pointed at the two heavy bags.

"That is the money from your yams," he said. "I sold the big ones as soon as you left. Later on I sold some of the seed-yams and gave out others to sharecroppers. I shall do that every year until you return. But I thought you would need the money now and so I brought it. Who knows what may happen tomorrow? Perhaps green men will come to our clan and shoot us."

"God will not permit it," said Okonkwo. "I do not know how to thank you."

"I can tell you," said Obierika. "Kill one of your sons for me."

"That will not be enough," said Okonkwo.

"Then kill yourself," said Obierika.

"Forgive me," said Okonkwo, smiling. "I shall not talk about thanking you any more."

Chapter Sixteen

WHEN NEARLY TWO YEARS LATER Obierika paid another visit to his friend in exile the circumstances were less happy. The missionaries had come to Umuofia. They had built their church there, won a handful of converts and were already sending evangelists to the surrounding towns and villages. That was a source of great sorrow to the leaders of the clan; but many of them believed that the strange faith and the white man's god would not last. None of his converts was a man whose word was heeded in the assembly of the people. None of them was a man of title. They were mostly the kind of people that were called *efulefu*, worthless, empty men. The imagery of an *efulefu* in the language of the clan was a man who sold his machete and wore the sheath to battle. Chielo, the priestess of Agbala, called the converts the excrement of the clan, and the new faith was a mad dog that had come to eat it up.

What moved Obierika to visit Okonkwo was the sudden appearance of the latter's son, Nwoye, among the missionaries in Umuofia.

"What are you doing here?" Obierika had asked when after many difficulties the missionaries had allowed him to speak to the boy.

"I am one of them," replied Nwoye.

"How is your father?" Obierika asked, not knowing what else to say.

"I don't know. He is not my father," said Nwoye, unhappily.

And so Obierika went to Mbanta to see his friend. And he found that Okonkwo did not wish to speak about Nwoye. It was only from Nwoye's mother that he heard scraps of the story.

The arrival of the missionaries had caused a considerable stir in the village of Mbanta. There were six of them and one was a white man. Every man and woman came out to see the white man. Stories about these strange men had grown since one of them had been killed in Abame and his iron horse tied to the sacred silk-cotton tree. And so everybody came to see the white man. It was the time of the year when everybody was at home. The harvest was over.

When they had all gathered, the white man began to speak to them. He spoke through an interpreter who was an Ibo man, though his dialect was different and harsh to the ears of Mbanta. Many people laughed at his dialect and the way he used words strangely. Instead of saying "myself" he always said "my buttocks." But he was a man of commanding presence and the clansmen listened to him. He said he was one of them, as they could see from his color and his language. The other four black men were also their brothers, although one of them did not speak Ibo. The white man was also their brother because they were all sons of God. And he told them about this new God, the Creator of all the world and all the men and women. He told them that they worshipped false gods, gods of wood and stone. A deep murmur went through the crowd when he said this. He told them that the true God lived on high and that all men when they died went before Him for judgment. Evil men and all the heathens who in their blindness bowed to wood and stone were thrown into a fire that burned like palm-oil. But good men who worshipped the true God lived forever in His happy kingdom. "We have been sent by this great God to ask you to leave your wicked ways and false gods and turn to Him so that you may be saved when you die," he said.

"Your buttocks understand our language," said someone light-heartedly and the crowd laughed.

"What did he say?" the white man asked his interpreter. But before he could answer, another man asked a question. "Where is the white man's horse?" he asked. The Ibo evangelists consulted among themselves and decided that the man probably meant bicycle. They told the white man and he smiled benevolently.

"Tell them," he said, "that I shall bring many iron horses when we have settled down among them. Some of them will even ride the iron horse themselves." This was interpreted to them but very few of them heard. They were talking excitedly among themselves because the white man had said he was going to live among them. They had not thought about that.

At this point an old man said he had a question. "Which is this god of yours," he asked, "the goddess of the earth, the god of the sky, Amadiora or the thunderbolt, or what?"

The interpreter spoke to the white man and he immediately gave his answer. "All the gods you have named are not gods at all. They are gods of deceit who tell you to kill your fellows and destroy innocent children. There is only one true God and He has the earth, the sky, you and me and all of us."

"If we leave our gods and follow your god," asked another man, "who will protect us from the anger of our neglected gods and ancestors?"

"Your gods are not alive and cannot do you any harm," replied the white man. "They are pieces of wood and stone."

When this was interpreted to the men of Mbanta they broke into derisive laughter. These men must be mad, they said to themselves. How else could they say that Ani and Amadiora were harmless? And Idemili and Ogwugwu too? And some of them began to go away.

Then the missionaries burst into song. It was one of those gay and rollicking tunes of evangelism which had the power of plucking at silent and dusty chords in the heart of an Ibo man. The interpreter explained each verse to the audience, some of whom now stood enthralled. It was a story of brothers who lived in darkness and in fear, ignorant of the love of God. It told of one sheep out on the hills, away from the gates of God and from the tender shepherd's care.

After the singing the interpreter spoke about the Son of God whose name was Jesu Kristi. Okonkwo, who only stayed in the hope that it might come to chasing the men out of the village or whipping them, now said:

"You told us with your own mouth that there was only one god. Now you talk about his son. He must have a wife, then." The crowd agreed.

"I did not say He had a wife," said the interpreter, somewhat lamely.

"Your buttocks said he had a son," said the joker. "So he must have a wife and all of them must have buttocks."

The missionary ignored him and went on to talk about the Holy Trinity. At the end of it Okonkwo was fully convinced that the man was mad. He shrugged his shoulders and went away to tap his afternoon palm-wine.

But there was a young lad who had been captivated. His name was Nwoye, Okonkwo's first son. It was not the mad logic of the Trinity that captivated him. He did not understand it. It was the poetry of the new religion, something felt in the marrow. The hymn about brothers who sat in darkness and in fear seemed to answer a vague and persistent question that haunted his young soul—the question of the twins crying in the bush and the question of Ikemefuna who was killed. He felt a relief within as the hymn poured into his parched soul. The words of the hymn were like the drops of frozen rain melting on the dry palate of the panting earth. Nwoye's callow mind was greatly puzzled.

Chapter Seventeen

THE MISSIONARIES SPENT THEIR FIRST four or five nights in the market-place, and went into the village in the morning to preach the gospel. They asked who the king of the village was, but the villagers told them that there was no king. "We have men of high title and the chief priests and the elders," they said.

It was not very easy getting the men of high title and the elders together after the excitement of the first day. But the missionaries persevered, and in the end they were received by the rulers of Mbanta. They asked for a plot of land to build their church.

Every clan and village had its "evil forest." In it were buried all those who died of the really evil diseases, like leprosy and smallpox. It was also the dumping ground for the potent fetishes of great medicine men when they died. An "evil forest" was, therefore, alive with sinister forces and powers of darkness. It was such a forest that the rulers of Mbanta gave to the missionaries. They did not really want them in their clan, and so they made them that offer which nobody in his right senses would accept.

"They want a piece of land to build their shrine," said Uchendu to his peers when they consulted among themselves. "We shall give them a piece of land." He paused, and there was a murmur of surprise and disagreement. "Let us give them a portion of the Evil Forest. They boast about victory over death. Let us give them a real battlefield in which to show their victory." They laughed and agreed, and sent for the missionaries, whom they had asked to leave them for a while so that they might "whisper together." They offered them as much of the Evil Forest as they cared to take. And to their greatest amazement the missionaries thanked them and burst into song.

"They do not understand," said some of the elders. "But they will understand when they go to their plot of land tomorrow morning." And they dispersed.

The next morning the crazy men actually began to clear a part of the forest and to build their house. The inhabitants of Mbanta expected them all to be dead within four days. The first day passed and the second and third and fourth, and none of them died. Everyone was puzzled. And then it became known that the white man's fetish had unbelievable power. It was said that he wore glasses on his eyes so that he could see and talk to evil spirits. Not long after, he won his first three converts.

Although Nwoye had been attracted to the new faith from the very first day, he kept it secret. He dared not go too near the missionaries for fear of his father. But whenever they came to preach in the open marketplace or the village playground, Nwoye was there. And he was already beginning to know some of the simple stories they told.

"We have now built a church," said Mr. Kiaga, the interpreter, who was now in charge of the infant congregation. The white man had gone back to Umuofia, where he built his headquarters and from where he paid regular visits to Mr. Kiaga's congregation at Mbanta.

"We have now built a church," said Mr. Kiaga, "and we want you all to come in every seventh day to worship the true God."

On the following Sunday, Nwoye passed and repassed the little red-earth and thatch building without summoning enough courage to enter. He heard the voice of singing and although it came from a handful of men it was loud and confident. Their church stood on a circular clearing that looked like the open mouth of the Evil Forest. Was it waiting to snap its teeth together? After passing and re-passing by the church, Nwoye returned home.

It was well known among the people of Mbanta that their gods and ancestors were sometimes long-suffering and would deliberately allow a man to go on defying them. But even in such cases they set their limit at seven market weeks or twenty-eight days. Beyond that limit no man was suffered to go. And so excitement mounted in the village as the seventh week approached since the impudent missionaries built their church in the Evil Forest. The villagers were so certain about the doom that awaited these men that one or two converts thought it wise to suspend their allegiance to the new faith.

At last the day came by which all the missionaries should have died. But they were still alive, building a new red-earth and thatch house for their teacher, Mr. Kiaga. That week they won a handful more converts. And for the first time they had a woman. Her name was Nneka, the wife of Amadi, who was a prosperous farmer. She was very heavy with child.

Nneka had had four previous pregnancies and childbirths. But each time she had borne twins, and they had been immediately thrown away. Her husband and his family were already becoming highly critical of such a woman and were not unduly perturbed when they found she had fled to join the Christians. It was a good riddance.

One morning Okonkwo's cousin, Amikwu, was passing by the church on his way from the neighboring village, when he saw Nwoye among the

Christians. He was greatly surprised, and when he got home he went straight to Okonkwo's hut and told him what he had seen. The women began to talk excitedly, but Okonkwo sat unmoved.

It was late afternoon before Nwoye returned. He went into the *obi* and saluted his father, but he did not answer. Nwoye turned round to walk into the inner compound when his father, suddenly overcome with fury, sprang to his feet and gripped him by the neck.

"Where have you been?" he stammered.

Nwoye struggled to free himself from the choking grip.

"Answer me," roared Okonkwo, "before I kill you!" He seized a heavy stick that lay on the dwarf wall and hit him two or three savage blows.

"Answer me!" he roared again. Nwoye stood looking at him and did not say a word. The women were screaming outside, afraid to go in.

"Leave that boy at once!" said a voice in the outer compound. It was Okonkwo's uncle, Uchendu. "Are you mad?"

Okonkwo did not answer. But he left hold of Nwoye, who walked away and never returned.

He went back to the church and told Mr. Kiaga that he had decided to go to Umuofia where the white missionary had set up a school to teach young Christians to read and write.

Mr. Kiaga's joy was very great. "Blessed is he who forsakes his father and his mother for my sake," he intoned. "Those that hear my words are my father and my mother."

Nwoye did not fully understand. But he was happy to leave his father. He would return later to his mother and his brothers and sisters and convert them to the new faith.

As Okonkwo sat in his hut that night, gazing into a log fire, he thought over the matter. A sudden fury rose within him and he felt a strong desire to take up his machete, go to the church and wipe out the entire vile and miscreant gang. But on further thought he told himself that Nwoye was not worth fighting for. Why, he cried in his heart, should he, Okonkwo, of all people, be cursed with such a son? He saw clearly in it the finger of his personal god or *chi*. For how else could he explain his great misfortune and exile and now his despicable son's behavior? Now that he had time to think of it, his son's crime stood out in its stark enormity. To abandon the gods of one's father and go about with a lot of effeminate men clucking like old hens was the very depth of abomination. Suppose when he died all his male children decided to follow Nwoye's steps and abandon their ancestors? Okonkwo felt a cold shudder run through him at the terrible prospect, like the prospect of annihilation. He saw himself and his fathers crowding round their ancestral shrine waiting in vain for worship and sacrifice and finding nothing but ashes of bygone days, and his children the while praying to the white man's god. If such a thing were ever to happen, he, Okonkwo, would wipe them off the face of the earth.

Okonkwo was popularly called the "Roaring Flame." As he looked into the log fire he recalled the name. He was a flaming fire. How then could he have begotten a son like Nwoye, degenerate and effeminate? Perhaps he was not his son. No! he could not be. His wife had played him false. He would teach her! But Nwoye resembled his grandfather, Unoka, who was Okonkwo's father. He pushed the thought out of his mind. He, Okonkwo, was called a flaming fire. How could he have begotten a woman for a son? At Nwoye's age Okonkwo had already become famous throughout Umuofia for his wrestling and his fearlessness.

He sighed heavily, and as if in sympathy the smoldering log also sighed. And immediately Okonkwo's eyes were opened and he saw the whole matter clearly. Living fire begets cold, impotent ash. He sighed again, deeply.

Chapter Eighteen

THE YOUNG CHURCH IN MBANTA had a few crises early in its life. At first the clan had assumed that it would not survive. But it had gone on living and gradually becoming stronger. The clan was worried, but not overmuch. If a gang of *efulefu* decided to live in the Evil Forest it was their own affair. When one came to think of it, the Evil Forest was a fit home for such undesirable people. It was true they were rescuing twins from the bush, but they never brought them into the village. As far as the villagers were concerned, the twins still remained where they had been thrown away. Surely the earth goddess would not visit the sins of the missionaries on the innocent villagers?

But on one occasion the missionaries had tried to overstep the bounds. Three converts had gone into the village and boasted openly that all the gods were dead and impotent and that they were prepared to defy them by burning all their shrines.

"Go and burn your mothers' genitals," said one of the priests. The men were seized and beaten until they streamed with blood. After that nothing happened for a long time between the church and the clan.

But stories were already gaining ground that the white man had not only brought a religion but also a government. It was said that they had built a place of judgment in Umuofia to protect the followers of their religion. It was even said that they had hanged one man who killed a missionary.

Although such stories were now often told they looked like fairy-tales in Mbanta and did not as yet affect the relationship between the new church and the clan. There was no question of killing a missionary here, for Mr. Kiaga, despite his madness, was quite harmless. As for his converts, no one could kill them without having to flee from the clan, for in spite of their worthlessness they still belonged to the clan. And so nobody gave serious thought to the stories about the white man's government or the consequences of killing the Christians. If they became more troublesome than they already were they would simply be driven out of the clan.

And the little church was at that moment too deeply absorbed in its own troubles to annoy the clan. It all began over the question of admitting outcasts.

These outcasts, or *osu*, seeing that the new religion welcomed twins and such abominations, thought that it was possible that they would also be received. And so one Sunday two of them went into the church. There was an immediate stir; but so great was the work the new religion had done among the converts that they did not immediately leave the church when the outcasts came in. Those who found themselves nearest to them merely moved to another seat. It was a miracle. But it only lasted till the end of the service. The whole church raised a protest and was about to drive these people out, when Mr. Kiaga stopped them and began to explain.

"Before God," he said, "there is no slave or free. We are all children of God and we must receive these our brothers."

"You do not understand," said one of the converts. "What will the heathen say of us when they hear that we receive *osu* into our midst? They will laugh."

"Let them laugh," said Mr. Kiaga. "God will laugh at them on the judgment day. Why do the nations rage and the peoples imagine a vain thing? He that sitteth in the heavens shall laugh. The Lord shall have them in derision."

"You do not understand," the convert maintained. "You are our teacher, and you can teach us the things of the new faith. But this is a matter which we know." And he told him what an *osu* was.

He was a person dedicated to a god, a thing set apart—a taboo for ever, and his children after him. He could neither marry nor be married by the free-born. He was in fact an outcast, living in a special area of the village, close to the Great Shrine. Wherever he went he carried with him the mark of his forbidden caste—long, tangled and dirty hair. A razor was taboo to him. An *osu* could not attend an assembly of the free-born, and they, in turn, could not shelter under his roof. He could not take any of the four titles of the clan, and when he died he was buried by his kind in the Evil Forest. How could such a man be a follower of Christ?

"He needs Christ more than you and I," said Mr. Kiaga.

"Then I shall go back to the clan," said the convert. And he went. Mr. Kiaga stood firm, and it was his firmness that saved the young church. The wavering converts drew inspiration and confidence from his unshakable faith. He ordered the outcasts to shave off their long, tangled hair. At first they were afraid they might die.

"Unless you shave off the mark of your heathen belief I will not admit you into the church," said Mr. Kiaga. "You fear that you will die. Why should that be? How are you different from other men who shave their hair?

The same God created you and them. But they have cast you out like lepers. It is against the will of God, who has promised everlasting life to all who believe in His holy name. The heathen say you will die if you do this or that, and you are afraid. They also said I would die if I built my church on this ground. Am I dead? They said I would die if I took care of twins. I am still alive. The heathen speak nothing but falsehood. Only the word of our God is true."

The two outcasts shaved off their hair, and soon they were the strongest adherents of the new faith. And what was more, nearly all the osu in Mbanta followed their example. It was in fact one of them who in his zeal brought the church into serious conflict with the clan a year later by killing the sacred python, the emanation of the god of water.

The royal python was the most revered animal in Mbanta and all the surrounding clans. It was addressed as "Our Father," and was allowed to go wherever it chose, even into people's beds. It ate rats in the house and sometimes swallowed hens' eggs. If a clansman killed a royal python accidentally, he made sacrifices of atonement and performed an expensive burial ceremony such as was done for a great man. No punishment was prescribed for a man who killed the python knowingly. Nobody thought that such a thing could ever happen.

Perhaps it never did happen. That was the way the clan at first looked at it. No one had actually seen the man do it. The story had arisen among the Christians themselves.

But, all the same, the rulers and elders of Mbanta assembled to decide on their action. Many of them spoke at great length and in fury. The spirit of wars was upon them. Okonkwo, who had begun to play a part in the affairs of his motherland, said that until the abominable gang was chased out of the village with whips there would be no peace.

But there were many others who saw the situation differently, and it was their counsel that prevailed in the end.

"It is not our custom to fight for our gods," said one of them. "Let us not presume to do so now. If a man kills the sacred python in the secrecy of his hut, the matter lies between him and the god. We did not see it. If we put ourselves between the god and his victim we may receive blows intended for the offender. When a man blasphemes, what do we do? Do we go and stop his mouth? No. We put our fingers into our ears to stop us hearing. That is a wise action."

"Let us not reason like cowards," said Okonkwo. "If a man comes into my hut and defecates on the floor, what do I do? Do I shut my eyes? No! I take a stick and break his head. That is what a man does. These people are daily pouring filth over us, and Okeke says we should pretend not to see."

Okonkwo made a sound full of disgust. This was a womanly clan, he thought. Such a thing could never happen in his fatherland, Umuofia.

"Okonkwo has spoken the truth," said another man. "We should do something. But let us ostracize these men. We would then not be held accountable for their abominations."

Everybody in the assembly spoke, and in the end it was decided to ostracize the Christians. Okonkwo ground his teeth in disgust.

That night a bell-man went through the length and breadth of Mbanta proclaiming that the adherents of the new faith were thenceforth excluded from the life and privileges of the clan.

The Christians had grown in number and were now a small community of men, women and children, self-assured and confident. Mr. Brown, the white missionary, paid regular visits to them. "When I think that it is only eighteen months since the Seed was first sown among you," he said, "I marvel at what the Lord hath wrought."

It was Wednesday in Holy Week and Mr. Kiaga had asked the women to bring red earth and white chalk and water to scrub the church for Easter; and the women had formed themselves into three groups for this purpose. They set out early that morning, some of them with their water-pots to the stream, another group with hoes and baskets to the village red-earth pit, and the others to the chalk quarry.

Mr. Kiaga was praying in the church when he heard the women talking excitedly. He rounded off his prayer and went to see what it was all about. The women had come to the church with empty waterpots. They said that some young men had chased them away from the stream with whips. Soon after, the women who had gone for red earth returned with empty baskets. Some of them had been heavily whipped. The chalk women also returned to tell a similar story.

"What does it all mean?" asked Mr. Kiaga, who was greatly perplexed.

"The village has outlawed us," said one of the women. "The bell-man announced it last night. But it is not our custom to debar anyone from the stream or the quarry."

Another woman said, "They want to ruin us. They will not allow us into the markets. They have said so."

Mr. Kiaga was going to send into the village for his men-converts when he saw them coming on their own. Of course they had all heard the bell-man, but they had never in all their lives heard of women being debarred from the stream.

"Come along," they said to the women. "We will go with you to meet those cowards." Some of them had big sticks and some even machetes.

But Mr. Kiaga restrained them. He wanted first to know why they had been outlawed.

"They say that Okoli killed the sacred python," said one man.

"It is false," said another. "Okoli told me himself that it was false."

Okoli was not there to answer. He had fallen ill on the previous night. Before the day was over he was dead. His death showed that the gods were still able to fight their own battles. The clan saw no reason then for molesting the Christians.

Chapter Nineteen

THE LAST BIG RAINS OF THE YEAR WERE FALLING. It was the time for treading red earth with which to build walls. It was not done earlier because the rains were too heavy and would have washed away the heap of trodden earth; and it could not be done later because harvesting would soon set in, and after that the dry season.

It was going to be Okonkwo's last harvest in Mbanta. The seven wasted and weary years were at last dragging to a close. Although he had prospered in his motherland Okonkwo knew that he would have prospered even more in Umuofia, in the land of his fathers where men were bold and warlike. In these seven years he would have climbed to the utmost heights. And so he regretted every day of his exile. His mother's kinsmen had been very kind to him, and he was grateful. But that did not alter the facts. He had called the first child born to him in exile Nneka—"Mother is Supreme"—out of politeness to his mother's kinsmen. But two years later when a son was born he called him Nwofia—"Begotten in the Wilderness."

As soon as he entered his last year in exile Okonkwo sent money to Obierika to build him two huts in his old compound where he and his family would live until he built more huts and the outside wall of his compound. He could not ask another man to build his own *obi* for him, nor the walls of his compound. Those things a man built for himself or inherited from his father.

As the last heavy rains of the year began to fall, Obierika sent word that the two huts had been built and Okonkwo began to prepare for his return, after the rains. He would have liked to return earlier and build his compound that year before the rains stopped, but in doing so he would have taken something from the full penalty of seven years. And that could not be. So he waited impatiently for the dry season to come.

It came slowly. The rain became lighter and lighter until it fell in slanting showers. Sometimes the sun shone through the rain and a light breeze blew. It was a gay and airy kind of rain. The rainbow began to appear, and sometimes two rainbows, like a mother and her daughter, the one young and beautiful, and the other an old and faint shadow. The rainbow was called the python of the sky.

Okonkwo called his three wives and told them to get things together for a great feast. "I must thank my mother's kinsmen before I go," he said.

Ekwefi still had some cassava left on her farm from the previous year. Neither of the other wives had. It was not that they had been lazy, but that they had many children to feed. It was therefore understood that Ekwefi would provide cassava for the feast. Nwoye's mother and Ojiugo would provide the other things like smoked fish, palm-oil and pepper for the soup. Okonkwo would take care of meat and yams.

Ekwefi rose early on the following morning and went to her farm with her daughter, Ezinma, and Ojiugo's daughter, Obiageli, to harvest cassava tubers. Each of them carried a long cane basket, a machete for cutting down the soft cassava stem, and a little hoe for digging out the tuber. Fortunately, a light rain had fallen during the night and the soil would not be very hard.

"It will not take us long to harvest as much as we like," said Ekwefi.

"But the leaves will be wet," said Ezinma. Her basket was balanced on her head, and her arms folded across her breasts. She felt cold. "I dislike cold water dropping on my back. We should have waited for the sun to rise and dry the leaves."

Obiageli called her "Salt" because she said that she disliked water. "Are you afraid you may dissolve?"

The harvesting was easy, as Ekwefi had said. Ezinma shook every tree violently with a long stick before she bent down to cut the stem and dig out the tuber. Sometimes it was not necessary to dig. They just pulled the stump, and earth rose, roots snapped below, and the tuber was pulled out.

When they had harvested a sizable heap they carried it down in two trips to the stream, where every woman had a shallow well for fermenting her cassava.

"It should be ready in four days or even three," said Obiageli. "They are young tubers."

"They are not all that young," said Ekwefi. "I planted the farm nearly two years ago. It is a poor soil and that is why the tubers are so small."

Okonkwo never did things by halves. When his wife Ekwefi protested that two goats were sufficient for the feast he told her that it was not her affair.

"I am calling a feast because I have the wherewithal. I cannot live on the bank of a river and wash my hands with spittle. My mother's people have been good to me and I must show my gratitude."

And so three goats were slaughtered and a number of fowls. It was like a wedding feast. There was foo-foo and yam pottage, egusi soup and bitter-leaf soup and pots and pots of palm-wine.

All the *umunna* were invited to the feast, all the descendants of Okolo, who had lived about two hundred years before. The oldest member of this extensive family was Okonkwo's uncle, Uchendu. The kola nut was given him to break, and he prayed to the ancestors. He asked them for health and children. "We do not ask for wealth because he that has health and children will also have wealth. We do not pray to have more money but to have more kinsmen. We are better than animals because we have kinsmen. An animal rubs its itching flank against a tree, a man asks his kinsman to scratch him." He prayed especially for Okonkwo and his family. He then broke the kola nut and threw one of the lobes on the ground for the ancestors.

As the broken kola nuts were passed round, Okonkwo's wives and children and those who came to help them with the cooking began to bring out the food. His sons brought out the pots of palm-wine. There was so much food and drink that many kinsmen whistled in surprise. When all was laid out, Okonkwo rose to speak.

"I beg you to accept this little kola," he said. "It is not to pay you back for all you did for me in these seven years. A child cannot pay for its mother's milk. I have only called you together because it is good for kinsmen to meet."

Yam pottage was served first because it was lighter than foo-foo and because yam always came first. Then the foo-foo was served. Some kinsmen ate it with egusi soup and others with bitter-leaf soup. The meat was then shared so that every member of the *umunna* had a portion. Every man rose in order of years and took a share. Even the few kinsmen who had not been able to come had their shares taken out for them in due term.

As the palm-wine was drunk one of the oldest members of the *umunna* rose to thank Okonkwo:

"If I say that we did not expect such a big feast I will be suggesting that we did not know how openhanded our son, Okonkwo, is. We all know him, and we expected a big feast. But it turned out to be even bigger than we expected. Thank you. May all you took out return again tenfold. It is good in these days when the younger generation consider themselves wiser than their sires to see a man doing things in the grand, old way. A man who calls his kinsmen to a feast does not do so to save them from starving. They all have food in their own homes. When we gather together in the moonlit village ground it is not because of the moon. Every man can see it in his own compound. We come together because it is good for kinsmen to do so. You may ask why I am saying all this. I say it because I fear for the younger generation, for you people." He waved his arm where most of the young men sat. "As for me, I have only a short while to live, and so have Uchendu and Unachukwu and Emefo. But I fear for you young people because you do not understand how strong is the bond of kinship. You do not know what it is to speak with one voice. And what is the result? An abominable religion has settled among you. A man can now leave his father and his brothers. He can curse the gods of his fathers and his ancestors, like a hunter's dog that suddenly goes mad and turns on his master. I fear for you; I fear for the clan."

He turned again to Okonkwo and said, "Thank you for calling us together."

Part Three

Chapter Twenty

SEVEN YEARS was a long time to be away from one's clan. A man's place was not always there, waiting for him. As soon as he left, someone else rose and filled it. The clan was like a lizard; if it lost its tail it soon grew another.

Okonkwo knew these things. He knew that he had lost his place among the nine masked spirits who administered justice in the clan. He had lost the chance to lead his warlike clan against the new religion, which, he was told, had gained ground. He had lost the years in which he might have taken the highest titles in the clan. But some of these losses were not irreparable. He was determined that his return should be marked by his people. He would return with a flourish, and regain the seven wasted years.

Even in his first year in exile he had begun to plan for his return. The first thing he would do would be to rebuild his compound on a more magnificent scale. He would build a bigger barn than he had had before and he would build huts for two new wives. Then he would show his wealth by initiating his sons into the *ozo* society. Only the really great men in the clan were able to do this. Okonkwo saw clearly the high esteem in which he would be held, and he saw himself taking the highest title in the land.

As the years of exile passed one by one it seemed to him that his *chi* might now be making amends for the past disaster. His yams grew abundantly, not only in his motherland but also in Umuofia, where his friend gave them out year by year to sharecroppers.

Then the tragedy of his first son had occurred. At first it appeared as if it might prove too great for his spirit. But it was a resilient spirit, and in the end Okonkwo overcame his sorrow. He had five other sons and he would bring them up in the way of the clan.

He sent for the five sons and they came and sat in his *obi*. The youngest of them was four years old.

"You have all seen the great abomination of your brother. Now he is no longer my son or your brother. I will only have a son who is a man, who will hold his head up among my people. If any one of you prefers to be a woman, let him follow Nwoye now while I am alive so that I can curse him. If you turn against me when I am dead I will visit you and break your neck."

Okonkwo was very lucky in his daughters. He never stopped regretting that Ezinma was a girl. Of all his children she alone understood his every mood. A bond of sympathy had grown between them as the years had passed.

Ezinma grew up in her father's exile and became one of the most beautiful girls in Mbanta. She was called Crystal of Beauty, as her mother had been called in her youth. The young ailing girl who had caused her mother so much heartache had been transformed, almost overnight, into a healthy, buoyant maiden. She had, it was true, her moments of depression when she would snap at everybody like an angry dog. These moods descended on her suddenly and for no apparent reason. But they were very rare and short-lived. As long as they lasted, she could bear no other person but her father.

Many young men and prosperous middle-aged men of Mbanta came to marry her. But she refused them all, because her father had called her one evening and said to her: "There are many good and prosperous people here, but I shall be happy if you marry in Umuofia when we return home."

That was all he had said. But Ezinma had seen clearly all the thought and hidden meaning behind the few words. And she had agreed.

"Your half-sister, Obiageli, will not understand me," Okonkwo said. "But you can explain to her."

Although they were almost the same age, Ezinma wielded a strong influence over her half-sister. She explained to her why they should not marry yet, and she agreed also. And so the two of them refused every offer of marriage in Mbanta.

"I wish she were a boy," Okonkwo thought within himself. She understood things so perfectly. Who else among his children could have read his thoughts so well? With two beautiful grown-up daughters his return to Umuofia would attract considerable attention. His future sons-in-law would be men of authority in the clan. The poor and unknown would not dare to come forth.

Umuofia had indeed changed during the seven years Okonkwo had been in exile. The church had come and led many astray. Not only the low-born and the outcast but sometimes a worthy man had joined it. Such a man was Ogbuefi Ugonna, who had taken two titles, and who like a madman had cut the anklet of his titles and cast it away to join the Christians. The white missionary was very proud of him and he was one of the first men in Umuofia to receive the sacrament of Holy Communion, or Holy Feast as it was called in Ibo. Ogbuefi Ugonna had thought of the Feast in terms of eating and drinking, only more holy than the village variety. He had therefore put his drinking-horn into his goatskin bag for the occasion.

But apart from the church, the white men had also brought a government. They had built a court where the District Commissioner judged cases in ignorance. He had court messengers who brought men to him for trial. Many of these messengers came from Umuru on the bank of the Great River, where the white men first came many years before and where they had built the center of their religion and trade and government. These court messengers were greatly hated in Umuofia because they were foreigners and also arrogant and high-handed. They were called *kotma*, and because of their ash-colored shorts they earned the additional name of Ashy-Buttocks. They guarded the prison, which was full of men who had offended against the white man's law. Some of these prisoners had thrown away their twins and some had molested the Christians. They were beaten in the prison by the *kotma* and made to work every morning clearing the government compound and fetching wood for the white Commissioner and the court messengers. Some of these prisoners were men of title who should be above such mean occupation. They were grieved by the indignity and mourned for their neglected farms. As they cut grass in the morning the younger men sang in time with the strokes of their machetes:

"Kotma *of the ash buttocks,*
  He is fit to be a slave.
The white man has no sense,
  He is fit to be a slave."

The court messengers did not like to be called Ashy-Buttocks, and they beat the men. But the song spread in Umuofia.

Okonkwo's head was bowed in sadness as Obierika told him these things.

"Perhaps I have been away too long," Okonkwo said, almost to himself. "But I cannot understand these things you tell me. What is it that has happened to our people? Why have they lost the power to fight?"

"Have you not heard how the white man wiped out Abame?" asked Obierika.

"I have heard," said Okonkwo. "But I have also heard that Abame people were weak and foolish. Why did they not fight back? Had they no guns and machetes? We would be cowards to compare ourselves with the men of Abame. Their fathers had never dared to stand before our ancestors. We must fight these men and drive them from the land."

"It is already too late," said Obierika sadly. "Our own men and our sons have joined the ranks of the stranger. They have joined his religion and they help to uphold his government. If we should try to drive out the white men in Umuofia we should find it easy. There are only two of them. But what of our own people who are following their way and have been given power? They would go to Umuru and bring the soldiers, and we would be like Abame." He paused for a long time and then said: "I told you on my last visit to Mbanta how they hanged Aneto."

"What has happened to that piece of land in dispute?" asked Okonkwo.

"The white man's court has decided that it should belong to Nnama's family, who had given much money to the white man's messengers and interpreter."

"Does the white man understand our custom about land?"

"How can he when he does not even speak our tongue? But he says that our customs are bad; and our own brothers who have taken up his religion also say that our customs are bad. How do you think we can fight when our own brothers have turned against us? The white man is very clever. He came quietly and peaceably with his religion. We were amused at his foolishness and allowed him to stay. Now he has won our brothers, and our clan can no longer act like one. He has put a knife on the things that held us together and we have fallen apart."

"How did they get hold of Aneto to hang him?" asked Okonkwo.

"When he killed Oduche in the fight over the land, he fled to Aninta to escape the wrath of the earth. This was about eight days after the fight, because Oduche had not died immediately from his wounds. It was on the seventh day that he died. But everybody knew that he was going to die and Aneto got his belongings together in readiness to flee. But the Christians had told the white man about the accident, and he sent his *kotma* to catch Aneto. He was imprisoned with all the leaders of his family. In the end Oduche died and Aneto was taken to Umuru and hanged. The other people were released, but even now they have not found the mouth with which to tell of their suffering.

The two men sat in silence for a long while afterwards.

Chapter Twenty-One

THERE WERE MANY MEN AND WOMEN in Umuofia who did not feel as strongly as Okonkwo about the new dispensation. The white man had indeed brought a lunatic religion, but he had also built a trading store and for the first time palm-oil and kernel became things of great price, and much money flowed into Umuofia.

And even in the matter of religion there was a growing feeling that there might be something in it after all, something vaguely akin to method in the overwhelming madness.

This growing feeling was due to Mr. Brown, the white missionary, who was very firm in restraining his flock from provoking the wrath of the clan. One member in particular was very difficult to restrain. His name was Enoch and his father was the priest of the snake cult. The story went around that Enoch had killed and eaten the sacred python, and that his father had cursed him.

Mr. Brown preached against such excess of zeal. Everything was possible, he told his energetic flock, but everything was not expedient. And so Mr. Brown came to be respected even by the clan, because he trod softly on its faith. He made friends with some of the great men of the clan and on one of his frequent visits to the neighboring villages he had been presented with a carved elephant tusk, which was a sign of dignity and rank. One of the great men in that village was called Akunna and he had given one of his sons to be taught the white man's knowledge in Mr. Brown's school.

Whenever Mr. Brown went to that village he spent long hours with Akunna in his *obi* talking through an interpreter about religion. Neither of them succeeded in converting the other but they learned more about their different beliefs.

"You say that there is one supreme God who made heaven and earth," said Akunna on one of Mr. Brown's visits. "We also believe in Him and call Him Chukwu. He made all the world and the other gods."

"There are no other gods," said Mr. Brown. "Chukwu is the only God and all others are false. You carve a piece of wood—like that one" (he pointed at the rafters from which Akunna's carved *Ikenga* hung), "and you call it a god. But it is still a piece of wood."

"Yes," said Akunna. "It is indeed a piece of wood. The tree from which it came was made by Chukwu, as indeed all minor gods were. But He made them for His messengers so that we could approach Him through them. It is like yourself. You are the head of your church."

"No," protested Mr. Brown. "The head of my church is God Himself."

"I know," said Akunna, "but there must be a head in this world among men. Somebody like yourself must be the head here."

"The head of my church in that sense is in England."

"That is exactly what I am saying. The head of your church is in your country. He has sent you here as his messenger. And you have also appointed your own messengers and servants. Or let me take another example, the District Commissioner. He is sent by your king."

"They have a queen," said the interpreter on his own account.

"Your queen sends her messenger, the District Commissioner. He finds that he cannot do the work alone and so he appoints *kotma* to help him. It is the same with God, or Chukwu. He appoints the smaller gods to help Him because His work is too great for one person."

"You should not think of Him as a person," said Mr. Brown. "It is because you do so that you imagine He must need helpers. And the worst thing about it is that you give all the worship to the false gods you have created."

"That is not so. We make sacrifices to the little gods, but when they fail and there is no one else to turn to we go to Chukwu. It is right to do so. We approach a great man through his servants. But when his servants fail to help us, then we go to the last source of hope. We appear to pay greater attention to the little gods but that is not so. We worry them more because we are afraid to worry their Master. Our fathers knew that Chukwu was the Overlord and that is why many of them gave their children the name Chukwuka—'Chukwu is Supreme.' "

"You said one interesting thing," said Mr. Brown. "You are afraid of Chukwu. In my religion Chukwu is a loving Father and need not be feared by those who do His will."

"But we must fear Him when we are not doing His will," said Akunna. "And who is to tell His will? It is too great to be known."

In this way Mr. Brown learned a good deal about the religion of the clan and he came to the conclusion that a frontal attack on it would not succeed. And so he built a school and a little hospital in Umuofia. He went from family to family begging people to send their children to his school. But at first they only sent their slaves or sometimes their lazy children. Mr. Brown begged and argued and prophesied. He said that the leaders of the land in the future would be men and women who had learned to read and write. If Umuofia failed to send her children to the school, strangers would come from other places to rule them. They could already see that happening in the Native Court, where the D.C. was surrounded by strangers who spoke his tongue. Most of these strangers came from the distant town of Umuru on the bank of the Great River where the white man first went.

In the end Mr. Brown's arguments began to have an effect. More people came to learn in his school, and he encouraged them with gifts of singlets and towels. They were not all young, these people who came to learn. Some of them were thirty years old or more. They worked on their farms in the morning and went to school in the afternoon. And it was not long before the people began to say that the white man's medicine was quick in working. Mr. Brown's school produced quick results. A few months in it were enough to make one a court messenger or even a court clerk. Those who stayed longer became teachers; and from Umuofia laborers went forth into the Lord's vineyard. New churches were established in the surrounding villages and a few schools with them. From the very beginning religion and education went hand in hand.

Mr. Brown's mission grew from strength to strength, and because of its link with the new administration it earned a new social prestige. But Mr. Brown himself was breaking down in health. At first he ignored the warning signs. But in the end he had to leave his flock, sad and broken.

It was in the first rainy season after Okonkwo's return to Umuofia that Mr. Brown left for home. As soon as he had learned of Okonkwo's return five months earlier, the missionary had immediately paid him a visit. He had just sent Okonkwo's son, Nwoye, who was now called Isaac, to the new training college for teachers in Umuru. And he had hoped that Okonkwo would be happy to hear of it. But Okonkwo had driven him away with the threat that if he came into his compound again, he would be carried out of it.

Okonkwo's return to his native land was not as memorable as he had wished. It was true his two beautiful daughters aroused great interest among suitors and marriage negotiations were soon in progress, but, beyond that, Umuofia did not appear to have taken any special notice of the warrior's return. The clan had undergone such profound change during his exile that it was barely recognizable. The new religion and government and the trading stores were very much in the people's eyes and minds. There were still many who saw these new institutions as evil, but even they talked and thought about little else, and certainly not about Okonkwo's return.

And it was the wrong year too. If Okonkwo had immediately initiated his two sons into the *ozo* society as he had planned he would have caused a stir. But the initiation rite was performed once in three years in Umuofia, and he had to wait for nearly two years for the next round of ceremonies.

Okonkwo was deeply grieved. And it was not just a personal grief. He mourned for the clan, which he saw breaking up and falling apart, and he mourned for the warlike men of Umuofia, who had so unaccountably become soft like women.

Chapter Twenty-Two

M<small>R</small>. B<small>ROWN'S</small> <small>SUCCESSOR</small> was the Reverend James Smith, and he was a different kind of man. He condemned openly Mr. Brown's policy of compromise and accommodation. He saw things as black and white. And black was evil. He saw the world as a battlefield in which the children of light were locked in mortal conflict with the sons of darkness. He spoke in his sermons about sheep and goats and about wheat and tares. He believed in slaying the prophets of Baal.

Mr. Smith was greatly distressed by the ignorance which many of his flock showed even in such things as the Trinity and the Sacraments. It only showed that they were seeds sown on a rocky soil. Mr. Brown had thought of nothing but numbers. He should have known that the kingdom of God did not depend on large crowds. Our Lord Himself stressed the importance of fewness. Narrow is the way and few the number. To fill the Lord's holy temple with an idolatrous crowd clamoring for signs was a folly of everlasting consequence. Our Lord used a whip only once in His life—to drive the crowd away from His church.

Within a few weeks of his arrival in Umuofia Mr. Smith suspended a young woman from the church for pouring new wine into old bottles. This woman had allowed her heathen husband to mutilate her dead child. The child had been declared an *ogbanje*, plaguing its mother by dying and entering her womb to be born again. Four times this child had run its evil round. And so it was mutilated to discourage it from returning.

Mr. Smith was filled with wrath when he heard of this. He disbelieved the story which even some of the most faithful confirmed, the story of really evil children who were not deterred by mutilation, but came back with all the scars. He replied that such stories were spread in the world by the Devil to lead men astray. Those who believed such stories were unworthy of the Lord's table.

There was a saying in Umuofia that as a man danced so the drums were beaten for him. Mr. Smith danced a furious step and so the drums went mad. The over-zealous converts who had smarted under Mr. Brown's restraining hand now flourished in full favor. One of them was Enoch, the son of the snake-priest who was believed to have killed and eaten the sacred python. Enoch's devotion to the new faith had seemed so much greater than Mr. Brown's that the villagers called him the outsider who wept louder than the bereaved.

Enoch was short and slight of build, and always seemed in great haste. His feet were short and broad, and when he stood or walked his heels came together and his feet opened outwards as if they had quarreled and meant to go in different directions. Such was the excessive energy bottled up in Enoch's small body that it was always erupting in quarrels and fights. On Sundays he always imagined that the sermon was preached for the benefit of his enemies. And if he happened to sit near one of them he would occasionally turn to give him a meaningful look, as if to say, "I told you so." It was Enoch who touched off the great conflict between church and clan in Umuofia which had been gathering since Mr. Brown left.

It happened during the annual ceremony which was held in honor of the earth deity. At such times the ancestors of the clan who had been committed to Mother Earth at their death emerged again as *egwugwu* through tiny ant-holes.

One of the greatest crimes a man could commit was to unmask an *egwugwu* in public, or to say or do anything which might reduce its immortal prestige in the eyes of the uninitiated. And this was what Enoch did.

The annual worship of the earth goddess fell on a Sunday, and the masked spirits were abroad. The Christian women who had been to church could not therefore go home. Some of their men had gone out to beg the *egwugwu* to retire for a short while for the women to pass. They agreed and were already retiring, when Enoch boasted aloud that they would not dare to touch a Christian. Whereupon they all came back and one of them gave Enoch a good stroke of the cane, which was always carried. Enoch fell on him and tore off his mask. The other *egwugwu* immediately surrounded their desecrated companion, to shield him from the profane gaze of women and children, and led him away. Enoch had killed an ancestral spirit, and Umuofia was thrown into confusion.

That night the Mother of the Spirits walked the length and breadth of the clan, weeping for her murdered son. It was a terrible night. Not even the oldest man in Umuofia had ever heard such a strange and fearful sound, and it was never to be heard again. It seemed as if the very soul of the tribe wept for a great evil that was coming—its own death.

On the next day all the masked *egwugwu* of Umuofia assembled in the marketplace. They came from all the quarters of the clan and even from the neighboring villages. The dreaded Otakagu came from Imo, and Ekwensu, dangling a white cock, arrived from Uli. It was a terrible gathering. The eerie voices of countless spirits, the bells that clattered behind some of them, and the clash of machetes as they ran forwards and backwards and saluted one another, sent tremors of fear into every heart. For the first time in living memory the sacred bull-roarer was heard in broad daylight.

From the marketplace the furious band made for Enoch's compound. Some of the elders of the clan went with them, wearing heavy protections of charms and amulets. These were men whose arms were strong in *ogwu*, or medicine. As for the ordinary men and women, they listened from the safety of their huts.

The leaders of the Christians had met together at Mr. Smith's parsonage on the previous night. As they deliberated they could hear the Mother of Spirits wailing for her son. The chilling sound affected Mr. Smith, and for the first time he seemed to be afraid.

"What are they planning to do?" he asked. No one knew, because such a thing had never happened before. Mr. Smith would have sent for the District Commissioner and his court messengers, but they had gone on tour on the previous day.

"One thing is clear," said Mr. Smith. "We cannot offer physical resistance to them. Our strength lies in the Lord." They knelt down together and prayed to God for delivery.

"O Lord, save Thy people," cried Mr. Smith.

"And bless Thine inheritance," replied the men.

They decided that Enoch should be hidden in the parsonage for a day or two. Enoch himself was greatly disappointed when he heard this, for he had hoped that a holy war was imminent; and there were a few other Christians who thought like him. But wisdom prevailed in the camp of the faithful and many lives were thus saved.

The band of *egwugwu* moved like a furious whirlwind to Enoch's compound and with machete and fire reduced it to a desolate heap. And from there they made for the church, intoxicated with destruction.

Mr. Smith was in his church when he heard the masked spirits coming. He walked quietly to the door which commanded the approach to the church compound, and stood there. But when the first three or four *egwugwu* appeared on the church compound he nearly bolted. He overcame this impulse and instead of running away he went down the two steps that led up to the church and walked towards the approaching spirits.

They surged forward, and a long stretch of the bamboo fence with which the church compound was surrounded gave way before them. Discordant bells clanged, machetes clashed and the air was full of dust and weird sounds. Mr. Smith heard a sound of footsteps behind him. He turned round and saw Okeke, his interpreter. Okeke had not been on the best of terms with his master since he had strongly condemned Enoch's behavior at the meeting of the leaders of the church during the night. Okeke had gone as far as to say that Enoch should not be hidden in the parsonage, because he would only draw the wrath of the clan on the pastor. Mr. Smith had rebuked him in very strong language, and had not sought his advice that morning. But now, as he came up and stood by him confronting the angry spirits, Mr. Smith looked at him and smiled. It was a wan smile, but there was deep gratitude there.

For a brief moment the onrush of the *egwugwu* was checked by the unexpected composure of the two men. But it was only a momentary check, like the tense silence between blasts of thunder. The second onrush was greater than the first. It swallowed up the two men. Then an unmistakable voice rose above the tumult and there was immediate silence. Space was made around the two men, and Ajofia began to speak.

Ajofia was the leading *egwugwu* of Umuofia. He was the head and spokesman of the nine ancestors who administered justice in the clan. His voice was unmistakable and so he was able to bring immediate peace to the agitated spirits. He then addressed Mr. Smith, and as he spoke clouds of smoke rose from his head.

"The body of the white man, I salute you," he said, using the language in which immortals spoke to men.

"The body of the white man, do you know me?" he asked.

Mr. Smith looked at his interpreter, but Okeke, who was a native of distant Umuru, was also at a loss.

Ajofia laughed in his guttural voice. It was like the laugh of rusty metal. "They are strangers," he said, "and they are ignorant. But let that pass." He turned round to his comrades and saluted them, calling them the fathers of Umuofia. He dug his rattling spear into the ground and it shook with metallic life. Then he turned once more to the missionary and his interpreter.

"Tell the white man that we will not do him any harm," he said to the interpreter. "Tell him to go back to his house and leave us alone. We liked his brother who was with us before. He was foolish, but we liked him, and for his sake we shall not harm his brother. But this shrine which he built must be destroyed. We shall no longer allow it in our midst. It has bred untold abominations and we have come to put an end to it." He turned to his comrades. "Fathers of Umuofia, I salute you;" and they replied with one guttural voice. He turned again to the missionary. "You can stay with us if you like our ways. You can worship your own god. It is good that a man should worship the gods and the spirits of his fathers. Go back to your house so that you may not be hurt. Our anger is great but we have held it down so that we can talk to you."

Mr. Smith said to his interpreter: "Tell them to go away from here. This is the house of God and I will not live to see it desecrated."

Okeke interpreted wisely to the spirits and leaders of Umuofia: "The white man says he is happy you have come to him with your grievances, like friends. He will be happy if you leave the matter in his hands."

"We cannot leave the matter in his hands because he does not understand our customs, just as we do not understand his. We say he is foolish because he does not know our ways, and perhaps he says we are foolish because we do not know his. Let him go away."

Mr. Smith stood his ground. But he could not save his church. When the *egwugwu* went away the red-earth church which Mr. Brown had built was a pile of earth and ashes. And for the moment the spirit of the clan was pacified.

Chapter Twenty-Three

For the first time in many years Okonkwo had a feeling that was akin to happiness. The times which had altered so unaccountably during his exile seemed to be coming round again. The clan which had turned false on him appeared to be making amends.

He had spoken violently to his clansmen when they had met in the marketplace to decide on their action. And they had listened to him with respect. It was like the good old days again, when a warrior was a warrior. Although they had not agreed to kill the missionary or drive away the Christians, they had agreed to do something substantial. And they had done it. Okonkwo was almost happy again.

For two days after the destruction of the church, nothing happened. Every man in Umuofia went about armed with a gun or a machete. They would not be caught unawares, like the men of Abame.

Then the District Commissioner returned from his tour. Mr. Smith went immediately to him and they had a long discussion. The men of Umuofia did not take any notice of this, and if they did, they thought it was not important. The missionary often went to see his brother white man. There was nothing strange in that.

Three days later the District Commissioner sent his sweet-tongued messenger to the leaders of Umuofia asking them to meet him in his headquarters. That also was not strange. He often asked them to hold such palavers, as he called them. Okonkwo was among the six leaders he invited.

Okonkwo warned the others to be fully armed. "An Umuofia man does not refuse a call," he said. "He may refuse to do what he is asked; he does not refuse to be asked. But the times have changed, and we must be fully prepared."

And so the six men went to see the District Commissioner, armed with their machetes. They did not carry guns, for that would be unseemly. They were led into the courthouse where the District Commissioner sat. He received them politely. They unslung their goatskin bags and their sheathed machetes, put them on the floor, and sat down.

"I have asked you to come," began the Commissioner, "because of what happened during my absence. I have been told a few things but I cannot believe them until I have heard your own side. Let us talk about it like friends and find a way of ensuring that it does not happen again."

Ogbuefi Ekwueme rose to his feet and began to tell the story.

"Wait a minute," said the Commissioner. "I want to bring in my men so that they too can hear your grievances and take warning. Many of them come from distant places and although they speak your tongue they are ignorant of your customs. James! Go and bring in the men." His interpreter left the courtroom and soon returned with twelve men. They sat together with the men of Umuofia, and Ogbuefi Ekwueme began to tell the story of how Enoch murdered an *egwugwu*.

It happened so quickly that the six men did not see it coming. There was only a brief scuffle, too brief even to allow the drawing of a sheathed machete. The six men were handcuffed and led into the guardroom.

"We shall not do you any harm," said the District Commissioner to them later, "if only you agree to cooperate with us. We have brought a peaceful administration to you and your people so that you may be happy. If any man ill-treats you we shall come to your rescue. But we will not allow you to ill-treat others. We have a court of law where we judge cases and administer justice just as it is done in my own country under a great queen. I have brought you here because you joined together to molest others, to burn people's houses and their place of worship. That must not happen in the dominion of our queen, the most powerful ruler in the world. I have decided that you will pay a fine of two hundred bags of cowries. You will be released as soon as you agree to this and undertake to collect that fine from your people. What do you say to that?"

The six men remained sullen and silent and the Commissioner left them for a while. He told the court messengers, when he left the guardroom, to treat the men with respect because they were the leaders of Umuofia. They said, "Yes, sir," and saluted.

As soon as the District Commissioner left, the head messenger, who was also the prisoners' barber, took down his razor and shaved off all the hair on the men's heads. They were still handcuffed, and they just sat and moped.

"Who is the chief among you?" the court messengers asked in jest. "We see that every pauper wears the anklet of title in Umuofia. Does it cost as much as ten cowries?"

The six men ate nothing throughout that day and the next. They were not even given any water to drink, and they could not go out to urinate or go into the bush when they were pressed. At night the messengers came in to taunt them and to knock their shaven heads together.

Even when the men were left alone they found no words to speak to one another. It was only on the third day, when they could no longer bear the hunger and the insults, that they began to talk about giving in.

"We should have killed the white man if you had listened to me," Okonkwo snarled.

"We could have been in Umuru now waiting to be hanged," someone said to him.

"Who wants to kill the white man?" asked a messenger who had just rushed in. Nobody spoke.

"You are not satisfied with your crime, but you must kill the white man on top of it." He carried a strong stick, and he hit each man a few blows on the head and back. Okonkwo was choked with hate.

As soon as the six men were locked up, court messengers went into Umuofia to tell the people that their leaders would not be released unless they paid a fine of two hundred and fifty bags of cowries.

"Unless you pay the fine immediately," said their headman, "we will take your leaders to Umuru before the big white man, and hang them."

This story spread quickly through the villages, and was added to as it went. Some said that the men had already been taken to Umuru and would be hanged on the following day. Some said that their families would also be hanged. Others said that soldiers were already on their way to shoot the people of Umuofia as they had done in Abame.

It was the time of the full moon. But that night the voice of children was not heard. The village *ilo* where they always gathered for a moon-play was empty. The women of Iguedo did not meet in their secret enclosure to learn a new dance to be displayed later to the village. Young men who were always abroad in the moonlight kept their huts that night. Their manly voices were not heard on the village paths as they went to visit their friends and lovers. Umuofia was like a startled animal with ears erect, sniffing the silent, ominous air and not knowing which way to run.

The silence was broken by the village crier beating his sonorous *ogene*. He called every man in Umuofia, from the Akakanma age group upwards, to a meeting in the marketplace after the morning meal. He went from one end of the village to the other and walked all its breadth. He did not leave out any of the main footpaths.

Okonkwo's compound was like a deserted homestead. It was as if cold water had been poured on it. His family was all there, but everyone spoke in whispers. His daughter Ezinma had broken her twenty-eight day visit to the family of her future husband, and returned home when she heard that her father had been imprisoned, and was going to be hanged. As soon as she got home she went to Obierika to ask what the men of Umuofia were going to do about it. But Obierika had not been home since morning. His wives thought he had gone to a secret meeting. Ezinma was satisfied that something was being done.

On the morning after the village crier's appeal the men of Umuofia met in the marketplace and decided to collect without delay two hundred and fifty bags of cowries to appease the white man. They did not know that fifty bags would go to the court messengers, who had increased the fine for that purpose.

Chapter
Twenty-Four

Okonkwo and his fellow prisoners were set free as soon as the fine was paid. The District Commissioner spoke to them again about the great queen, and about peace and good government. But the men did not listen. They just sat and looked at him and at his interpreter. In the end they were given back their bags and sheathed machetes and told to go home. They rose and left the courthouse. They neither spoke to anyone nor among themselves.

The courthouse, like the church, was built a little way outside the village. The footpath that linked them was a very busy one because it also led to the stream, beyond the court. It was open and sandy. Footpaths were open and sandy in the dry season. But when the rains came the bush grew thick on either side and closed in on the path. It was now dry season.

As they made their way to the village the six men met women and children going to the stream with their waterpots. But the men wore such heavy and fearsome looks that the women and children did not say "*nno*" or "welcome" to them, but edged out of the way to let them pass. In the village little groups of men joined them until they became a sizable company. They walked silently. As each of the six men got to his compound, he turned in, taking some of the crowd with him. The village was astir in a silent, suppressed way.

Ezinma had prepared some food for her father as soon as news spread that the six men would be released. She took it to him in his *obi*. He ate absent-mindedly. He had no appetite, he only ate to please her. His male relations and friends had gathered in his *obi*, and Obierika was urging him to eat. Nobody else spoke, but they noticed the long stripes on Okonkwo's back where the warder's whip had cut into his flesh.

The village crier was abroad again in the night. He beat his iron gong and announced that another meeting would be held in the morning. Everyone knew that Umuofia was at last going to speak its mind about the things that were happening.

Okonkwo slept very little that night. The bitterness in his heart was now mixed with a kind of childlike excitement. Before he had gone to bed he had brought down his war dress, which he had not touched since his return from exile. He had shaken out his smoked raffia skirt and examined his tall feather head-gear and his shield. They were all satisfactory, he had thought.

As he lay on his bamboo bed he thought about the treatment he had received in the white man's court, and he swore vengeance. If Umuofia decided on war, all would be well. But if they chose to be cowards he would go out and avenge himself. He thought about wars in the past. The noblest, he thought, was the war against Isike. In those days Okudo was still alive. Okudo sang a war song in a way that no other man could. He was not a fighter, but his voice turned every man into a lion.

"Worthy men are no more," Okonkwo sighed as he remembered those days. "Isike will never forget how we slaughtered them in that war. We killed twelve of their men and they killed only two of ours. Before the end of the fourth market week they were suing for peace. Those were the days when men were men."

As he thought of these things he heard the sound of the iron gong in the distance. He listened carefully, and could just hear the crier's voice. But it was very faint. He turned on his bed and his back hurt him. He ground his teeth. The crier was drawing nearer and nearer until he passed by Okonkwo's compound.

"The greatest obstacle in Umuofia," Okonkwo thought bitterly, "is that coward, Egonwanne. His sweet tongue can change fire into cold ash. When he speaks he moves our men to impotence. If they had ignored his woman-ish wisdom five years ago, we would not have come to this." He ground his teeth. "Tomorrow, he will tell them that our fathers never fought a 'war of blame.' If they listen to him I shall leave them and plan my own revenge."

The crier's voice had once more become faint, and the distance had taken the harsh edge off his iron gong. Okonkwo turned from one side to the other and derived a kind of pleasure from the pain his back gave him. "Let Egonwanne talk about a 'war of blame' tomorrow and I shall show him my back and head." He ground his teeth.

The marketplace began to fill as soon as the sun rose. Obierika was waiting in his *obi* when Okonkwo came along and called him. He hung his goatskin bag and his sheathed machete on his shoulder and went out to join him. Obierika's hut was close to the road and he saw every man who passed to the marketplace. He had exchanged greetings with many who had already passed that morning.

When Okonkwo and Obierika got to the meeting place there were already so many people that if one threw up a grain of sand it would not find its way to the earth again. And many more people were coming from every quarter of the nine villages. It warmed Okonkwo's heart to see such strength of numbers. But he was looking for one man in particular, the man whose tongue he dreaded and despised so much.

"Can you see him?" he asked Obierika.

"Who?"

"Egonwanne," he said, his eyes roving from one corner of the huge marketplace to the other. Most of the men sat on wooden stools they had brought with them.

"No," said Obierika, casting his eyes over the crowd. "Yes, there he is, under the silk-cotton tree. Are you afraid he would convince us not to fight?"

"Afraid? I do not care what he does to *you.* I despise him and those who listen to him. I shall fight alone if I choose."

They spoke at the top of their voices because everybody was talking, and it was like the sound of a great market.

"I shall wait till he has spoken," Okonkwo thought. "Then I shall speak."

"But how do you know he will speak against war?" Obierika asked after a while.

"Because I know he is a coward," said Okonkwo. Obierika did not hear the rest of what he said because at that moment somebody touched his shoulder from behind and he turned round to shake hands and exchange greetings with five or six friends. Okonkwo did not turn round even though he knew the voices. He was in no mood to exchange greetings. But one of the men touched him and asked about the people of his compound.

"They are well," he replied without interest.

The first man to speak to Umuofia that morning was Okika, one of the six who had been imprisoned. Okika was a great man and an orator. But he did not have the booming voice which a first speaker must use to establish silence in the assembly of the clan. Onyeka had such a voice; and so he was asked to salute Umuofia before Okika began to speak.

"*Umuofia kwenu!*" he bellowed, raising his left arm and pushing the air with his open hand.

"*Yaa!*" roared Umuofia.

"*Umuofia kwenu!*" he bellowed again, and again and again, facing a new direction each time. And the crowd answered, "*Yaa!*"

There was immediate silence as though cold water had been poured on a roaring flame.

Okika sprang to his feet and also saluted his clansmen four times. Then he began to speak:

"You all know why we are here, when we ought to be building our barns or mending our huts, when we should be putting our compounds in order. My father used to say to me: 'Whenever you see a toad jumping in broad daylight, then know that something is after its life.' When I saw you all pouring into this meeting from all the quarters of our clan so early in the morning, I knew that something was after our life." He paused for a brief moment and then began again:

"All our gods are weeping. Idemili is weeping, Ogwugwu is weeping, Agbala is weeping, and all the others. Our dead fathers are weeping because of the shameful sacrilege they are suffering and the abomination we have all seen with our eyes." He stopped again to steady his trembling voice.

"This is a great gathering. No clan can boast of greater numbers or greater valor. But are we all here? I ask you: Are all the sons of Umuofia with us here?" A deep murmur swept through the crowd.

"They are not," he said. "They have broken the clan and gone their several ways. We who are here this morning have remained true to our fathers, but our brothers have deserted us and joined a stranger to soil their fatherland. If we fight the stranger we shall hit our brothers and perhaps shed the blood of a clansman. But we must do it. Our fathers never dreamed of such a thing, they never killed their brothers. But a white man never came to them. So we must do what our fathers would never have done. Eneke the bird was asked why he was always on the wing and he replied: 'Men have learned to shoot without missing their mark and I have learned to fly without perching on a twig.' We must root out this evil. And if our brothers take the side of evil we must root them out too. And we must do it *now*. We must bale this water now that it is only ankle-deep. . . ."

At this point there was a sudden stir in the crowd and every eye was turned in one direction. There was a sharp bend in the road that led from the marketplace to the white man's court, and to the stream beyond it. And so no one had seen the approach of the five court messengers until they had come round the bend, a few paces from the edge of the crowd. Okonkwo was sitting at the edge.

He sprang to his feet as soon as he saw who it was. He confronted the head messenger, trembling with hate, unable to utter a word. The man was fearless and stood his ground, his four men lined up behind him.

In that brief moment the world seemed to stand still, waiting. There was utter silence. The men of Umuofia were merged into the mute backcloth of trees and giant creepers, waiting.

The spell was broken by the head messenger. "Let me pass!" he ordered.

"What do you want here?"

"The white man whose power you know too well has ordered this meeting to stop."

In a flash Okonkwo drew his machete. The messenger crouched to avoid the blow. It was useless. Okonkwo's machete descended twice and the man's head lay beside his uniformed body.

The waiting backcloth jumped into tumultuous life and the meeting was stopped. Okonkwo stood looking at the dead man. He knew that Umuofia would not go to war. He knew because they had let the other messengers escape. They had broken into tumult instead of action. He discerned fright in that tumult. He heard voices asking: "Why did he do it?"

He wiped his machete on the sand and went away.

Chapter Twenty-Five

W HEN THE DISTRICT COMMISSIONER ARRIVED at Okonkwo's compound at the head of an armed band of soldiers and court messengers he found a small crowd of men sitting wearily in the *obi*. He commanded them to come outside, and they obeyed without a murmur.

"Which among you is called Okonkwo?" he asked through his interpreter.

"He is not here," replied Obierika.

"Where is he?"

"He is not here!"

The Commissioner became angry and red in the face. He warned the men that unless they produced Okonkwo forthwith he would lock them all up. The men murmured among themselves, and Obierika spoke again.

"We can take you where he is, and perhaps your men will help us."

The Commissioner did not understand what Obierika meant when he said, "Perhaps your men will help us." One of the most infuriating habits of these people was their love of superfluous words, he thought.

Obierika with five or six others led the way. The Commissioner and his men followed their firearms held at the ready. He had warned Obierika that if he and his men played any monkey tricks they would be shot. And so they went.

There was a small bush behind Okonkwo's compound. The only opening into this bush from the compound was a little round hole in the red-earth wall through which fowls went in and out in their endless search for food. The hole would not let a man through. It was to this bush that Obierika led the Commissioner and his men. They skirted round the compound, keeping close to the wall. The only sound they made was with their feet as they crushed dry leaves.

Then they came to the tree from which Okonkwo's body was dangling, and they stopped dead.

"Perhaps your men can help us bring him down and bury him," said Obierika. "We have sent for strangers from another village to do it for us, but they may be a long time coming."

The District Commissioner changed instantaneously. The resolute administrator in him gave way to the student of primitive customs.

"Why can't you take him down yourselves?" he asked.

"It is against our custom," said one of the men. "It is an abomination for a man to take his own life. It is an offense against the Earth, and a man who commits it will not be buried by his clansmen. His body is evil, and only strangers may touch it. That is why we ask your people to bring him down, because you are strangers."

"Will you bury him like any other man?" asked the Commissioner.

"We cannot bury him. Only strangers can. We shall pay your men to do it. When he has been buried we will then do our duty by him. We shall make sacrifices to cleanse the desecrated land."

Obierika, who had been gazing steadily at his friend's dangling body, turned suddenly to the District Commissioner and said ferociously: "That man was one of the greatest men in Umuofia. You drove him to kill himself; and now he will be buried like a dog. . . ." He could not say any more. His voice trembled and choked his words.

"Shut up!" shouted one of the messengers, quite unnecessarily.

"Take down the body," the Commissioner ordered his chief messenger, "and bring it and all these people to the court."

"Yes, sah," the messenger said, saluting.

The Commissioner went away, taking three or four of the soldiers with him. In the many years in which he had toiled to bring civilization to different parts of Africa he had learned a number of things. One of them was that a District Commissioner must never attend to such undignified details as cutting a hanged man from the tree. Such attention would give the natives a poor opinion of him. In the book which he planned to write he would stress that point. As he walked back to the court he thought about that book. Every day brought him some new material. The story of this man who had killed a messenger and hanged himself would make interesting reading. One could almost write a whole chapter on him. Perhaps not a whole chapter but a reasonable paragraph, at any rate. There was so much else to include, and one must be firm in cutting out details. He had already chosen the title of the book, after much thought: *The Pacification of the Primitive Tribes of the Lower Niger.*

A Glossary of Ibo Words and Phrases

agadi-nwayi: old woman.

agbala: woman; also used of a man who has taken no title.

chi: personal god.

efulefu: worthless man.

egwugwu: a masquerader who impersonates one of the ancestral spirits of the village.

ekwe: a musical instrument; a type of drum made from wood.

eneke-nti-oba: a kind of bird.

eze-agadi-nwayi: the teeth of an old woman.

iba: fever.

ilo: the village green, where assemblies for sports, discussions, etc., take place.

inyanga: showing off, bragging.

isa-ifi: a ceremony. If a wife had been separated from her husband for some time and were then to be re-united with him, this ceremony would be held to ascertain that she had not been unfaithful to him during the time of their separation.

iyi-uwa: a special kind of stone which forms the link between an *ogbanje* and the spirit world. Only if the *iyi-uwa* were discovered and destroyed would the child not die.

jigida: a string of waist beads.

kotma: court messenger. The word is not of Ibo origin but is a corruption of "court messenger."

kwenu: a shout of approval and greeting.

ndichie: elders.

nna ayi: our father.

nno: welcome.

nso-ani: a religious offence of a kind abhorred by everyone, literally earth's taboo.

nza: a very small bird.

obi: the large living quarters of the head of the family.

obodo dike: the land of the brave.

ochu: murder or manslaughter.

ogbanje: a changeling; a child who repeatedly dies and returns to its mother to be reborn. It is almost impossible to bring up an *ogbanje* child without it dying, unless its *iyi-uwa* is first found and destroyed.

ogene: a musical instrument; a kind of gong.

oji odu achu-ijiji-o: (cow i.e., the one that uses its tail to drive flies away).

osu: outcast. Having been dedicated to a god, the *osu* was taboo and was not allowed to mix with the freeborn in any way.

Oye: the name of one of the four market days.

ozo: the name of one of the titles or ranks.

tufia: a curse or oath.

udu: a musical instrument; a type of drum made from pottery.

uli: a dye used by women for drawing patterns on the skin.

umuada: a family gathering of daughters, for which the female kinsfolk return to their village of origin.

umunna: a wide group of kinsmen (the masculine form of the word *umuada*).

Uri: part of the betrothal ceremony when the dowry is paid.

Related Readings

William Butler Yeats

The Second Coming

William Butler Yeats saw history as a series of two-thousand-year cycles, during each of which a civilization emerges, flourishes, decays and is destroyed. Yeats, writing in the 1920s, believed that the Christian civilization was in decline. In this poem he refers to the biblical prophecy that Jesus Christ will return to the earth at the end of the world.

Turning and turning in the widening gyre
The falcon cannot hear the falconer;
Things fall apart; the center cannot hold;
Mere anarchy is loosed upon the world,
5   The blood-dimmed tide is loosed, and everywhere
The ceremony of innocence is drowned;
The best lack all conviction, while the worst
Are full of passionate intensity.

Surely some revelation is at hand;
10   Surely the Second Coming is at hand.
The Second Coming! Hardly are those words out
When a vast image out of *Spiritus Mundi*
Troubles my sight: somewhere in sands of the desert
A shape with lion body and the head of a man,
15   A gaze blank and pitiless as the sun,
Is moving its slow thighs, while all about it
Reel shadows of the indignant desert birds.
The darkness drops again; but now I know
That twenty centuries of stony sleep
20   Were vexed to nightmare by a rocking cradle,
And what rough beast, its hour come round at last,
Slouches towards Bethlehem to be born?

Somini Sengupta

Chinua Achebe: A Storyteller Far from Home

For some, the creative act of writing grows from roots deep in the soil of the homeland. For such writers, exile can be especially painful. At the time of this interview, in January 2000, Chinua Achebe was living in the United States.

To BE HUMAN, the writer Chinua Achebe has said, one must have a story. "It's one of the things humans do," he insists. "Not just have a story, but tell a story."

For more than four decades Mr. Achebe, the man widely regarded as the progenitor of the modern African novel and the author of the groundbreaking 1958 book "Things Fall Apart," has been telling the story of his native Nigeria, before and after its encounter with European colonialism.

But these days, as Nigeria takes its first steps toward democracy after a long spell of political repression, Mr. Achebe is not in place to tell the tale. Since 1990, when a car accident outside Lagos left him paralyzed from the waist down, he has made a modest wood-frame house on the Bard College campus, Annandale-on-Hudson, N.Y., his improbable, and, he maintains, his impermanent home.

He has been unable to move back to Nigeria not just because the country was, until recently, in the grip of a corrupt dictatorship, but also because the essentials of civil order—including a health-care system that can tend to his needs—has all but collapsed.

Now 69, he waits for things to fall into place in Nigeria again. And he waits to go home. "I have chosen a particular story, or maybe that story has chosen me," he says. "I just find it useful, fruitful to be in that community, as a writer, as a human being. There is so much to do."

That apparently came into sharp relief in August when, for the first time in nine years, Mr. Achebe went home to Nigeria for a visit. One evening at a talk at Bard College, where he has taught since 1990, he spoke of that visit publicly for the first time.

Speaking softly and with remarkable modesty, peppering his lecture with metaphors, Mr. Achebe talked with his hands, sweeping the air in an arc when referring to Nigeria, sometimes clasping his hands as though in prayer, pointing a long finger when speaking of the reign of dictators. The country, he said at one point, is like a wobbly tripod, and its three major ethnic groups—the Hausa, Igbo and Yoruba, who frequently contest one another for power and turf—are its three unwieldy legs. "Nigeria," he observed, "refuses to stand on three legs."

"I'm still very emotional about it," he said of his five-week sojourn. "It's really a wonderful experience to connect again to people who share this culture, this land of Igbo, and to be with people who have been treated very badly by rulers."

In an interview later that evening he tried to explain the conditions of his strange exile here by turning to the novel *Ambiguous Adventure*, by the Senegalese writer Cheik A. Kane. Its protagonist, a young African aristocrat, goes to France, seeking to master French philosophy. When he gets there, he discovers how unnecessary he is.

"They're not saying, 'You can't stay here,' " Mr. Achebe explains. "There's no work for you. That's a terrible thing for an artist—to be trying to work, trying to scratch around for work, when at home work is all over."

Does he feel like this sometimes?

He nods wordlessly.

Will he return to Nigeria?

"Sure, sure," comes the unequivocal answer. "I will go back as soon as I can, as soon as I think it's safe, which means if I need to go to hospital, there will be a hospital."

Mr. Achebe's coming to Bard College for so long a stay was wholly unexpected. He was flown to London for surgery immediately after his accident. Six months later he was invited to Bard. At the time, Mr. Achebe says, he and his wife, Christie, who now teaches psychology at Bard, thought they would be here for a year or two.

But their stay dragged on as political conditions in Nigeria deteriorated. Elections were held and annulled. Gen. Sani Abacha—"that hideous tyrant," in Mr. Achebe's words—took power. In 1995 the writer Ken Saro-Wiwa was hanged. Nigerians, Mr. Achebe is fond of saying, saw how far the bottom really was.

In all these years Mr. Achebe has not lost touch with Nigeria. People call, they write. But it doesn't make it easier to be away.

"It's almost like, 'Come and help!'" he says. "For me it begins to sound like, 'Am I running away?'"

At Bard Mr. Achebe spends much of his day reading in the college library or writing letters by longhand, which a colleague transcribes. Usually he teaches a class on African literature each semester, though he had the fall term off to work on a book of essays, *Home and Exile*. He writes when the spirit moves him, he says. He calls himself "a lazy writer."

Assessing Mr. Achebe's work is a daunting task for many scholars of African literature. *Things Fall Apart*, the story of the Igbo people of Nigeria just before British arrival and the first African novel to enjoy a wide international audience, became a seminal text of postcolonial literature. It was one of the first books to present European colonialism from an African point of view and to express in English the way Africans spoke in their native tongues.

The book has been translated into 50 languages and has sold more than 8 million copies worldwide. Altogether he has written five novels, four books of nonfiction, numerous books of short stories, children's books and poems.

"In the English language, he is the founding father of modern African literature," says K. Anthony Appiah, a Harvard University philosophy professor who grew up in Ghana. "'Things Fall Apart' is the beginning of the modern canon. You can't imagine the rest of the literature without it."

The Somalian writer Nuruddin Farah calls him "the most singular contribution Africa has made to world literature."

For Mr. Achebe, an Igbo by ethnicity and the son of a Christian evangelist, writing in English was never a conscious choice. English was the language of his education; Igbo was for conversation. English was the language of the novel; Igbo, the medium of poetry. "I have two hands," he says simply. "So I give them different things to do."

His novelist's hand has been in repose awhile. Perhaps it, too, is waiting to go home. "Anthills of the Savannah," published in 1987, was Mr. Achebe's last novel. Shortly after it was published he made a prescient observation.

"I would be very, very sad to have to live in Europe or America," he said in an interview in February 1988, two years before his accident. "The relationship between me and the society I write about is so close and so necessary."

Has it been difficult to write away from home?

Yes, he confesses, adding that he hopes Bard College does not feel too bad about it. Of course he can conjure pictures from memory. But "you need to have continuous contact if this is what you've elected to talk about," he says.

"You don't want to miss any important event in that life."

That he was missing many events in that life became all the more plain on this last trip home.

He recalls landing at the Lagos airport and there being no wheelchair anywhere, until his family complained vigorously and a wheelchair suddenly arrived. He speaks of people milling about at the airport, apparently aimlessly. He describes the main thoroughfare through Ogidi, his hometown 400 miles east of Lagos, as a road so rutted that his car had to snake its way around, practically through people's homes. And he remembers that at home the electrical generator designed to be a backup during power failures became the main source of power. "This is a country that has ceased to work," he says.

Yet he also speaks of the festive cannon fire announcing his arrival, when his car pulled into Ogidi, and of the six young men who appointed themselves his bodyguards, to protect him from ruffians known to rob visitors from abroad. All through his stay, he recalls with relish, a stream of guests arrived: journalists seeking interviews, relatives coming to share a meal, political leaders coming to chat.

Mr. Achebe's recollections sounded like those of an elder, pleased to be wanted. Or perhaps of a man who feels not quite so paralyzed.

It seemed like people were saying: " 'Oh, you've come home! Talk to us!' " he remembers. "You realize you serve a certain need. And that is to be around."

Thanks in part to the trip, he says, a new novel may be on its way soon.

The homecoming also included a meeting with the new president, Olusegun Obasanjo, Nigeria's first civilian ruler in 16 years. For him Mr. Achebe offers guarded praise.

"Of all the possibilities we had," he says, "Obasanjo is probably, well, probably the best at this time."

For the prospects of democracy Mr. Achebe is remarkably optimistic, but characteristically cautious, too.

"All we have done is turn around," he insists. "We were facing the wrong direction before."

Mr. Achebe and his wife seem to have been reluctant to recreate their Nigerian home in Annandale. There are few mementos of Nigeria in their house: a Yoruba carving of a horse sits above the television, and some of his manuscripts have been shipped over.

"It's almost pathetic to create an atmosphere of home in this situation," he says, looking around his living room. "You make a new home where you go."

He hasn't become an American citizen, nor does he plan to. He says he is superstitious about these things.

"There's a reason we were planted in a certain place," he observes. "Our people have a saying: The whole essence of travel is to go back home."

Jomo Kenyatta

The Gentlemen of the Jungle

In this fable, the former Prime Minister of Kenya expresses some beliefs about power and politics.

ONCE UPON A TIME an elephant made a friendship with a man. One day a heavy thunderstorm broke out, the elephant went to his friend, who had a little hut at the edge of the forest, and said to him: 'My dear good man, will you please let me put my trunk inside your hut to keep it out of this torrential rain?' The man, seeing what situation his friend was in, replied: 'My dear good elephant, my hut is very small, but there is room for your trunk and myself. Please put your trunk in gently.' The elephant thanked his friend, saying: 'You have done me a good deed and one day I shall return your kindness.' But what followed? As soon as the elephant put his trunk inside the hut, slowly he pushed his head inside, and finally flung the man out in the rain, and then lay down comfortably inside his friend's hut, saying: 'My dear good friend, your skin is harder than mine, and as there is not enough room for both of us, you can afford to remain in the rain while I am protecting my delicate skin from the hailstorm.'

The man, seeing what his friend had done to him, started to grumble; the animals in the nearby forest heard the noise and came to see what was the matter. All stood around listening to the heated argument between the man and his friend the elephant. In this turmoil the lion came along roaring, and said in a loud voice: 'Don't you all know that I am the King of the Jungle! How dare any one disturb the peace of my kingdom?' On hearing this the elephant, who was one of the high ministers in the jungle kingdom, replied in a soothing voice, and said: 'My lord, there is no disturbance of the peace in your kingdom. I have only been having a little discussion with my friend here as to the possession of this little hut which your lordship sees me occupying.' The lion, who wanted to have 'peace and tranquillity' in his kingdom, replied in a noble voice, saying: 'I command my ministers to appoint a Commission of Enquiry to go thoroughly into this matter and report accordingly.' He then turned to the man and said: 'You have done well by establishing friendship with my people, especially with the elephant, who is one of my honourable ministers of state. Do not grumble any more, your hut is not lost to you. Wait until the sitting of my Imperial Commission, and there you will be given plenty of opportunity to state your case. I am sure that you will be pleased with the findings of the Commission.' The man was very pleased by these sweet words from the King of the Jungle, and innocently waited for his opportunity, in the belief that naturally the hut would be returned to him.

The elephant, obeying the command of his master, got busy with other ministers to appoint the Commission of Enquiry. The following elders of the jungle were appointed to sit in the Commission: (1) Mr Rhinoceros; (2) Mr Buffalo; (3) Mr Alligator; (4) The Rt Hon. Mr Fox to act as chairman; and (5) Mr Leopard to act as Secretary to the Commission. On seeing the personnel, the man protested and asked if it was not necessary to include in this Commission a member from his side. But he was told that it was impossible, since no one from his side was well enough educated to understand the intricacy of jungle law. Further, that there was nothing to fear, for the members of the Commission were all men of repute for their impartiality in justice, and as they were gentlemen chosen by God to look after the interests of races less adequately endowed with teeth and claws, he might rest assured that they would investigate the matter with the greatest care and report impartiality.

The Commission sat to take the evidence. The Rt Hon. Mr Elephant was first called. He came along with a superior air, brushing his tusks with a sapling which Mrs Elephant had provided, and in an authoritative voice said: 'Gentlemen of the Jungle, there is no need for me to waste your valuable time in relating a story which I am sure you all know. I have always regarded it as my duty to protect the interests of my friends, and this appears to have caused the misunderstanding between myself and my friend here. He invited me to save his hut from being blown away by a hurricane. As the hurricane had gained access owing to the unoccupied space in the hut, I considered it necessary, in my friend's own interests, to turn the undeveloped space to a more economic use by sitting in it myself; a duty which any of you would undoubtedly have performed with equal readiness in similar circumstances.'

After hearing the Rt Hon. Mr Elephant's conclusive evidence, the Commission called Mr Hyena and other elders of the jungle, who all supported what Mr Elephant had said. They then called the man, who began to give his own account of the dispute. But the Commission cut him short, saying: 'My good man, please confine yourself to relevant issues. We have already heard the circumstances from various unbiased sources; all we wish you to tell us is whether the undeveloped space in your hut was occupied by any one else before Mr Elephant assumed his position?' The man began to say: 'No, but—' But at this point the Commission declared that they had heard sufficient evidence from both sides and retired to consider their decision. After enjoying a delicious meal at the expense of the Rt Hon. Mr Elephant, they reached their verdict, called the man, and declared as follows: 'In our opinion this dispute has arisen through a regrettable misunderstanding due to the backwardness of your ideas. We consider that Mr Elephant has fulfilled his sacred duty of protecting your interests. As it is clearly for your good that the space should be put to its most economic use, and as you yourself have not reached the stage of expansion which would enable you to fill it, we consider it necessary to arrange a compromise to suit both parties. Mr Elephant shall continue his occupation of your hut, but we give you permission to look for a site where you can build another hut more suited to your needs, and we will see that you are well protected.'

The man, having no alternative, and fearing that his refusal might expose him to the teeth and claws of members of the Commission, did as they suggested. But no sooner had he built another hut than Mr Rhinoceros charged in with his horn lowered and ordered the man to quit. A Royal Commission was again appointed to look into the matter, and the same finding was given. This procedure was repeated until Mr Buffalo, Mr Leopard, Mr Hyena and the rest were all accommodated with new huts. Then the man decided that he must adopt an effective method of protection, since Commissions of Enquiry did not seem to be of any use to him. He sat down and said, 'Ng'enda thi ndagaga motegi,' which literally means 'there is nothing that treads on the earth that cannot be trapped,' or in other words, you can fool people for a time, but not for ever.

Early one morning, when the huts already occupied by the jungle lords were all beginning to decay and fall to pieces, he went out and built a bigger and better hut a little distance away. No sooner had Mr Rhinoceros seen it than he came rushing in, only to find that Mr Elephant was already inside, sound asleep. Mr Leopard next came to the window, Mr Lion, Mr Fox and Mr Buffalo entered the doors, while Mr Hyena howled for a place in the shade and Mr Alligator basked on the roof. Presently they all began disputing about their rights of penetration, and from disputing they came to fighting, and while they were all embroiled together the man set the hut on fire and burnt it to the ground, jungle lords and all. Then he went home, saying: 'Peace is costly, but it's worth the expense,' and lived happily ever after.

David Diop

He Who Has Lost All

Sometimes change is so great and terrible that even nature appears to mourn.

The sun shone in my hut
And my wives were fair and supple
Like the palms in the night breeze.
My children passed over the wide river
5   Deep as death
And my canoes vied with the crocodiles.
The motherly moon attended our dances
The wild and heavy rhythm of the tom-tom,
Tom-tom of joy, tom-tom of recklessness
        Midst fires of freedom.

10   Then one day, the Silence . . .
The sun's rays seemed to die out
In my hut empty of meaning.
My wives crushed their reddened mouths
Against the thin hard lips of steel-eyed conquerors
15   And my children left their calm nudity
For the uniform of iron and blood.
Your voice, too, died out.
The irons of slavery have rent my heart
Tom-toms of my nights, tom-toms of my fathers.

Translated from the French by Anne Atik

from

West with the Night

Beryl Markham

Message from Nungwe

A pilot who flies frequently across Africa, Beryl Markham writes of her view of the enormous continent.

COMPETITORS IN CONQUEST have overlooked the vital soul of Africa herself, from which emanates the true resistance to conquest. The soul is not dead, but silent, the wisdom not lacking, but of such simplicity as to be counted non-existent in the tinker's mind of modern civilization. Africa is of an ancient age and the blood of many of her peoples is as venerable and as chaste as truth. What upstart race, sprung from some recent, callow century to arm itself with steel and boastfulness, can match in purity the blood of a single Masai Murani whose heritage may have stemmed not far from Eden? It is not the weed that is corrupt; roots of the weed sucked first life from the genesis of earth and hold the essence of it still. Always the weed returns; the cultured plant retreats before it. Racial purity, true aristocracy, devolve not from edict, nor from rote, but from the preservation of kinship with the elemental forces and purposes of life whose understanding is not farther beyond the mind of a Native shepherd than beyond the cultured fumblings of a mortar-board intelligence.

Whatever happens, armies will continue to rumble, colonies may change masters, and in the face of it all Africa lies, and will lie, like a great, wisely somnolent giant unmolested by the noisy drum-rolling of bickering empires. It is not only a land; it as an entity born of one man's hope and another man's fancy.

So there are many Africas. There are as many Africas as there are books about Africa—and as many books about it as you could read in a leisurely lifetime. Whoever writes a new one can afford a certain complacency in the knowledge that his is a new picture agreeing with no one else's, but likely to be haughtily disagreed with by all those who believe in some other Africa.

Doctor Livingstone's Africa was a pretty dark one. There have been a lot of Africas since that, some darker, some bright, most of them full of animals and pygmies, and a few mildly hysterical about the weather, the jungle, and the trials of safari.

All of these books, or at least as many of them as I have read, are accurate in their various portrayals of Africa—not my Africa, perhaps, nor that of an early settler, nor of a veteran of the Boer War, nor of an American millionaire who went there and shot zebra and lion, but of an Africa true to each writer of each book. Being thus all things to all authors, it follows, I suppose, that Africa must be all things to all readers.

Africa is mystic; it is wild; it is a sweltering inferno; it is a photographer's paradise, a hunter's Valhalla, an escapist's Utopia. It is what you will, and it withstands all interpretations. It is the last vestige of a dead world or the cradle of a shiny new one. To a lot of people, as to myself, it is just 'home.' It is all these things but one thing—it is never dull.

* * *

Africa is never the same to anyone who leaves it and returns again. It is not a land of change, but it is a land of moods and its moods are numberless. It is not fickle, but because it has mothered not only men, but races, and cradled not only cities, but civilizations—and seen them die, and seen new ones born again—Africa can be dispassionate, indifferent, warm, or cynical, replete with the weariness of too much wisdom.

Today Africa may seem to be that ever-promised land, almost achieved; but tomorrow it may be a dark land again, drawn into itself, contemptuous, and impatient with the futility of eager men who have scrambled over it since the experiment of Eden. In the family of continents, Africa is the silent, the brooding sister, courted for centuries by knight-errant empires— rejecting them one by one and severally, because she is too sage and a little bored with the importunity of it all.

Imperious Carthage must once have looked upon Africa as its own province, its future empire; and the sons of the Romans who destroyed that hope, and are today no longer Romans, have retreated with a step rather less firm than Caesar's over routes that knew the rumble of cavalry long before Christ.

All nations lay claim to Africa, but none has wholly possessed her yet. In time she will be taken, yielding neither to Nazi nor to Fascist conquest, but to integrity equal to her own and to wisdom capable of understanding her wisdom and of discerning between wealth and fulfilment. Africa is less a wilderness than a repository of primary and fundamental values, and less a barbaric land than an unfamiliar voice. Barbarism, however bright its trappings, is still alien to her heart.

Athol Fugard

My Children! My Africa!

This play by renowned South African playwright Athol Fugard is set in a period when the fight against apartheid was at its peak. Conflicts over the means for ending this unjust political system often turned families, neighborhoods, and generations against one another.

CHARACTERS

MR. M (ANELA MYALATYA)

ISABEL DYSON

THAMI MBIKWANA

TIME AND PLACE

The action takes place in a small Eastern Cape Karoo town in the autumn of 1984.

Act One

SCENE 1

Classroom of the Zolile High School. Mr. M is at a table with Thami and Isabel on either side of him. A lively interschool debate is in progress. Everybody is speaking at the same time.

MR. M: Order please!

ISABEL: I never said anything of the kind.

THAMI: Yes you did. You said that women were more—

MR. M: I call you both to order!

ISABEL: What I said was that women—

THAMI: —were more emotional than men—

ISABEL: Correction! That women were more intuitive than men—

MR. M: Miss Dyson and Mr. Mbikwana! Will you both please—

ISABEL: You are twisting my words and misquoting me.

THAMI: I am not. I am simply asking you—

MR. M: Come to order!

Grabs the school bell and rings it violently. This works. Silence.

I think it is necessary for me to remind all of you exactly what a debate is supposed to be.

(*Opens and reads from a little black dictionary that is at hand on the table*) My dictionary defines it as follows: "The orderly and regulated discussion of an issue with opposing viewpoints receiving equal time and consideration." Shouting down the opposition so that they cannot be heard does not comply with that definition.

Enthusiasm for your cause is most commendable but without personal discipline it is as useless as having a good donkey and a good cart but no harness.

We are now running out of time. I am therefore closing the open section of our debate. No more interruptions from the floor please. We'll bring our proceedings to a close with a brief, I repeat *brief,* three minutes at the most, summing up of our arguments.

Starting with the proposers of the motion: Mr. Thami Mbikwana of the Zolile High School, will you please make your concluding statement.

Thami stands up. Wild round of applause from the audience. He is secure and at ease. He is speaking to an audience of schoolmates. His "concluding statement" is outrageous and he knows it and enjoys it.

THAMI: I don't stand here now and speak to you as your friend and schoolmate. That would lessen the seriousness of my words to you. No! Close your eyes, forget that you know my face and voice, forget that you know anything about Thami Mbikwana. Think of me rather as an oracle, of my words as those of the great ancestors of our traditional African culture, which we turn our back on and desert to our great peril!

The opposition has spoken about sexual exploitation and the need for women's liberation. Brothers and sisters these are foreign ideas. Do not listen to them. They come from a culture, the so-called Western Civilization, that has meant only misery to Africa and its people. It is the same culture that shipped away thousands of our ancestors as slaves, the same culture that has exploited Africa with the greed of a vulture during the period of Colonialism and the same culture which continues to exploit us in the twentieth century under the disguise of concern for our future.

The opposition has not been able to refute my claim that women cannot do the same jobs as men because they are not the equals of us physically and that a woman's role in the family, in society is totally different to that of a man's. These facts taken together reinforce what our fathers, and our grandfathers and our great-grandfathers knew; namely that happiness and prosperity for the tribe and the nation is achieved when education of the little ladies takes these facts into consideration. Would it be right for a woman to go to war while the man sits at the sewing machine? I do not have milk in my breasts to feed the baby while my wife is out digging up roads for the Divisional Council.

Wild laughter.

Brothers and sisters, it is obvious that you feel the same as I do about this most serious matter. I hope that at the end of this debate, your vote will reflect your agreement with me.

Wild applause and whistles.

MR. M: Thank you Mr. Mbikwana.

Thami sits.

And now finally, a last statement from the captain of the visiting team, Miss Isabel Dyson of Camdeboo Girls High.

Polite applause. Isabel stands. She takes on the audience with direct unflinching eye contact. She is determined not to be intimidated.

ISABEL: You have had to listen to a lot of talk this afternoon about traditional values, traditional society, your great ancestors, your glorious past. In spite of what has been implied I want to start off by telling you that I have as much respect and admiration for your history and tradition as anybody else. I believe most strongly that there are values and principles in traditional African society which could be studied with great profit by the Western Civilization so scornfully rejected by the previous speaker. But at the same time, I know, and you know, that Africa no longer lives in that past. For better or for worse it is part now of the twentieth century and all the nations on this continent are struggling very hard to come to terms with that reality. Arguments about sacred traditional values, the traditional way of life et cetera and et cetera, are used by those who would like to hold back Africa's progress and keep it locked up in the past.

Maybe there was a time in the past when a woman's life consisted of bearing children and hoeing the fields while men sharpened their spears and sat around waiting for another war to start. But it is a silly argument that relies on that old image of primitive Africa for its strength. It is an argument that insults your intelligence. Times have changed. Sheer brute strength is not the determining factor anymore. You do not need the muscles of a prize fighter when you sit down to operate the computers that control today's world. The American space program now has women astronauts on board the space shuttles doing the same jobs as men. As for the difference in the emotional and intellectual qualities of men and women, remember that it is a question of difference and not inferiority and that with those differences go strengths which compensate for weaknesses in the opposite sex.

And lastly, a word of warning. The argument against equality for women, in education or any other field, based on alleged "differences" between the two sexes, is an argument that can very easily be used against any other "different" group. It is an argument based on prejudice, not fact. I ask you not to give it your support. Thank you.

She sits. Polite applause.

MR. M: Thank you Miss Dyson. We come now to the vote. But before we do that, a word of caution. We have had a wonderful experience this afternoon. Don't let it end on a frivolous and irresponsible note. Serious issues have been debated. Vote accordingly. To borrow a phrase from Mr. Mbikwana, forget the faces, remember the words. If you believe that we have the right to vote out there in the big world, then show here, in the classroom, that you know how to use it.

We'll take it on a count of hands, and for the benefit of any over-enthusiastic supporters, only one hand per person please. Let me read the proposal once again: "That in view of the essential physical and psychological differences between men and women, there should be correspondingly different educational syllabuses for the two sexes."

All those in favor raise a hand.

Mr. M, Thami and Isabel count hands.

Seventeen?

Thami and Isabel nod agreement.

All those against.

They all count again.

Twenty-four?

Reactions from Thami and Isabel.

The proposal is defeated by twenty-four votes to seventeen. Before we break just a reminder about the special choir practice this afternoon. Members of the choir must please join Mrs. Magada in Number Two Classroom after school. *(To Isabel and Thami)* Allow me to offer you my congratulations Miss Dyson on a most well-deserved victory. What do you say Mbikwana?

THAMI: *(To Isabel)*: Your concluding statement was a knockout.

MR. M: You didn't do too badly yourself.

ISABEL: You made me so angry!

THAMI (*All innocence*): I did?

ISABEL: *Ja* you did. (*Thami laughs*) I was beginning to think you actually believed what you were saying.

THAMI: But I do!

ISABEL: Oh, come on . . . !

MR. M (*Rubbing his hands with pleasure*): All I can say is . . . Splendid! Splendid! Splendid! The intellect in action. Challenge and response. That is what a good debate is all about. And whatever you do young lady, don't underestimate your achievement in winning the popular vote. It wasn't easy for that audience to vote against Mbikwana. He's one of them, and a very popular "one of them" I might add. (*Waving a finger at Thami*) You were quite shameless in the way you tried to exploit that loyalty.

THAMI (*Another laugh*): Was that wrong?

MR. M: No. As the saying goes, all is fair in love, war and debating. But the fact that you didn't succeed is what makes me really happy. I am very proud of our audience. In my humble opinion they are the real winners this afternoon. You two just had to talk and argue. Anybody can do that. They had to listen . . . intelligently!

ISABEL: They certainly gave me a good time.

MR. M: That was very apparent, if I may say so Miss Dyson. I can't thank you enough for coming to us today. I sincerely hope there'll be another occasion.

ISABEL: Same here.

MR. M: Good! (*Consults his watch*) Now you must excuse me. There is a staff meeting waiting for me. Will you look after Miss Dyson please Mbikwana?

THAMI: Yes teacher.

Mr. M leaves. Isabel and Thami pack away into their bookbags the papers and books they used in the debate. Without the mediating presence of Mr. M they are both a little self-conscious. First moves in the ensuing conversation are awkward.

ISABEL: I wish we had a teacher like . . . Mr. . . . . (*Pronouncing the name carefully*) M-ya-lat-ya. Did I say it right?

THAMI: Yes you did, but nobody calls him that. He's just plain Mr. M to everybody.

ISABEL: Mr. M.

THAMI: That's right.

ISABEL: Well I think he's wonderful.

THAMI: He's okay.

ISABEL: I had a geography teacher in Standard Seven who was a little bit like him. Full of fun and lots of energy.

THAMI: *Ja*, that's Mr. M all right.

Pause.

ISABEL: I meant what I said to him. I really did have a good time.

THAMI: Same here.

ISABEL: You did? Because to be honest with you, I wasn't expecting it.

THAMI: Me neither.

ISABEL: No?

THAMI: Nope.

ISABEL: Why not?

THAMI (*Embarrassed*): Well . . . you know . . .

ISABEL: Let me guess. You've never debated with girls before.

He nods, smiling sheepishly.

And white girls at that! I don't believe it. You boys are all the same.

THAMI: But you were good!

ISABEL: Because I happen to feel very strongly about what we were debating. But it was also the whole atmosphere you know. It was so . . . so free and easy. The debates at my school are such stuffy affairs. And so boring most of the time. Everything is done according to the rules with everybody being polite and nobody getting excited . . . lots of discipline but very little enthusiasm. This one was a riot!

THAMI (*Finger to his lips*): Be careful.

ISABEL: Of what?

THAMI: That word.

ISABEL: Which one?

THAMI: Riot! Don't say it in a black township. Police start shooting as soon as they hear it.

ISABEL: Oh. I'm sorry.

THAMI (*Having a good laugh*): It's a joke Isabel.

ISABEL: Oh . . . you caught me off guard. I didn't think you would joke about those things.

THAMI: Riots and police? Oh yes, we joke about them. We joke about everything.

ISABEL: Okay, then I'll say it again: this afternoon was a riot.

THAMI: Good! Try that one on your folks when you get home tonight. Say the newspapers have got it all wrong. You had a wonderful time taking part in a little township riot.

This time Isabel does get the joke. A good laugh.

ISABEL: Oh *ja*, I can just see my mom and dad cracking up at that one.

THAMI: They wouldn't think it was funny? (*The idea of whites reacting to township humor amuses him enormously*)

ISABEL: Are you kidding? They even take the Marx Brothers seriously. I can just hear my mom: "Isabel, I think it is very wrong to joke about those things!"

THAMI: Dyson! That's an English name.

ISABEL: Sober, sensible, English-speaking South African. I'm the third generation.

THAMI: What does your dad do?

ISABEL: He's a chemist. The chemist shop in town. Karoo Pharmacy. That's ours. My mother and sister work in it as well, and on Saturdays, provided there isn't a hockey match, so do I.

THAMI: Any brothers?

ISABEL: No. Just the four of us.

THAMI: A happy family.

ISABEL: *Ja*, I suppose you could call us that. Mind you, Lucille would say it would be a lot happier if only her little sister would be, as she puts it, "more accommodating of others."

THAMI: What does she mean?

ISABEL: She means she doesn't like the fact that I've got opinions of my own. I'm the rebel in the family.

THAMI: That sounds interesting.

ISABEL: I can't help it. Whenever it's time for a family *indaba* . . . you know, when we sit down in the living room to discuss family business and things . . . I just always seem to end up disagreeing with everybody and wanting to do things differently.

But other than that, *ja*, an average sort of happy family. What else do you want to know. Go ahead, anything . . . provided I also get a turn to ask questions.

Thami studies her.

Eighteen years old. I think I want to be a writer. My favorite subject is English and my favorite sport, as you might have guessed, is hockey. Anything else?

THAMI: Yes. What did you have for breakfast this morning?

ISABEL: Auntie, our maid, put down in front of me a plate of steaming, delicious jungle oats over which I sprinkled a crust of golden brown sugar, and while that was melting on top I added a little moat of chilled milk all around the side. That was followed by brown-bread toast, quince jam and lots and lots of tea.

THAMI: Yes, you're a writer.

ISABEL: You think so?

THAMI: You made me hungry.

ISABEL: My turn now?

THAMI: Yep.

ISABEL: Let's start with your family.

THAMI: Mbikwana! *(He clears his throat)* Mbikwana is an old Bantu name and my mother and my father are good, reliable, ordinary, hardworking Bantu-speaking black South African natives. I am the one-hundred-thousandth generation.

ISABEL: You really like teasing, don't you.

THAMI: Amos and Lilian Mbikwana. They're in Cape Town. My mother is a domestic and my father works for the railways. I stay here with my grandmother and married sister. I was sent to school in the peaceful *platteland* because it is so much safer you see than the big city with all its temptations and troubles. *(He laughs)* Another Bantu joke.

ISABEL: You're impossible!

They are now beginning to relax with each other. Isabel finds the class register on the desk.

"Zolile High School. Standard Ten." *(She opens it and reads)* Awu.

THAMI: *(Pointing to the appropriate desk in the classroom):* There. Johnny. Center forward in our soccer team.

ISABEL: Bandla.

THAMI: There.

ISABEL: Cwati.

THAMI: Cwati. There.

ISABEL: Who was the chap sitting there who laughed at *all* your jokes and applauded *everything* you said.

THAMI: Stephen Gaika. He's mad!

ISABEL: And your best friend?

THAMI: They are all my friends.

ISABEL: And where does . . . *(She finds his name in the register)* Thami Mbikwana sit?

Thami points. Isabel goes to the desk and sits.

THAMI: Yes that's the one. For nearly two years I've sat there . . . being educated!

ISABEL *(Reading names carved into the wood of the desk):* John, Bobby, Zola, Bo . . . Boni . . .

THAMI: Bonisile.

ISABEL: Where's your name?

THAMI: You won't find it there. I don't want to leave any part of me in this classroom.

ISABEL: That sounds heavy.

THAMI: It's been heavy. You've got no problems with it, hey.

ISABEL: With school? No not really. Couple of teachers have tried their best to spoil it for me, but they haven't succeeded. I've had a pretty good time in fact. I think I might even end up with the old cliché . . . you know, school years, best years, happiest years . . . whatever it is they say.

THAMI: No. I won't be saying that.

ISABEL: That surprises me.

THAMI: Why?

ISABEL: *Ja,* come on, wouldn't you be if I said it? You're obviously clever. I'll bet you sail through your exams.

THAMI: It's not as simple as just passing exams, Isabel. School doesn't mean the same to us that it does to you.

ISABEL: Go on.

THAMI: I used to like it. Junior school? You should have seen me. I wanted to have school on Saturdays and Sundays as well. Yes, I did. Other boys wanted to kill me. I hated the holidays.

ISABEL: So what happened?

THAMI: I changed.

ISABEL: *Ja,* I'm listening.

THAMI (*A shrug*): That's all. I changed. Things changed. Everything changed.

ISABEL (*Realizing she is not going to get any more out of him*): Only five months to go.

THAMI: I'm counting.

ISABEL: What then?

THAMI: After school? (*Another shrug*) I don't know yet. Do you?

ISABEL: *Ja.* Rhodes University. I want to study journalism.

THAMI: Newspaper reporter.

ISABEL: And radio, TV. It's a very wide field now. You can specialize in all sorts of things. *(Perplexed)* Don't you want to study further Thami?

THAMI: I told you, I'm not sure about anything yet.

ISABEL: What does Mr. M say?

THAMI: It's got nothing to do with him.

ISABEL: But you're his favorite, aren't you?

Noncommittal shrug from Thami.

I bet you are. And I also bet you anything you like that he's got a career planned out for you.

THAMI *(Sharply)*: What I do with my life has got nothing to do with him.

ISABEL: Sorry.

THAMI: I don't listen to what he says and I don't do what he says.

ISABEL: I said I'm sorry, I didn't mean to interfere.

THAMI: That's all right. It's just that he makes me so mad sometimes. He always thinks *he* knows what is best for me. He never asks me how I feel about things. I know he means well, but I'm not a child anymore. I've got ideas of my own now.

ISABEL *(Placating)*: *Ja,* I know what you mean. I've had them in my life as well. They always know what is best for you, don't they. So anyway, listen . . . I'm going to write up the debate for our school newspaper. I'll send you a copy if you like.

THAMI: You got a school newspaper! How about that!

ISABEL: It's a bit unethical reporting on a contest in which I took part, and won, but I promise to be objective. I made notes of most of your main points.

THAMI: You can have my speech if you want it.

ISABEL: Hell, thanks. That will make it much easier . . . and guarantee there won't be any misquotes!

Thami hands over the speech. It is obvious that they both want to prolong the conversation, but this is prevented by the sound of Mr. M's bell being rung vigorously in the distance. They check wristwatches.

ISABEL: Oh my God, look at the time!

They grab their bookbags and run.

SCENE 2

Isabel alone. She speaks directly to the audience.

ISABEL: It's on the edge of town, on the right-hand side when you drive out to join the National Road going north to Middleberg. Unfortunately, as most of Camdeboo would say, you can't miss it. I discovered the other day that it has actually got a name . . . Brakwater . . . from the old farm that used to be there. Now everybody just calls it "the location." There's been a lot of talk lately about moving it to where it can't be seen. Our mayor, Mr. Pienaar, was in our shop the other day and I heard him say to my dad that it was "very much to be regretted" that the first thing that greeted any visitor to the town was the "terrible mess of the location." To be fair to old Pienaar he has got a point you know. Our town is very pretty. We've got a lot of nicely restored National Monument houses and buildings. Specially in the Main Street. Our shop is one of them. The location is quite an eyesore by comparison. Most of the houses—if you can call them that!—are made of bits of old corrugated iron or anything else they could find to make four walls and a roof. There are no gardens or anything like that. You've got to drive in first gear all the time because of the potholes and stones, and when the wind is blowing and all the dust and rubbish flying around . . . ! I think you'd be inclined to agree with our mayor.

I've actually been into it quite a few times. With my mom to visit Auntie, our maid, when she was sick. And with my dad when he had to take emergency medicines to the clinic. I can remember one visit, just sitting in the car and staring out of the window trying to imagine what it would be like to live my whole life in one of those little *pondoks*. No electricity, no running water, no privacy! Auntie's little house has only got two small rooms and nine of them sleep there. I ended up being damn glad I was born with a white skin.

But don't get the wrong idea. I'm not saying I've spent a lot of time thinking about it seriously or anything like that.

It's just been there, you know, on the edge of my life, the way it is out there on the edge of town. So when Miss Brockway, our principal, called me in and told me that the black school had started a debating society and had invited us over for a debate, I didn't have any objections. She said it was a chance for a "pioneering intellectual exchange" between the two schools.

She also said she had checked with the police and they had said it would be all right provided we were driven straight to the school and then straight out afterwards. There's been a bit of trouble in the location again and people are starting to get nervous about it. So off we went . . . myself, Renee Vermaas and Cathy Bullard, the C.G.H. Debating Team . . . feeling very virtuous about our "pioneering" mission into the location. As Renee tactfully put it: "Shame! We must remember that English isn't their home language. So don't use too many big words and speak slowly and carefully."

They were waiting for us in what they called Number One Classroom. (*Shaking her head*) Honestly, I would rate it as the most bleak, depressing, dingy classroom I have ever been in. Everything about it was gray—the cement floor, the walls, the ceiling. When I first saw it I thought to myself, how in God's name does anybody study or learn anything in here. But there they were, about forty of them, my age, mostly boys, not one welcoming smile among the lot of them. And they *were* studying something and very intently . . . three privileged and uncomfortable white girls, in smart uniforms, from a posh school, who had come to give them a lesson in debating. I know I'm a good debater and one of the reasons for that is that I always talk very directly to the audience and the opposition. I am not shy about making eye contact. Well, when I did it this time, when it was my turn to speak and I stood up and looked at those forty unsmiling faces, I suddenly realized that I hadn't prepared myself for one simple but all-important fact: they had no intention of being grateful to me. They were sitting there waiting to judge me, what I said and how I said it, on the basis of total equality. Maybe it doesn't sound like such a big thing to you, but you must understand I had never really confronted that before, and I don't just mean in debates. I mean in my life!

I'm not saying I've had no contact across the color line. Good heavens no! I get as much of that as any average young white South African. I have a great time every morning with Auntie in the kitchen when she's cooking breakfast and we gossip about everything and everybody in town. And then there's Samuel with his crash helmet and scooter . . . he delivers medicines for my dad . . . I have wonderful long conversations with him about religion and the meaning of life generally. He's a very staunch Zionist. Church every Sunday. But it's always "Miss Isabel," the *baas*'s daughter, that he's talking to. When I stood up in front of those black matric pupils in Number One Classroom it was a very different story. I wasn't at home or in my dad's shop or in my school or any of the other safe places in my life.

I was in Brakwater! It was *their* school. It was *their* world. I was the outsider and I was being asked to prove myself. Standing there in front of them like that I felt . . . exposed! . . . in a way that has never happened to me before. Cathy told me afterwards that she's never heard me start a debate *so* badly and finish it *so* strongly.

God, it was good! I don't know when exactly it happened, but about halfway through my opening address, I realized that everything about that moment . . . the miserable little classroom, myself, my voice, what I was saying and them hearing and understanding me, because I knew they understood me—they were staring and listening so hard I could feel it on my skin!—all of it had become one of the most real experiences I have ever had. I have never before had so . . . so exciting . . . a sense of myself! Because that *is* what we all want, isn't it? For things to be real, our lives, our thoughts, what we say and do? That's what I want, now. I didn't really know it before that debate, but I do now. You see I finally worked out what happened to me in the classroom. I discovered a new world! I've always thought about the location as just a sort of embarrassing backyard to our neat and proper little white world, where our maids and our gardeners and our delivery boys went at the end of the day. But it's not. It's a whole world of its own with its own life that has nothing to do with us. If you put together all the Brakwaters in the country, then it's a pretty big one—and if you'll excuse my language—there's a hell of a lot of people living in it! That's quite a discovery you know. But it's also a little—what's the word?—disconcerting! You see, it means that what I thought was out there for me . . . no! it's worse that that! it's what I was made to believe was out there for me . . . the ideas, the chances, the people . . . specially the people! . . . all of that is only a small fraction of what it could be.

(*Shaking her head*) No. Or as Auntie says in the kitchen when she's not happy about something: *Aikona!* Not good enough. I'm greedy. I want more. I want as much as I can get.

SCENE 3

Isabel alone. Mr. M enters, hat in hand, mopping his brow with a handkerchief.

MR. M: Miss Dyson! There you are.

ISABEL (*Surprised*): Hello!

MR. M: My apologies for descending on you out of the blue like this but I've been looking for you high and low. One of your schoolmates said I would find you here.

ISABEL: Don't apologize. It's a pleasure to see you again Mr. M.

MR. M (*Delighted*): Mr. M! How wonderful to hear you call me that.

ISABEL: You must blame Thami for my familiarity.

MR. M: Blame him? On the contrary, I will thank him most gratefully. Hearing you call me Mr. M like all the others at the school gives me a happy feeling that you are also a member of my very extended family.

ISABEL: I'd like to be.

MR. M: Then welcome to my family Miss . . .

ISABEL (*Before he can say it*): "Isabel" if you please Mr. M, just plain "Isabel."

MR. M (*Bowing*): Then doubly welcome young Isabel.

ISABEL (*Curtsy*): I thank you kind sir.

MR. M: You have great charm young lady. I can understand now how you managed to leave so many friends behind you after only one visit to the school. Hardly a day passes without someone stopping me and asking: When is Isabel Dyson and her team coming back?

ISABEL: Well? When are we?

MR. M: You would still welcome a return visit?

ISABEL: But of course.

MR. M: Why so emphatically "of course"?

ISABEL: Because I enjoyed the first one so emphatically very much.

MR. M: The unruly behavior of my young family wasn't too much for you?

ISABEL: Didn't I also get a little unruly once or twice, Mr. M?

MR. M: Yes, now that you mention it. You certainly gave as good as you got.

ISABEL (*With relish*): And that is precisely why I enjoyed myself . . .

MR. M: You like a good fight.

ISABEL: *Ja.* Specially the ones I win!

MR. M: Splendid! Splendid! Splendid! Because that is precisely what I have come to offer you.

ISABEL: Your Thami wants a return bout, does he?

MR. M: He will certainly welcome the opportunity to salvage his pride when it comes along . . . his friends are teasing him mercilessly . . . but what I have come to talk to you about is a prospect even more exciting than that. I have just seen Miss Brockway and she has given it her official blessing. It was her suggestion that I approach you directly. So here I am. Can you spare a few minutes?

ISABEL: As many as you like.

MR. M: It came to me as I sat there in Number One trying to be an impartial referee while you and Thami went for each other hammer and tongs, no holds barred and no quarter given or asked. I don't blame our audience for being so unruly. Once or twice I felt like doing some shouting myself. What a contest! But at the same time, what a waste I thought! Yes you heard me correctly. A waste! They shouldn't be fighting each other. They should be fighting together! If the sight of them as opponents is so exciting, imagine what it would be like if they were allies. If those two stood side by side and joined forces, they could take on anybody . . . and win! For the next few days that is all I could think of. It tormented me. When I wrote my report about the debate in the school diary, that was the last sentence. "But oh!, what a waste!"

The truth is, I've seen too much of it Isabel. Wasted people! Wasted chances! It's become a phobia with me now. It's not easy you know to be a teacher, to put your heart and soul into educating an eager young mind which you know will never get a chance to develop further and realize its full potential. The thought that you and Thami would be another two victims of this country's lunacy, was almost too much for me.

The time for lamentations is passed. (*Takes an envelope from his pocket*) Two days ago I received this in the mail. It's the program for this year's Grahamstown Schools Festival. It has given me what I was looking for . . . an opportunity to fight the lunacy. The Standard Bank is sponsoring a new event: an interschool English literature quiz. Each team to consist of two members. I'll come straight to the point. I have suggested to Miss Brockway that Zolile High and Camdeboo High join forces and enter a combined team. As I have already told you, she has agreed and so has the Festival director who I spoke to on the telephone this morning. There you have it Isabel Dyson. I anxiously await your response.

ISABEL: I'm in the team?

MR. M: Yes.

ISABEL: And . . . ? (*Her eyes brighten with anticipation*)

MR. M: That's right.

ISABEL: Thami!

MR. M: Correct!

ISABEL: Mr. M, you're a genius!

MR. M (*Holding up a hand to stop what was obviously going to be a very enthusiastic response*): Wait! Wait! Before you get carried away and say yes, let me warn you about a few things. It's going to mean a lot of very hard work. I am appointing myself team coach and as Thami will tell you, I can be a very hard taskmaster. You'll have to give up a lot of free time young lady.

ISABEL: Anything else?

MR. M: Not for the moment.

ISABEL: Then I'll say it again. Mr. M, you're a genius! (*Her joy is enormous, and she shows it*) How's that for unruly behavior?

MR. M: The very worst! They couldn't do it better on the location streets. What a heartwarming response Isabel.

ISABEL: What were you expecting? That I would say no?

MR. M: I didn't know what to expect. I knew that you would give me a sympathetic hearing, but that I would be swept off my feet, literally and figuratively . . . no. I was most certainly not prepared for that. Does my silly little idea really mean that much to you?

ISABEL: None of that, Mr. M! It's not silly and it's not little and you know it.

MR. M: All right. But does it really mean that much to you?

ISABEL: Yes it does.

MR. M (*Persistent*):   But why?

ISABEL: That visit to Zolile was one of the best things that has happened to me. I don't want it to just end there. One visit and that's it.

Mr. M listens quietly, attentively, an invitation to Isabel to say more.

It feels like it could be the beginning of something. I've met you and Thami and all the others and I would like to get to know you all better. But how do I do that? I can't just go after you chaps like . . . well, you know what I mean. Roll up and knock on your doors like you were neighbors or just living down the street. It's not as easy as that with us is it. You're in the location I'm in the town . . . and all the rest of it. So there I was feeling more and more frustrated about it all when along you come with your "silly little" idea. It's perfect! Do I make sense?

MR. M: Most definitely. Make some more.

ISABEL: I've been thinking about it you see. When I told my mom and dad about the debate and what a good time I'd had, I could see that they didn't really understand what I was talking about. Specially my mom. I ended up getting very impatient with her which wasn't very smart of me because the harder I tried to make her understand the more nervous she got. Anyway, I've cooled off now and I realize why she was like that. Being with black people on an equal footing, you know . . . as equals, because that is how I ended up feeling with Thami and his friends . . . that was something that had never happened to her. She didn't know what I was talking about. And because she knows nothing about it, she's frightened of it.

MR. M: You are not.

ISABEL: No. Not anymore.

MR. M: So you were.

ISABEL: Well, not so much frightened as sort of uncertain. You see, I thought I knew what to expect, but after a few minutes in Number One Classroom I realized I was wrong by a mile.

MR. M: What had you expected, Isabel?

ISABEL: You know, that everybody would be nice and polite and very, very grateful.

MR. M: And we weren't?

ISABEL: You were, but not them. Thami and his friends. (*She laughs at the memory*) Ja, to be honest Mr. M, that family of yours *was* a bit scary at first. But not anymore! I feel I've made friends with Thami . . . and the others, so now it's different.

MR. M: Simple as that.

ISABEL: Simple as that.

MR. M: Knowledge has banished fear.

ISABEL: That's right.

MR. M: Bravo. Bravo. And yet again Bravo! If you knew what it meant to me to hear you speak like that. I wasn't wrong. From the moment I first shook hands with you I knew you were a kindred spirit.

ISABEL: Tell me more about the competition.

MR. M: First prize is five thousand rand which the bank has stipulated must be spent on books for the school library. We will obviously divide it equally between Camdeboo and Zolile when you and Thami win.

ISABEL: Yes, what about my teammate. What does he say? Have you asked him yet?

MR. M: No, I haven't *asked* him Isabel, and I won't. I will *tell* him, and when I do I trust he will express as much enthusiasm for the idea as you have. I am an old-fashioned traditionalist in most things young lady, and my classroom is certainly no exception. I Teach, Thami Learns. He understands and accepts that that is the way it should be. You don't like the sound of that do you.

ISABEL: Does sound a bit dictatorial you know.

MR. M: It might sound that way but I assure you it isn't. We do not blur the difference between the generations in the way that you white people do. Respect for authority, right authority, is deeply ingrained in the African soul. It's all I've got when I stand there in Number One. Respect for my authority is my only teaching aid. If I ever lost it those young people will abandon their desks and take to the streets. I expect Thami to trust my judgment of what is best for him, and he does. That trust is the most sacred responsibility in my life.

ISABEL: He's your favorite, isn't he?

MR. M: Good Heavens! A good teacher doesn't have favorites! Are you suggesting that I might be a bad one? Because if you are . . . (Looking around) you would be right young lady. Measured by that yardstick I am a very bad teacher indeed. He *is* my favorite. Thami Mbikwana! Yes, I have waited a long time for him. To tell you the truth I had given up all hope of him ever coming along. Any teacher who takes his calling seriously dreams about that one special pupil, that one eager and gifted young head into which he can pour all that he knows and loves and who will justify all the years of frustration in the classroom. There have been pupils that I'm proud of, but I've always had to bully them into doing their schoolwork. Not with Thami. *He* wants to learn the way other boys want to run out of the classroom and make mischief. If he looks after himself he'll go far and do big things. He's a born leader Isabel, and that is what your generation needs. Powerful forces are fighting for the souls of you young people. You need *real* leaders. Not rabble-rousers. I know Thami is meant to be one. I know it with such certainty it makes me frightened. Because it is a responsibility. Mine and mine alone.

I've got a small confession to make. In addition to everything I've already said, there's another reason for this idea of mine. When you and Thami shine at the Festival, as I know you will, and win first prize and we've pocketed a nice little check for five thousand rand, I am going to point to Thami and say: And now ladies and gentlemen, a full university scholarship if you please.

ISABEL: And you'll get it. We'll shine, we'll win, we'll pocket that check and Thami will get a scholarship.

Mr. M's turn for an enthusiastic response.

MR. M (*Embarrassment and laughter*): Your unruly behavior is very infectious!

ISABEL: My unruly behavior? I like that! I caught that disease in the location I'll have you know.

MR. M: The future is ours Isabel. We'll show this stupid country how it is done.

ISABEL: When do we start?

MR. M: Next week. We need to plan our campaign very carefully.

ISABEL: I'll be ready.

SCENE 4

Mr. M alone. He talks directly to the audience.

MR. M: "I am a man who in the eager pursuit of knowledge forgets his food and in the joy of its attainment forgets his sorrows, and who does not perceive that old age is coming on."
    (*He shakes his head*) No. As I'm sure you have already guessed, that is not me. My pursuit of knowledge is eager, but I do perceive, and only too clearly, that old age is coming on, and at the best of times I do a bad job of forgetting my sorrows. Those wonderful words come from the finest teacher I have ever had, that most wise of all the ancient philosophers . . . Confucius! Yes. I am a Confucian. A black Confucian! There are not many of us. In fact I think there's a good chance that the only one in the country is talking to you at this moment.
    I claim him as my teacher because I have read very carefully, and many times, and I will read it many times more, a little book I have about him, his life, his thoughts and utterances. Truly, they *are* wonderful words my friends, wonderful, wonderful words! My classroom motto comes from its pages: "Learning undigested by thought is labor lost. Thought unassisted by learning is perilous!"

But the words that challenge me most these days, is something he said towards the end of his life. At the age of seventy he turned to his pupils one day and said that he could do whatever his heart prompted, without transgressing what was right.

What do you say to that?

Think about it. *Anything* his heart prompted, *anything* that rose up as a spontaneous urge in his soul, *without* transgressing what was right!

What a heart my friends! Aren't you envious of old Confucius? Wouldn't it be marvelous to have a heart you could trust like that? Imagine being able to wake up in the morning in your little room, yawn and stretch, scratch a few fleabites and then jump out of your bed and eat your bowl of *mealie-pap* and sour milk with a happy heart because you know that when you walk out into the world you will be free to obey and act out, with a clear conscience, all the promptings of your heart. No matter what you see out there on the battle grounds of location streets, and believe me, there are days now when my eyesight feels more like a curse than a blessing, no matter what stories of hardship and suffering you hear, or how bad the news you read in the newspaper, knowing that the whole truth, which can't be printed, is even worse . . . in spite of all that, you need have no fear of your spontaneous urges, because in obeying them you will not transgress what is right.

(*Another shake of his head, another rueful smile*) No yet again. Not in this life, and most certainly not in this world where I find myself, will those wonderful words of Confucius ever be mine. Not even if I lived to be one hundred and seventy will I end up a calm, gentle Chinese heart like his. I wish I could. Believe me, I really wish I could. Because I am frightened of the one I've got. I don't get gentle promptings from it my friends. I get heart attacks. When I walk out into those streets, and I see what is happening to my people, it jumps out and savages me like a wild beast. (*Thumping his chest with a clenched fist*) I've got a whole zoo in here, a mad zoo of hungry animals . . . and the keeper is frightened! All of them. Mad and savage!

Look at me! I'm sweating today. I've been sweating for a week. Why? Because one of those animals, the one called Hope, has broken loose and is looking for food. Don't be fooled by its gentle name. It is as dangerous as Hate and Despair would be if they ever managed to break out. You think I'm exaggerating? Pushing my metaphor a little too far? Then I'd like to put you inside a black skin and ask you to keep Hope alive, find food for it on these streets where our children, our loved and precious children go hungry and die of malnutrition. No, believe me, it is a dangerous animal for a black man to have prowling around in his heart. So how do I manage to keep mine alive, you ask. Friends, I am going to let you in on a terrible secret. That is why I am a teacher.

It is all part of a secret plan to keep alive this savage Hope of mine. The truth is that I am worse than Nero feeding Christians to the lions. I feed young people to my Hope. Every young body behind a school desk keeps it alive.

So you've been warned! If you see a hungry gleam in my eyes when I look at your children . . . you know what it means. That is the monster that stands here before you. Full name: Anela Myalatya. Age: fifty-seven. Marital status: bachelor. Occupation: teacher. Address: the back room of the Reverend Mbopa's house next to the Anglican Church of St. Mark. It's a little on the small side. You know those big kitchen-size boxes of matches they sell these days . . . well if you imagine one of those as Number One Classroom at Zolile High, then the little matchbox you put in your pocket is my room at the Reverend Mbopa's. But I'm not complaining. It has got all I need . . . a table and chair where I correct homework and prepare lessons, a comfortable bed for a good night's insomnia and a reserved space for my chair in front of the television set in the Reverend Mbopa's lounge.

So there you have it. What I call my life rattles around in these two matchboxes . . . the classroom and the back room. If you see me hurrying along the streets you can be reasonably certain that one of those two is my urgent destination. The people tease me. "Faster Mr. M" they shout to me from their front doors. "You'll be late." They think it's a funny joke. They don't know how close they are to a terrible truth . . .

Yes! The clocks are ticking my friends. History has got a strict timetable. If we're not careful we might be remembered as the country where everybody arrived too late.

SCENE 5

Mr. M waiting. Isabel hurries on, carrying hockey stick and togs, and her bookbag. She is hot and exhausted.

ISABEL: Sorry Mr. M, sorry. The game started late.

MR. M: I haven't been waiting long.

Isabel unburdens herself and collapses with a groan.

Did you win?

ISABEL: No. We played a team of friendly Afrikaans-speaking young Amazons from Jansenville and they licked us hollow. Four-one! It was brutal! God they were fit. And fast. They ran circles around us on that hockey field. I felt so stupid. I kept saying to myself "It's only a game Isabel. Relax! Enjoy it! Have a good time!" But no, there I was swearing under my breath at poor little Hilary Castle for being slow and not getting into position for my passes.
(Laughing at herself) You want to know something really terrible? A couple of times I actually wanted to go over and hit her with my hockey stick. Isn't that awful? It's no good Mr. M, I've got to face it: I'm a bad loser. Got any advice for me?

MR. M: On how to be a good one?

ISABEL: *Ja.* How to lose graciously. With dignity. I mean it. I really wish I could.

MR. M: If I did have advice for you Isabel, I think I would be well advised to try it out on myself first . . .

ISABEL: Why? You one as well?

Mr. M nods.

I don't believe it.

MR. M: It's true, Isabel. I'm ashamed to say it but when I lose I also want to grab my hockey stick and hit somebody.

A good laugh from Isabel.

Believe me I can get very petty and mean if I'm not on the winning side. I suppose most bachelors end up like that. We get so used to having everything our own way that when something goes wrong . . . !

So there's my advice to you. Get married! If what I've heard is true, holy matrimony is the best school of all for learning how to lose.

ISABEL: I don't think it's something you can learn. You've either got it or you haven't. Like Thami. Without even thinking about it I know *he's* a good loser.

MR. M: Maybe.

ISABEL: No. No maybes about it. He'd never grab his hockey stick and take it out on somebody else if he didn't win.

MR. M: You're right. I can't see him doing that. You've become good friends, haven't you?

ISABEL: The best. These past few weeks have been quite an education. I owe you a lot you know. I think Thami would say the same . . . if you would only give him the chance to do so.

MR. M: What do you mean by that remark, young lady?

ISABEL: You know what I mean by that remark, *Mr. Teacher!* It's called Freedom of Speech.

MR. M: I've given him plenty of Freedom, within reasonable limits, but he never uses it.

ISABEL: Because you're *always* the teacher and he's *always* the pupil. Stop teaching him all the time Mr. M. Try just talking to him for a change . . . you know, like a friend. I bet you in some ways I already know more about Thami than you.

MR. M: I don't deny that. In which case tell me, is he happy?

ISABEL: What do you mean? Happy with what? Us? The competition?

MR. M: Yes, and also his schoolwork and . . . everything else.

ISABEL: Why don't you ask him?

MR. M: Because all I'll get is another polite "Yes Teacher." I thought maybe he had said something to you about the way he really felt.

ISABEL (*Shaking her head*): The two of you! It's crazy!
But *ja*, he's happy. At least I think he is. He's not a blabbermouth like me, Mr. M. He doesn't give much away . . . even when we talk about ourselves. I don't know what it was like in your time, but being eighteen years old today is a pretty complicated

MR. M: Thami has told you he's got problems?

ISABEL: Come on, Mr. M! We've all got problems. I've got problems, you've got problems, Thami's got problems.

MR. M: But did he say what they were?

ISABEL: You're fishing for something, Mr. M. What is it?

MR. M: Trouble, Isabel. I'm sorry to say it, but I'm fishing for Trouble and I'm trying to catch it before it gets too big.

ISABEL: Thami is in trouble?

MR. M: Not yet, but he will be if he's not careful. And all his friends as well. It's swimming around everywhere trying to stir up things. In the classroom, out on the streets.

ISABEL: Oh, you mean that sort of trouble. Is it really as bad as people are saying?

MR. M: There's a dangerous, reckless mood in the location. Specially among the young people. Very silly things are being said Isabel, and I've got a suspicion that even sillier things are being whispered among themselves. I know Thami trusts you. I was wondering if he had told you what they were whispering about.

ISABEL (*Shocked by what Mr. M is asking of her*): Wow! That's a hard one you're asking for Mr. M. Just suppose he had, do you think it would be right for me to tell you? *We* call that splitting, you know, and you're not very popular if you're caught doing it.

MR. M: It would be for his own good Isabel.

ISABEL: Well he hasn't . . . thank God! So I don't have to deal with that one. (*Pause*) If I ever did that to him, and he found out, that would be the end of our friendship you know. I wish you hadn't asked me.

MR. M (*Realizing his mistake*): Forgive me Isabel. I'm just overanxious on his behalf. One silly mistake now could ruin everything. Forget that I asked you and . . . please . . . don't mention anything about our little chat to Thami. I'll find time to have a word with him myself.

Thami appears, also direct from the sports field.

THAMI: Hi folks. Sorry I'm late.

ISABEL: I've just got here myself. Mr. M is the one who's been waiting.

THAMI: Sorry teacher. The game went into extra time.

ISABEL: Did you win?

THAMI: No. We lost one-nil.

ISABEL: Good.

THAMI: But it was a good game. We're trying out some new combinations and they nearly worked. The chaps are really starting to come together as a team. A little more practice, that's all we need.

ISABEL: Hear that, Mr. M? What did I tell you. And look at him. Smiling! Happy! Even in defeat, a generous word for his teammates.

THAMI: What's going on?

ISABEL: Don't try to look innocent Mbikwana. Your secret is out. Your true identity has been revealed. You are a good loser, and don't try to deny it.

THAMI: Me? You're wrong. I don't like losing.

ISABEL: It's not a question of liking or not liking, but of being able to do so without a crooked smile on your face, a knot in your stomach and murder in your heart.

THAMI: You lost your game this afternoon.

ISABEL: Whatever made you guess! We were trounced. So be careful. I'm looking for revenge.

MR. M: Good! Then let's see if you can get it in the arena of English literature. What do we deal with today?

THAMI: Nineteenth-century poetry.

MR. M (*With relish*): Beautiful! Beautiful! Beautiful! (*Making himself comfortable*) Whose service?

Thami picks up a stone, hands behind his back, then clenched fists for Isabel to guess. She does. She wins. Their relationship is now obviously very relaxed and easy.

ISABEL: Gird your loins, Mbikwana. I want blood.

THAMI: I wish you the very best of luck.

ISABEL:	God, I hate you.
MR. M:	First service, please.
ISABEL:	Right. I'll give you an easy one to start with. The Lake Poets. Name them.
THAMI:	Wordsworth . . .
ISABEL:	Yes, he was one. Who else?
THAMI:	Wordsworth and . . .
ISABEL:	There was only one Wordsworth.
THAMI:	I pass.
ISABEL:	Wordsworth, Southey and Coleridge.
THAMI:	I should have guessed Coleridge!
MR. M:	One-love.
ISABEL:	First line of a poem by each of them please.
THAMI:	Query Mr. Umpire . . . how many questions is that?
MR. M:	One at a time please Isabel.
ISABEL:	Coleridge.
THAMI:	"In Xanadu did Kubla Khan A stately pleasure dome decree . . . " And if you don't like that one what about: " 'Tis the middle of the night by the castle clock, And the owls have awakened the crowing cock; Tu—whit! Tu—whoo!" And if you're still not satisfied . . .
ISABEL:	Stop showing off young man.
MR. M:	One-all.
ISABEL:	Wordsworth.
THAMI:	"Earth has not anything to show more fair: Dull would he be of soul who could pass by A sight so touching in its majesty . . . "
MR. M:	One-two.

ISABEL: Southey.

THAMI: Pass.

ISABEL: "From his brimstone bed at break of day
A-walking the Devil is gone . . .
His jacket was red and his breeches were blue,
And there was a hole where the tail came through."

THAMI: Hey, I like that one!

ISABEL: A poet laureate to boot.

MR. M: Two-all.

ISABEL: One of them was expelled from school. Who was it and why?

THAMI: Wordsworth. For smoking in the lavatory.

ISABEL (*After a good laugh*): You're terrible Thami. He should be penalized
Mr. Umpire . . . for irreverence! It was Southey and the reason he
was expelled—you're going to like this—was for writing a
"precocious" essay against flogging.

THAMI: How about that!

MR. M: Three-two. Change service.

THAMI: I am not going to show you any mercy. What poet was born with
deformed feet, accused of incest and died of fever while helping
the Greeks fight for freedom? "A love of liberty characterizes his
poems and the desire to see the fettered nations of Europe set
free."

ISABEL: Byron.

THAMI: Lord Byron if you please.

MR. M: Two-four.

ISABEL: One of your favorites.

THAMI: You bet.
"Yet, Freedom! yet thy banner, torn, but flying,
Streams like the thunder-storm *against* the wind."
Do you know the Christian names of Lord Byron?

ISABEL: Oh dammit! . . . It's on the tip of my tongue. Henry?

Thami shakes his head.

Herbert?

THAMI: How many guesses does she get, Mr. Umpire?

ISABEL: All right, give him the point. I pass.

THAMI: George Gordon.

MR. M: Three-four.

THAMI: To whom was he unhappily married for one long year?

ISABEL: Pass.

THAMI: Anne Isabella Milbanke.

MR. M: Four-all.

THAMI: Father's occupation?

ISABEL: Pass.

THAMI: John Byron was a captain in the army.

MR. M: Five-four.

THAMI: What other great poet was so overcome with grief when he heard news of Lord Byron's death, that he went out and carved into a rock: "Byron is dead."

ISABEL: Matthew Arnold?

THAMI: No. Another aristocrat . . . Alfred Lord Tennyson.

MR. M: Six-four. Change service.

ISABEL: Right. Whose body did your Lord Byron burn on a beach in Italy?

THAMI: Shelley.

MR. M: Four-seven.

ISABEL: And what happened to Mr. Shelley's ashes?

THAMI: In a grave beside John Keats in Rome.

MR. M: Four-eight.

ISABEL: Shelley's wife. What is she famous for?

THAMI: Which one? There were two. Harriet Westbrook, sixteen years old, who he abandoned after three years and who drowned herself?

Or number two wife—who I think is the one you're interested in—Mary Wollstonecraft, the author of *Frankenstein*.

MR. M: Four-nine.

ISABEL: How much?

MR. M: Four-nine.

ISABEL: I don't believe this! (*She grabs her hockey stick*)

THAMI (*Enjoying himself immensely*): I crammed in two poets last night, Isabel. Guess who they were?

ISABEL: Byron and Shelley. In that case we will deal with Mr. John Keats. What profession did he abandon in order to devote himself to poetry?

THAMI: Law.

ISABEL: You're guessing and you're wrong. He qualified as a surgeon.

MR. M: Five-nine.

ISABEL: What epitaph, composed by himself, is engraved on his tombstone in Rome?

THAMI: Pass.

ISABEL: "Here lies one whose name was writ on water."

MR. M: Six-nine. Let's leave the Births, Marriages and Deaths column please. I want to hear some more poetry.

THAMI: Whose service?

MR. M: Yours.

THAMI: "I must go down to the seas again, to the lonely sea and the sky,
And all I ask is a tall ship and a star to steer her by . . . "

ISABEL: "And the wheel's kick and the wind's song and the white sail's shaking,
And a grey mist on the sea's face and a grey dawn breaking . . .
I must go down to the seas again to the vagrant gypsy life,
To the gull's way and the whale's way where the wind's like a whetted knife . . . "

THAMI: "And all I ask is a merry yarn from a laughing fellow rover,

And quiet sleep and a sweet dream when the long trick's over."

MR. M: Bravo! Bravo! Bravo! But who gets the point?

ISABEL: Give it to John Masefield, Mr. Umpire. (*To Thami*) Nineteenth century?

THAMI: He was born in 1878. To tell you the truth I couldn't resist it. You choose one.

ISABEL: "I met a traveller from an antique land
Who said: Two vast and trunkless legs of stone
Stand in the desert . . . Near them, on the sand,
Half sunk, a shattered visage lies, whose frown,
And wrinkled lip, and sneer of cold command,
Tell that its sculptor well those passions read
Which yet survive, stamped on these lifeless things,
The hand that mocked them, and the heart that fed.
And on the pedestal these words appear:"

THAMI: "My name is Ozymandias, king of kings:
Look on my works, ye Mighty, and despair!"

ISABEL: "Nothing beside remains. Round the decay
Of that colossal wreck, boundless and bare
The lone and level sands stretch far away."

THAMI: And that point goes to Mr. Shelley.

ISABEL (*Takes notebook from her bookbag*): You'll be interested to know gentlemen that Ozymandias is not a fiction of Mr. Shelley's very fertile imagination. He was a real, live Egyptian king. Rameses the Second! According to *Everyman's Encyclopedia* . . . "One of the most famous of the Egyptian kings . . . erected many monuments . . . but his oppressive rule left Egypt impoverished and suffering from an incurable decline."

THAMI: What happened to the statue?

ISABEL: You mean how was it toppled?

THAMI: Yes.

ISABEL: Didn't say. Weather I suppose. And time. Two thousand four hundred B.C. . . . That's over four thousand years ago. Why? What were you thinking?

THAMI: I had a book of Bible stories when I was small, and there was a picture in it showing the building of the pyramids by the slaves. Thousands of them, like ants, pulling the big blocks of stone with ropes, being guarded by soldiers with whips and spears. According to that picture the slaves must have easily outnumbered the soldiers one hundred to one. I actually tried to count them all one day but the drawing wasn't good enough for that.

ISABEL: What are you up to, Mbikwana? Trying to stir up a little social unrest in the time of the Pharaohs, are you?

THAMI: Don't joke about it Miss Dyson. There are quite a few Ozymandiases in this country waiting to be toppled. And you'll see it happen. *We* won't leave it to Time to bring them down.

Mr. M has been listening to the exchange between Thami and Isabel very attentively.

MR. M (*Trying to put a smile on it*): Who is the *we* you speak of with such authority Thami?

THAMI: The People.

MR. M (*Recognition*): Yes, yes, yes, of course . . . I should have known. "The People" . . . with a capital P. Does that include me? Am I one of "The People"?

THAMI: If you choose to be.

MR. M: I've got to choose have I. My black skin doesn't confer automatic membership. So how do I go about choosing?

THAMI: By identifying with the fight for our Freedom.

MR. M: As simple as that? Then I am most definitely one of "The People." I want our Freedom as much as any of you. In fact, I was fighting for it in my own small way long before you were born! But I've got a small problem. Does that noble fight of ours really have to stoop to pulling down a few silly statues? Where do you get the idea that we, "The People," want you to do that for us?

THAMI (*Trying*): They are not our heroes, teacher.

MR. M: They are not our statues Thami! Wouldn't it be better for us to rather put our energies into erecting a few of our own? We've also got heroes, you know.

THAMI: Like who, Mr. M? Nelson Mandela? (*Shaking his head with disbelief*) Hey! *They* would pull *that* statue down so fast—

MR. M (*Cutting him off*):   In which case they would be just as guilty of gross vandalism . . . because that is what it will be, regardless of who does it to whom. Destroying somebody else's property is inexcusable behavior!

No Thami. As one of the People you claim to be acting for, I raise my hand in protest. Please don't pull down any statues on my behalf. Don't use me as an excuse for an act of Lawlessness. If you want to do something "revolutionary" for me let us sit down and discuss it, because I have a few constructive alternatives I would like to suggest. Do I make myself clear?

THAMI: Yes teacher.

MR. M: Good. I'm glad we understand each other.

ISABEL (*Intervening*):   So, what's next? Mr. M? How about singling out a few specific authors who we know will definitely come up. Like Dickens. I bet you anything you like there'll be questions about him and his work.

MR. M: Good idea. We'll concentrate on novelists. A short list of hot favorites.

ISABEL: Thomas Hardy . . . Jane Austen . . . who else, Thami?

MR. M: Put your heads together and make a list. I want twenty names. Divide it between the two of you and get to work. I must be on my way.

ISABEL: Just before you go Mr. M, I've got an invitation for you and Thami from my mom and dad. Would the two of you like to come to tea one afternoon?

MR. M: What a lovely idea!

ISABEL: They've had enough of me going on and on about the all-knowing Mr. M and his brilliant protégé Thami. They want to meet you for themselves. Thami? All right with you?

MR. M: Of course we accept Isabel. It will be a pleasure and a privilege for us to meet Mr. and Mrs. Dyson. Tell them we accept most gratefully.

ISABEL: Next Sunday.

MR. M: Perfect.

ISABEL: Thami?

MR. M: Don't worry about him, Isabel. I'll put it in my diary and remind him at school.

Mr. M leaves.

ISABEL *(Sensitive to a change of mood in Thami)*: I think you'll like my folks. My mom's a bit on the reserved side but that's just because she's basically very shy. But you and my dad should get on well. Start talking sport with him and he won't let you go. He played cricket for E.P. you know. *(Pause)* You will come, won't you?

THAMI *(Edge to his voice)*: Didn't you hear Mr. M? "A delight and a privilege! We accept most gratefully." *(Writing in his notebook)* Charles Dickens . . . Thomas Hardy . . . Jane Austen . . .

ISABEL: Was he speaking for you as well?

THAMI: He speaks for me on nothing!

ISABEL: Relax . . . I know that. That's why I tried to ask you separately and why I'll ask you again. Would you like to come to tea next Sunday to meet my family? It's not a polite invitation. They really want to meet you.

THAMI: Me? Why? Are they starting to get nervous?

ISABEL: Oh come off it Thami. Don't be like that. They're always nervous when it comes to me. But this time it happens to be genuine interest. I've told you. I talk about you at home. They know I have a good time with you . . . that we're a team . . . which they are now very proud of incidentally . . . and that we're cramming like lunatics so that we can put up a good show at the Festival. Is it so strange that they want to meet you after all that? Honestly, sometimes dealing with the two of you is like walking on a tightrope. I'm always scared I'm going to put a foot wrong and . . . well I just *hate* being scared like that.

A few seconds of truculent silence between the two of them.

What's going on Thami? Between you two? There's something very wrong isn't there?

THAMI: No more than usual.

ISABEL: No you don't. A hell of a lot more than usual and don't deny it because it's getting to be pretty obvious. I mean I know he gets on your nerves. I knew that the first day we met. But it's more than that now. These past couple of meetings I've caught you looking at him, watching him in a . . . I don't know . . . in a sort of hard way. Very critical. Not just once. Many times. Do you know you're doing it?

Shrug of the shoulders from Thami.

Well if you know it or not you are. And now he's started as well.

THAMI: What do you mean?

ISABEL: He's watching you.

THAMI: So? He can watch me as much as he likes. I've got nothing to hide. Even if I had he'd be the last person to find out. He sees nothing Isabel.

ISABEL: I think you are very wrong.

THAMI: No, I'm not. That's his trouble. He's got eyes and ears but he sees nothing and hears nothing.

ISABEL: Go on. Please. (*Pause*) I mean it Thami. I want to know what's going on.

THAMI: He is out of touch with what is really happening to us blacks and the way we feel about things. He thinks the world is still the way it was when he was young. It's not! It's different now, but he's too blind to see it. He doesn't open his eyes and ears and see what is happening around him or listen to what people are saying.

ISABEL: What are they saying?

THAMI: They've got no patience left, Isabel. They want change. They want it now!

ISABEL: But he agrees with that. He never stops saying it himself.

THAMI: No. His ideas about change are the old-fashioned ones. And what have they achieved? Nothing. We are worse off now than we ever were. The people don't want to listen to his kind of talk anymore.

ISABEL: I'm still lost, Thami. What kind of talk is that?

THAMI: You've just heard it, Isabel. It calls our struggle vandalism and lawless behavior. It's the sort of talk that expects us to do nothing and wait quietly for white South Africa to wake up. If we listen to it our grandchildren still won't know what it means to be Free.

ISABEL: And those old-fashioned ideas of his . . . are we one of them?

THAMI: What do you mean?

ISABEL: You and me. The competition.

THAMI: Let's change the subject, Isabel. *(From his notebook)* Charles Dickens . . . Thomas Hardy . . . Jane Austen . . .

ISABEL: No! You can't do that! I'm involved. I've got a right to know. Are we an old-fashioned idea?

THAMI: Not our friendship. That is our decision, our choice.

ISABEL: And the competition?

THAMI *(Uncertain of himself)*: Maybe . . . I'm not sure. I need time to think about it.

ISABEL *(Foreboding)*: Oh boy. This doesn't sound so good. You've got to talk to him Thami.

THAMI: He won't listen.

ISABEL: Make him listen!

THAMI: It doesn't work that way with us Isabel. You can't just stand up and tell your teacher he's got the wrong ideas.

ISABEL: Well that's just your bad luck because you are going to have to do it. Even if it means breaking sacred rules and traditions, you have got to stand up and have it out with him.

I don't think you realize what all of this means to him. It's a hell of a lot more than just an "old-fashioned idea" as far as he's concerned. This competition, you and me, but especially you, Thami Mbikwana, has become a sort of crowning achievement to his life as a teacher. It's become a sort of symbol for him, and if it were to all suddenly collapse . . . ! No. I don't want to think about it.

THAMI *(Flash of anger and impatience)*: Then don't! Please leave it alone now and just let's get on with whatever it is we've got to do.

ISABEL: Right, if that's the way you want it . . . *(From her notebook)* Charles Dickens, Thomas Hardy, Jane Austen . . . who else?

THAMI: I'm sorry. I know you're only trying to help but you've got to understand that it's not just a personal issue between him and me. That would be easy. I don't think I would care then. Just wait for the end of the year and then get out of that classroom and that school as fast as I can. But there is more to it than that. I've told you before: sitting in a classroom doesn't mean the same thing to me that it does to you. That classroom is a political reality in my life—it's a part of the whole political system we're up against and Mr. M has chosen to identify himself with it.

ISABEL (*Trying a new tack*): All right. I believe you. I accept everything you said . . . about him, your relationship, the situation . . . no arguments. Okay? But doesn't all of that only make it still more important that the two of you start talking to each other? I know *he* wants to, but he doesn't know how to start. It's *so* sad . . . because I can see him trying to reach out to you. Show him how it's done. Make the first move. Oh Thami, don't let it go wrong between the two of you. That's just about the worst thing I could imagine. We all need each other.

THAMI: I don't need him.

ISABEL: I think you do, just as much as he—

THAMI: Don't tell me what I need, Isabel! And stop telling me what to do! You don't know what my life is about, so keep your advice to yourself.

ISABEL: I'm sorry. I don't mean to interfere. I thought we were a team and that what involved you two concerned me as well. I'll mind my own business in future. (*She is deeply hurt. She collects her things*) Let's leave it at that then. See you next week . . . I hope!
(*Starts to leave, stops, returns and confronts him*) You used the word *friendship* a few minutes ago. It's a beautiful word and I'll do anything to make it true for us. But don't let's cheat Thami. If we can't be open and honest with each other and say what is in our hearts, we've got no right to use it. (*She leaves*)

Thami alone.

THAMI (*Singing*):

> *Masiye Masiye Skolweni*
>
> *Masiye Masiye Skolweni*
>
> *Eskolweni Sasakhaya*
>
> *Eskolweni Sasakhaya (Repeat)*

> *Gongo Gongo*
>
> *Iyakhala Intsimbi*
>
> *Gongo Gongo*
>
> *Iyakhala Intsimbi*

> (*Translating*)

> Come, come, let's go to school
>
> Let's go to our very own school

> *Gongo Gongo*
>
> The bell is ringing
>
> *Gongo Gongo*
>
> The bell is calling!

Singing that at the top of his voice and holding his slate under his arm, seven-year-old Thami Mbikwana marched proudly with the other children every morning into his classroom.

> *Gongo Gongo*
>
> The school bell is ringing!

And what a wonderful sound that was for me. Starting with the little farm school, I remember my school bells like beautiful voices calling to me all through my childhood . . . and I came running when they did. You should have seen me man. In junior school I was the first one at the gates every morning. I was waiting there when the caretaker came to unlock them. Oh yes! Young Thami was a very eager scholar. And what made it even better, he was also one of the clever ones. "A most particularly promising pupil" is how one of my school reports described me. My first real scholastic achievement was a composition I wrote about myself in

Standard Two. Not only did it get me top marks in the class, the teacher was so proud of me, she made me read it out to the whole school at assembly.

(His composition) "The story of my life so far. By Thami Mbikwana. The story of my life so far is not yet finished because I am only ten years old and I am going to live a long long time. I come from Kingwilliamstown. My father is Amos Mbikwana and he works very hard for the *baas* on the railway. I am also going to work very hard and get good marks in all my classes and make my teacher very happy. The story of my life so far has also got a very happy ending because when I am big I am going to be a doctor so that I can help my people. I will drive to the hospital every day in a big, white ambulance full of nurses. I will make black people better free of charge. The white people must pay me for my medicine because they have got lots of money. That way I will also get lots of money. My mother and my father will stop working and come and live with me in a big house. That is the story of my life up to where I am in Standard Two."

I must bring my story up to date because there have been some changes and developments since little Thami wrote those hopeful words eight years ago. To start with I don't think I want to be a doctor anymore. That praiseworthy ambition has unfortunately died in me. It still upsets me very much when I think about the pain and suffering of my people, but I realize now that what causes most of it is not an illness that can be cured by the pills and bottles of medicine they hand out at the clinic. I don't need to go to university to learn what my people really need is a strong double-dose of that traditional old Xhosa remedy called "*Inkululeko.*" Freedom. So right now I'm not sure what I want to be anymore. It's hard, you see, for us "bright young blacks" to dream about wonderful careers as doctors, or lawyers, when we keep waking up in a world which doesn't allow the majority of our people any dreams at all. But to get back to my composition, I did try my best to keep that promise I made in it. For a long time—Standard Three, Standard Four, Standard Five—I did work very hard and I did get good marks in all my subjects. This "most particularly promising pupil" made a lot of teachers very happy.

I'm sorry to say but I can't do it anymore. I have tried very hard, believe me, but it is not as simple and easy as it used to be to sit behind that desk and listen to the Teacher. That little world of the classroom where I used to be happy, where they used to pat me on the head and say: "Little Thami, you'll go far!"—that little room of wonderful promises, where I used to feel so safe, has become a place I don't trust anymore. Now I sit at my desk like an animal that has smelt danger, heard something moving in the bushes and knows it must be very, very careful.

At the beginning of this year the Inspector of Bantu Schools in the Cape Midlands Region, Mr. Dawid Grobbelaar—he makes us call him Oom Dawie—came to give us Standard Tens his usual pep talk. He does it every year. We know Oom Dawie well. He's been coming to Zolile for a long time. When he walked into our classroom we all jumped up as usual but he didn't want any of that. "Sit, sit. I'm not a bloody sergeant major." Oom Dawie believes he knows how to talk to us. He loosened his tie, took off his jacket and rolled up his sleeves. It was a very hot day.

"Dis better. *Nou kan ons lekker gesels.* Boys and girls or maybe I should say 'young men' and 'young women' now, because you are coming to the end of your time behind those desks . . . you are special! You are the elite! We have educated you because we want you to be major shareholders in the future of this wonderful Republic of ours. In fact, we want *all* the peoples of South Africa to share in that future . . . black, white, brown, yellow, and if there are some green ones out there, then them as well." Ho! Ho! Ho!

I don't remember much about what he said after that because my head was trying to deal with that one word: the Future! He kept using it . . . "our future," "the country's future," "a wonderful future of peace and prosperity." What does he really mean, I kept asking myself. Why does my heart go hard and tight as a stone when he says it? I look around me in the location at the men and women who went out into that "wonderful future" before me. What do I see? Happy and contented shareholders in this exciting enterprise called the Republic of South Africa? No. I see a generation of tired, defeated men and women crawling back to their miserable little *pondoks* at the end of a day's work for the white *baas* or madam. And those are the lucky ones. They've at least got work. Most of them are just sitting around wasting away their lives while they wait helplessly for a miracle to feed their families, a miracle that never comes.

Those men and women are our fathers and mothers. We have grown up watching their humiliation. We have to live every day with the sight of them begging for food in this land of their birth, and their parents' birth . . . all the way back to the first proud ancestors of our people. Black people lived on this land for centuries before any white settler had landed! Does Oom Dawie think we are blind? That when we walk through the streets of the white town we do not see the big houses and the beautiful gardens with their swimming pools full of laughing people, and compare it with what we've got, what we have to call home? Or does Oom Dawie just think we are very stupid? That in spite of the wonderful education he has given us, we can't use the simple arithmetic of add and subtract, multiply and divide to work out the rightful share of twenty-five million black people?

Do you understand me, good people? Do you understand now why it is not as easy as it used to be to sit behind that desk and learn only what Oom Dawie has decided I must know? My head is rebellious. It refuses now to remember when the Dutch landed, and the Huguenots landed, and the British landed. It has already forgotten when the Old Union became the proud young Republic. But it does know what happened in Kliptown in 1955, in Sharpeville on twenty-first March 1960 and in Soweto on the sixteenth of June 1976. Do you? Better find out because those are dates your children will have to learn one day. We don't need Zolile classrooms anymore. We know now what they really are—traps which have been carefully set to catch our minds, our souls. No, good people. We have woken up at last. We have found another school—the streets, the little rooms, the funeral parlors of the location—anywhere the people meet and whisper names we have been told to forget, the dates of events they try to tell us never happened, and the speeches they try to say were never made.

Those are the lessons we are eager and proud to learn, because they are lessons about *our* history, about *our* heroes. But the time for whispering them is past. Tomorrow we start shouting.

AMANDLA!

Act Two

Isabel and Thami. Isabel has books and papers. From behind a relaxed and easy manner, she watches Thami carefully.

ISABEL: What I've done is write out a sort of condensed biography of all of them . . . you know, the usual stuff . . . date of birth, where they were born, where they died, who they married . . . et cetera, et cetera. My dad made copies for you and Mr. M. Sit. *(Hands over a set of papers to Thami)* You okay?

THAMI: *Ja, ja.*

ISABEL: For example . . . *(Reading)* Bronte sisters . . . I lumped them all together . . . Charlotte 1816–1855; Emily 1818–1848; Anne 1820–1849. . . . Can you believe that? Not one of them reached the age of forty. Anne died when she was twenty-nine, Emily when she was thirty, and Charlotte reached the ripe old age of thirty-nine! Family home: Haworth, Yorkshire. First publication a joint volume of verse . . . *Poems by Currer, Ellis and Acton Bell*. All novels published under these nom de plumes. Charlotte the most prolific . . . *(Abandoning the notes)* Why am I doing this? You're not listening to me.

THAMI: Sorry.

ISABEL *(She waits for more, but that is all she gets)*: So? Should I carry on wasting my breath or do you want to say something?

THAMI: No, I must talk.

ISABEL: Good. I'm ready to listen.

THAMI: I don't know where to begin.

ISABEL: The deep end. Take my advice, go to the deep end and just jump right in. That's how I learnt to swim.

THAMI: No. I want to speak carefully because I don't want you to get the wrong ideas about what's happening and what I'm going to say. It's not like it's your fault, that it's because of anything you said or did . . . you know what I mean?

ISABEL: You don't want me to take personally whatever it is you are finding so hard to tell me.

THAMI: That's right. It's not about you and me personally. I've had a good time with you Isabel.

ISABEL: And I've had an important one with you.

THAMI: If it was just you and me, there wouldn't be a problem.

ISABEL: We've got a problem have we?

THAMI: I have.

ISABEL (*Losing patience*): Oh for God's sake Thami. Stop trying to spare my feelings and just say it. If you are trying to tell me that I've been wasting my breath for a lot longer than just this afternoon . . . just go ahead and say it! I'm not a child. I can take it. Because that is what you are trying to tell me isn't it? That it's all off.

THAMI: Yes.

ISABEL: The great literary quiz team is no more. You are pulling out of the competition.

THAMI: Yes.

ISABEL: You shouldn't have made it so hard for yourself Thami. It doesn't come as all that big a surprise. I've had a feeling that something was going to go wrong somewhere.

Been a strange time these past few weeks hasn't it? At home, at school, in the shop . . . everywhere! Things I've been seeing and doing my whole life, just don't feel right anymore. Like my Saturday chats with Samuel—I told you about him remember, he delivers for my dad—well you should have heard the last one. It was excruciating. It felt so false, and forced, and when I listened to what I was saying and how I was saying it . . . oh my God! Sounded as if I thought I was talking to a ten-year-old. Halfway through our misery my dad barged in and told me not to waste Samuel's time because he had work to do which of course led to a flaming row between me and my dad . . . Am I changing Thami? My dad says I am.

THAMI: In what way?

ISABEL: Forget it. The only thing I *do* know at this moment is that I don't very much like the way anything feels right now, starting with myself. So have you told Mr. M yet?

THAMI: No.

ISABEL: Good luck. I don't envy you that little conversation. If I'm finding the news a bit hard to digest, I don't know what he is going to do with it. I've just got to accept it. I doubt very much if he will.

THAMI: He's got no choice Isabel. I've decided and that's the end of it.

ISABEL: So do you think we can at least talk about it? Help me to understand? Because to be absolutely honest with you Thami I don't think I do. You're not the only one with a problem. What Mr. M had to say about the team and the whole idea made a hell of a lot of sense to me. You owe it to me Thami. A lot more than just my spare time is involved.

THAMI: Talk about what? Don't you know what is going on?

ISABEL: Don't be stupid Thami! Of course I do! You'd have to be pretty dumb not to know that the dreaded "unrest" has finally reached us as well.

THAMI: We don't call it that. Our word for it is *"Isiqalo"* . . . The Beginning.

ISABEL: All right then, "The Beginning." I don't care what it's called. All I'm asking you to do is explain to me how the two of us learning some poetry, cramming in potted bios . . . interferes with all of that.

THAMI: Please just calm down and listen to me! I know you're angry and I don't blame you. I would be as well. But you must understand that pulling out of this competition is just a small side issue. There was a meeting in the location last night. It was decided to call for a general stay-at-home. We start boycotting classes tomorrow as part of that campaign.

ISABEL: Does Mr. M know about all of this?

THAMI: I think he does now.

ISABEL: Wasn't he at that meeting?

THAMI: The meeting was organized by the Comrades. He wasn't welcome.

ISABEL: Because his ideas are old-fashioned.

THAMI: Yes.

ISABEL: School boycott! Comrades! So our safe, contented little Camdeboo is really going to find out what it's all about. How long do you think it will last?

THAMI: I don't know. It's hard to say.

ISABEL: A week.

THAMI: No. It will be longer.

ISABEL: A month? Two months?

THAMI: We'll go back to school when the authorities scrap Bantu Education and recognize and negotiate with Student Committees. That was the resolution last night.

ISABEL: But when the boycott and . . . you know . . . everything is all over could we carry on then, if there was still time?

THAMI: I haven't thought about that.

ISABEL: So think about it. Please.

THAMI (*Nervous about a commitment*): It's hard to say Isabel . . . but *ja* . . . maybe we could . . . I'm not sure.

ISABEL: Not much enthusiasm there, Mr. Mbikwana! You're right. Why worry about a stupid competition. It will most probably be too late anyway. So that's it then. Let's just say we gave ourselves a crash course in English literature.

    Could have done a lot worse with our spare time, couldn't we? I enjoyed myself. I read a lot of beautiful poetry I might never have got around to. (*Uncertain of herself*) It doesn't mean the end of everything though does it? I mean, we can go on meeting, just as friends?

THAMI (*Warily*): When?

ISABEL: Oh . . . I mean, you know, like anytime. Next week! (*Pause*) I'm not talking about the competition Thami. I accept that it's dead. I think it's a pity . . . but so what. I'm talking now about you and me just as friends.

    (*She waits. She realizes. She collects herself*) So our friendship *is* an old-fashioned idea after all. Well don't waste your time here. You better get going and look after . . . whatever it is that's beginning. And good luck!

Thami starts to go.

No! Thami come back here!! (*Struggling ineffectually to control her anger and pain*) There is something very stupid somewhere and it's most probably me but I can't help it . . . *it just doesn't make sense!* I know it does to you and I'm sure it's just my white selfishness and ignorance that is stopping me from understanding *but it still doesn't make sense*. Why can't we go on seeing each other and meeting as friends? Tell me what is wrong with our friendship?

THAMI: You're putting words in my mouth Isabel. I didn't say there was anything wrong with it. But others won't see it the way we do.

ISABEL: Who? Your Comrades?

THAMI: Yes.

ISABEL: And they are going to decide whether we can or can't be friends!

THAMI: I was right. You don't understand what's going on.

ISABEL: And you're certainly not helping me to.

THAMI (*Trying*): Visiting you like this is dangerous. People talk. U'sispumla . . . your maid . . . has seen me. She could mention, just innocently but to the wrong person, that Thami Mbikwana is visiting and having tea with the white people she works for.

ISABEL: And of course that is such a big crime!

THAMI: In the eyes of the location . . . yes! My world is also changing Isabel. I'm breaking the boycott by being here. The Comrades don't want any mixing with whites. They have ordered that contact must be kept at a minimum.

ISABEL: And you go along with that.

THAMI: Yes.

ISABEL: Happily!

THAMI (*Goaded by her lack of understanding*): Yes! I go along happily with that!!

ISABEL: Hell, Thami, this great Beginning of yours sounds like . . . (*Shakes her head*) I don't know. Other people deciding who can and who can't be your friends, what you must do and what you can't do. Is this the Freedom you've been talking to me about? That you were going to fight for?

Mr. M enters quietly. His stillness is in disturbing contrast to the bustle and energy we have come to associate with him.

MR. M: Don't let me interrupt you. Please carry on. *(To Thami)* I'm most interested in your reply to that question. *(Pause)* I think he's forgotten what it was Isabel. Ask him again.

ISABEL *(Backing out of the confrontation)*: No. Forget it.

MR. M *(Persisting)*: Isabel was asking you how you managed to reconcile your desire for Freedom with what the Comrades are doing.

ISABEL: I said forget it Mr. M. I'm not interested anymore.

MR. M *(Insistent)*: But I am.

THAMI: The Comrades are imposing a discipline which our struggle needs at this point. There is no comparison between that and the total denial of our Freedom by the white government. They have been forcing on us an inferior education in order to keep us permanently suppressed. When our struggle is successful there will be no more need for the discipline the Comrades are demanding.

MR. M *(Grudging admiration)*: Oh Thami . . . you learn your lessons so well! The "revolution" has only just begun and you are already word perfect. So then tell me, do you think I agree with this inferior "Bantu Education" that is being forced on you?

THAMI: You teach it.

MR. M: But unhappily so! Most unhappily, unhappily so! Don't you know that? Did you have your fingers in your ears the thousand times I've said so in the classroom? Where were you when I stood there and said I regarded it as my duty, my deepest obligation to you young men and women to sabotage it, and that my conscience would not let me rest until I had succeeded. And I have! Yes, I have succeeded! I have got irrefutable proof of my success. You! Yes. You can stand here and accuse me, unjustly, because I have also had a struggle and I have won mine. I have liberated your mind in spite of what the Bantu Education was trying to do to it. Your mouthful of big words and long sentences which the not-so-clever Comrades are asking you to speak and write for them, your wonderful eloquence at last night's meeting which got them all so excited—yes, I heard about it!—you must thank me for all of that, Thami.

THAMI: No I don't. You never taught me those lessons.

MR. M: Oh I see. You have got other teachers have you?

THAMI: Yes. Yours were lessons in whispering. There are men now who are teaching us to shout. Those little tricks and jokes of yours in the classroom liberated nothing. The struggle doesn't need the big English words you taught me how to spell.

MR. M: Be careful, Thami. Be careful! Be careful! Don't scorn words. They are sacred! Magical! Yes, they are. Do you know that without words a man can't think? Yes, it's true. Take that thought back with you as a present from the despised Mr. M and share it with the Comrades. Tell them the difference between a man and an animal is that Man thinks, and he thinks with words. Consider the mighty ox. Four powerful legs, massive shoulders, and a beautiful thick hide that gave our warriors shields to protect them when they went into battle. Think of his beautiful head, Thami, the long horns, the terrible bellow from his lungs when he charges a rival! *But it has got no words and therefore it is stupid!* And along comes that funny little hairless animal that has got only two thin legs, no horns and a skin worth nothing and he tells that ox what to do. He is its master and he is that because he can speak! If the struggle needs weapons give it words Thami. Stones and petrol bombs can't get inside those armored cars. Words can. They can do something even more devastating than that . . . they can get inside the heads of those inside the armored cars. I speak to you like this because if I have faith in anything, it is faith in the power of the word. Like my master, the great Confucius, I believe that, using only words, a man can right a wrong and judge and execute the wrongdoer. You are meant to use words like that.

Talk to others. Bring them back into the classroom. They will listen to you. They look up to you as a leader.

THAMI: No I won't. You talk about them as if they were a lot of sheep waiting to be led. They know what they are doing. They'd call me a traitor if I tried to persuade them otherwise.

MR. M: Then listen carefully Thami. I have received instructions from the department to make a list of all those who take part in the boycott. Do you know what they will do with that list when all this is over . . . because don't fool yourself Thami, it will be. When your boycott comes to an inglorious end like all the others . . . they will make all of you apply for readmission and if your name is on that list . . . (*He leaves the rest unspoken*)

THAMI: Will you do it? Will you make that list for them?

MR. M: That is none of your business.

THAMI: Then don't ask me questions about mine.

MR. M (*His control finally snaps. He explodes with anger and bitterness*): Yes, I will! I will ask you all the questions I like. And you know why? Because I am a man and you are a boy. And if you are not in that classroom tomorrow you will be a very, very silly boy.

THAMI: Then don't call me names, Mr. M.

MR. M: No? Then what must I call you? Comrade Thami? Never! You are a silly boy now, and without an education you will grow up to be a stupid man!

For a moment it looks as if Thami is going to leave without saying anything more, but he changes his mind and confronts Mr. M for the last time.

THAMI: The others called *you* names at the meeting last night. Did your spies tell you that? Government stooge, sellout, collaborator. They said you licked the white man's arse and would even eat his shit if it meant keeping your job. Did your spies tell you that I tried to stop them saying those things? Don't wait until tomorrow to make your list Mr. M. You can start now. Write down the first name: Thami Mbikwana.

He leaves. A few seconds of silence after Thami's departure. Isabel makes a move towards Mr. M, but he raises his hand sharply, stopping her, keeping her at a distance.

ISABEL: This fucking country! (*She leaves*)

Mr. M alone. His mood at the beginning of the scene is one of quiet, vacant disbelief.

MR. M: It was like being in a nightmare. I was trying to get to the school, I knew that if I didn't hurry I was going to be late so I *had to get to the school* . . . but every road I took was blocked by policemen and soldiers with their guns ready, or Comrades building barricades. First I tried Jabulani Street, then I turned into Kwaza Road and then Lamini Street . . . and then I gave up and just wandered around aimlessly, helplessly, watching my world go mad and set itself on fire. Everywhere I went . . . overturned buses, looted bread vans, the government offices . . . everything burning and the children dancing around rattling boxes of matches and shouting *"Tshisa! Qhumisa! Tshisa! Qhumisa! Qhumisa!"* . . . and then running for their lives when the police armored cars appeared. They were everywhere, crawling around in the smoke like giant dung beetles looking for shit to eat.

I ended up on the corner where Mrs. Makatini always sits selling *vetkoek* and prickly pears to people waiting for the bus. The only person there was little Sipho Fondini from Standard Six, writing on the wall: "Liberation First, then Education." He saw me and he called out: "Is the spelling right Mr. M?" And he meant it! The young eyes in that smoke-stained little face were terribly serious.

Somewhere else a police van raced past me crowded with children who should have also been in their desks in school. Their hands waved desperately through the bars, their voices called out: "Teacher! Teacher! Help us! Tell our mothers. Tell our fathers." "No, Anela," I said. "This is too much now. Just stand here and close your eyes and wait until you wake up and find your world the way it was." But that didn't happen. A police car came around the corner and suddenly there were children everywhere throwing stones and tear-gas bombs falling all around and I knew that I wasn't dreaming, that I was coughing and choking and hanging on to a lamppost in the real world. No! No!

Do something Anela. Do something. Stop the madness! Stop the madness.

SCENE 3

Mr. M alone in Number One Classroom. He is ringing his school bell wildly.

MR. M: Come to school! Come to school. Before they kill you all, come to school!

Silence. Mr. M looks around the empty classroom. He goes to his table, and after composing himself, opens the class register and reads out the names as he does every morning at the start of a new school day.

> Johnny Awu, living or dead? Christopher Bandla, living or dead? Zandile Cwati, living or dead? Semphiwe Dambuza . . . Ronald Gxasheka . . . Noloyiso Mfundweni . . . Steven Gaika . . . Zachariah Jabavu . . . Thami . . . Thami Mbikwana . . .
> (*Pause*) Living or dead?
> How many young souls do I have present this morning? There are a lot of well-aimed stray bullets flying around on the streets out there. Is that why this silence is so . . . heavy?
> But what can I teach you? (*Picks up his little black dictionary on the table*) My lessons were meant to help you in *this* world. I wanted you to know how to read and write and talk in *this* world of living, stupid, cruel men.
> (*Helpless gesture*) Now? Oh my children! I have no lessons that will be of any use to you now. Mr. M and all of his wonderful words are . . . useless, useless, useless!

The sound of breaking glass. Stones land in the classroom. Mr. M picks up one.

> No! One of you is still alive. Ghosts don't throw stones with hot, sweating young hands. (*Grabs the bell and rings it wildly again*) Come to school! Come to school!

Thami appears.

THAMI (*Quietly*): Stop ringing that bell, Mr. M.

MR. M: Why? It's only the school bell, Thami. I thought you liked the sound of it. You once told me it was almost as good as music . . . don't you remember?

THAMI: You are provoking the Comrades with it.

MR. M: No Thami. I am summoning the Comrades with it.

THAMI: They say you are ringing the bell to taunt them. You are openly defying the boycott by being here in the school.

MR. M: I ring this bell because according to my watch it is schooltime and I am a teacher and those desks are empty! I will go on ringing it as I have been doing these past two weeks, at the end of every lesson. And you can tell the Comrades that I will be back here ringing it tomorrow and the day after tomorrow and for as many days after that as it takes for this world to come to its senses.

Is that the only reason you've come? To tell me to stop ringing the school bell?

THAMI: No.

MR. M: You haven't come for a lesson have you?

THAMI: No I haven't.

MR. M: Of course not. What's the matter with me. Slogans don't need much in the way of grammar do they. As for these . . . (*The stone in his hand*) No, you don't need me for lessons in stone-throwing either. You've already got teachers in those very revolutionary subjects haven't you.

(*Picks up his dictionary. The stone in one hand, the book in the other*) You know something interesting, Thami . . . if you put these two on a scale I think you would find that they weighed just about the same. But in this hand I am holding the whole English language. This . . . (*The stone*) is just *one* word in that language. It's true! All that wonderful poetry that you and Isabel tried to cram into your beautiful heads . . . in here! Twenty-six letters, sixty thousand words. The greatest souls the world has ever known were able to open the floodgates of their ecstasy, their despair, their joy! . . . with the words in this little book! Aren't you tempted? I was.

(*Opens the book at the flyleaf and reads*) "Anela Myalatya. Cookhouse. 1947." One of the first books I ever bought. (*Impulsively*) I want you to have it.

THAMI (*Ignoring the offered book*): I've come here to warn you.

MR. M: You've already done that and I've already told you that you are wasting your breath. Now take your stones and go. There are a lot of unbroken windows left.

THAMI: I'm not talking about the bell now. It's more serious than that.

MR. M: In my life nothing is more serious than ringing the school bell.

THAMI: There was a meeting last night. Somebody stood up and denounced you as an informer.

Pause. Thami waits. Mr. M says nothing.

He said you gave names to the police.

Mr. M says nothing.

Everybody is talking about it this morning. You are in big danger.

MR. M: Why are you telling me all this?

THAMI: So that you can save yourself. There's a plan to march to the school and burn it down. If they find you here . . .

Pause.

MR. M: Go on. (*Violently*) If they find me here *what?*

THAMI: They will kill you.

MR. M: "They will kill me." That's better. Remember what I taught you . . . if you've got a problem, put it into words so that you can look at it, handle it, and ultimately solve it. They will kill me! You are right. That is very serious. So then . . . what must I do? Must I run away and hide somewhere?

THAMI: No, they will find you. You must join the boycott.

MR. M: I'm listening.

THAMI: Let me go back and tell them that we have had a long talk and that you have realized you were wrong and have decided to join us. Let me say that you will sign the declaration and that you won't have anything to do with the school until all demands have been met.

MR. M: And they will agree to that? Accept me as one of them even though it is believed that I am an informer?

THAMI: I will tell them you are innocent. That I confronted you with the charge and that you denied it and that I believe you.

MR. M: I see. (*Studying Thami intently*) You don't believe that I am an informer.

THAMI: No.

MR. M: Won't you be taking a chance in defending me like that? Mightn't they end up suspecting you?

THAMI: They'll believe me. I'll make them believe me.

MR. M: You can't be sure. Mobs don't listen to reason Thami. Hasn't your revolution already taught you that? Why take a chance like that to save a collaborator? Why do you want to do all this for me?

THAMI (*Avoiding Mr. M's eyes*): I'm not doing it for you. I'm doing it for the Struggle. Our Cause will suffer if we falsely accuse and hurt innocent people.

MR. M: I see. My "execution" would be an embarrassment to the Cause. I apologize Thami. For a moment I allowed myself to think that you were doing it because we were . . . who we are . . . the "all-knowing Mr. M and his brilliant protégé Thami"! I was so proud of us when Isabel called us that.

Well young Comrade, you have got nothing to worry about. Let them come and do whatever it is they want to. Your Cause won't be embarrassed, because you see, they won't be "hurting" an innocent man.

(*He makes his confession simply and truthfully*) That's right Thami. I am guilty. I did go to the police. I sat down in Captain Lategan's office and told him I felt it was my duty to report the presence in our community of strangers from the north. I told him that I had reason to believe that they were behind the present unrest. I gave the Captain names and addresses. He thanked me and offered me money for the information—which I refused.

(*Pause*) Why do you look at me like that? Isn't that what you expected from me? . . . a government stooge, a sellout, an arse-licker? Isn't that what you were all secretly hoping I would do . . . so that you could be proved right? (*Appalled*) Is that why I did it? Out of spite? Can a man destroy himself, his life for a reason as petty as that?

I sat here before going to the police station saying to myself that it was my duty, to my conscience, to you, to the whole community to do whatever I could to put an end to this madness of boycotts and arson, mob violence and lawlessness . . . and maybe that is true . . . but only maybe . . . because Thami, the truth is that I was so lonely! You had deserted me. I was so jealous of those who had taken you away. *Now*, I've *really* lost you, haven't I? Yes. I can see it in your eyes. You'll never forgive me for doing that, will you?

You know Thami, I'd sell my soul to have you all back behind your desks for one last lesson. Yes. If the devil thought it was worth having and offered me that in exchange—one lesson!—he could have my soul. So then it's all over! Because this . . . (*The classroom*) is all there was for me. This was my home, my life, my one and only ambition . . . to be a good teacher! (*His dictionary*) Anela Myalatya, twenty years old, from Cookhouse, wanted to be that the way your friends wanted to be big soccer stars playing for Kaizer Chiefs! That ambition goes back to when he was just a skinny little ten-year-old pissing on a small gray bush at the top of the Wapadsberg Pass.

We were on our way to a rugby match at Somerset East. The lorry stopped at the top of the mountain so that we could stretch our legs and relieve ourselves. It was a hard ride on the back of that lorry. The road hadn't been tarred yet. So there I was, ten years old and sighing with relief as I aimed for the little bush. It was a hot day. The sun right over our heads . . . not a cloud in the vast blue sky. I looked out . . . it's very high up there at the top of the pass . . . and there it was, stretching away from the foot of the mountain, the great pan of the Karoo . . . stretching away forever it seemed into the purple haze and heat of the horizon. Something grabbed my heart at that moment, my soul, and squeezed it until there were tears in my eyes. I had never seen anything so big, so beautiful in all my life. I went to the teacher who was with us and asked him: "Teacher, where will I come to if I start walking that way?" . . . and I pointed. He laughed. "Little man," he said, "that way is north. If you start walking that way and just keep on walking, and your legs don't give in, you will see all of Africa! Yes, Africa little man! You will see the great rivers of the continent: the Vaal, the Zambesi, the Limpopo, the Congo and then the mighty Nile. You will see the mountains: the Drakensberg, Kilimanjaro, Kenya and the Ruwenzori. And you will meet all our brothers: the little Pygmies of the forests, the proud Masai, the Watusi . . . tallest of the tall and the Kikuyu standing on one leg like herons in a pond waiting for a frog." "Has teacher seen all that?" I asked. "No," he said. "Then how does teacher know it's there?" "Because it is all in the books and I have read the books and if you work hard in school little man, you can do the same without worrying about your legs giving in."

He was right Thami. *I* have seen it. It is all there in the books just as he said it was and I have made it mine. I can stand on the banks of all those great rivers, look up at the majesty of all those mountains, whenever I want to. It is a journey I have made many times. Whenever my spirit was low and I sat alone in my room, I said to myself: Walk Anela! Walk! . . . and I imagined myself at the foot of the Wapadsberg setting off for that horizon that called me that day forty years ago. It always worked! When I left that little room, I walked back into the world a proud man, because I was an African and all the splendor was my birthright.

(*Pause*) I don't want to make that journey again Thami. There is someone waiting for me now at the end of it who has made a mockery of all my visions of splendor. He has in his arms my real birthright. I saw him on the television in the Reverend Mbopa's lounge. An Ethiopian tribesman, and he was carrying the body of a little child that had died of hunger in the famine . . . a small bundle carelessly wrapped in a few rags. I couldn't tell how old the man was. The lines of despair and starvation on his face made him look as old as Africa itself.

He held that little bundle very lightly as he shuffled along to a mass grave, and when he reached it, he didn't have the strength to kneel and lay it down gently . . . He just opened his arms and let it fall. I was very upset when the program ended. Nobody had thought to tell us his name and whether he was the child's father, or grandfather, or uncle. And the same for the baby! Didn't it have a name? How dare you show me one of our children being thrown away and not tell me its name! I demand to know who is in that bundle!

(*Pause*) Not knowing their names doesn't matter anymore. They are more than just themselves. The tribesmen and dead child do duty for all of us Thami. Every African soul is either carrying that bundle or in it.

What is wrong with this world that it wants to waste you all like that . . . my children . . . my Africa!

(*Holding out a hand as if he wanted to touch Thami's face*) My beautiful and proud young Africa!

More breaking glass and stones and the sound of a crowd outside the school. Mr. M starts to move. Thami stops him.

THAMI: No! Don't go out there. Let me speak to them first. Listen to me! I will tell them I have confronted you with the charges and that you have denied them and that I believe you. I will tell them you are innocent.

MR. M: You will lie for me, Thami?

THAMI: Yes.

MR. M (*Desperate to hear the truth*): Why?

Thami can't speak.

Why will you lie for me Thami?

THAMI: I've told you before.

MR. M: The "Cause"?

THAMI: Yes.

MR. M: Then I do not need to hide behind your lies.

THAMI: They will kill you.

MR. M: Do you think I'm frightened of them? Do you think I'm frightened of dying?

Mr. M breaks away from Thami. Ringing his bell furiously he goes outside and confronts the mob. They kill him.

SCENE 4

Thami waiting. Isabel arrives.

THAMI: Isabel.

ISABEL (*It takes her a few seconds to respond*): Hello Thami.

THAMI: Thank you for coming.

ISABEL (*She is tense. Talking to him is not easy*): I wasn't going to. Let me tell you straight out that there is nothing in this world . . . nothing! . . . that I want to see less at this moment than anything or anybody from the location. But you said in your note that it was urgent, so here I am. If you've got something to say, I'll listen.

THAMI: Are you in a hurry?

ISABEL: I haven't got to be somewhere else, if that's what you mean. But if you're asking because it looks as if I would like to run away from here, from you!—very fast—then the answer is yes. But don't worry I'll be able to control that urge for as long as you need to say what you want to.

THAMI (*Awkward in the face of Isabel's severe and unyielding attitude*): I just wanted to say good-bye.

ISABEL: Again?

THAMI: What do you mean?

ISABEL: You've already done that Thami. Maybe you didn't use that word, but you turned your back on me and walked out of my life that last afternoon the three of us . . . (*She can't finish*) How long ago was that?

THAMI: Three weeks I think.

ISABEL: So why do you want to do it again? Aren't you happy with the last time? It was so dramatic Thami!

THAMI (*Patiently*): I wanted to see you because I'm leaving the town, I'm going away for good.

ISABEL: Oh I see. This is meant to be a "sad" good-bye is it? (*She is on the edge*) I'm sorry if I'm hurting your feelings but I thought you wanted to see me because you had something to say about recent events in our little community . . . (*She takes a crumpled little piece of newspaper out of her pocket and opens it with unsteady hands*) a certain unrest-related . . . I think that is the phrase they use . . . yes . . . here it is . . . (*Reading*) ". . . unrest-related incident in which according to witnesses the defenseless teacher was attacked by a group of blacks who struck him over the head with an iron rod before setting him on fire."

THAMI: Stop it Isabel.

ISABEL (*Fighting hard for self-control*): Oh Thami, I wish I could! I've tried everything, but nothing helps. It just keeps going around and around inside my head. I've tried crying. I've tried praying! I've even tried confrontation. *Ja*, the day after it happened I tried to get into the location. I wanted to find the witnesses who reported it so accurately and ask them: "Why didn't you stop it!" There was a police roadblock at the entrance and they wouldn't let me in. They thought I was crazy or something and "escorted" me back into the safekeeping of two now very frightened parents.

There is nothing wrong with me! All I need is someone to tell me why he was killed. What madness drove those people to kill a man who had devoted his whole life to helping them. He was such a good man Thami! He was one of the most beautiful human beings I have ever known and his death is one of the ugliest things I have ever known.

Thami gives her a few seconds to calm down.

THAMI (*Gently*):   He was an informer Isabel. Somehow or the other somebody discovered that Mr. M was an informer.

ISABEL: You mean that list of pupils taking part in the boycott? You call that informing?

THAMI: No. It was worse than that. He went to the police and gave them the names and addresses of our political action committee. All of them were arrested after his visit. They are now in detention.

ISABEL: Mr. M did that?

THAMI: Yes.

ISABEL: I don't believe it.

THAMI: It's true Isabel.

ISABEL: No! What proof do you have?

THAMI: His own words. He told me so himself. I didn't believe it either when he was first accused, but the last time I saw him, he said it was true, that he had been to the police.

ISABEL (*Stunned disbelief*):   Mr. M? A police spy? For how long?

THAMI: No. It wasn't like that. He wasn't paid or anything. He went to the police just that one time. He said he felt it was his duty.

ISABEL: And what do you mean?

THAMI: Operation Qhumisa . . . the boycotts and strikes, the arson . . . you know he didn't agree with any of that. But he was also very confused about it all. I think he wished he had never done it.

ISABEL: So he went to the police just once.

THAMI: Yes.

ISABEL: As a matter of conscience.

THAMI: Yes.

ISABEL: That doesn't make him an "informer" Thami!

THAMI: Then what do you call somebody who gives information to the police?

ISABEL: No! You know what that word really means, the sort of person it suggests. Was Mr. M one of those? He was acting out of concern for his people . . . you said so yourself. He thought he was doing the right thing! You don't murder a man for that!

THAMI (*Near the end of his patience*): Be careful Isabel.

ISABEL: Of what?

THAMI: The words you use.

ISABEL: Oh? Which one don't you like? Murder? What do you want me to call it . . . "an unrest-related incident"? If you are going to call him an informer, then I am going to call his death murder!

THAMI: It was an act of self-defense.

ISABEL: By whom?

THAMI: The People.

ISABEL (*Almost speechless with outrage*): What? A mad mob attacks one unarmed defenseless man and you want me to call it—

THAMI (*Abandoning all attempts at patience. He speaks with the full authority of the anger inside him*): Stop Isabel! You just keep quiet now and listen to me. You're always saying you want to understand us and what it means to be black . . . well if you do, listen to me carefully now. I don't call it murder, and I don't call the people who did it a mad mob and yes, I do expect you to see it as an act of self-defense—listen to me!—blind and stupid but still self-defense.

He betrayed us and our fight for freedom. Five men are in detention because of Mr. M's visit to the police station. There have been other arrests and there will be more. Why do you think I'm running away?

How were those people to know he wasn't a paid informer who had been doing it for a long time and would do it again? They were defending themselves against what they thought was a terrible danger to themselves. What Anela Myalatya did to them and their cause is what your laws define as treason when it is done to you and threatens the safety and security of your comfortable white world. Anybody accused of it is put on trial in your courts and if found guilty they get hanged. Many of my people have been found guilty and have been hanged. Those hangings *we* call murder!

Try to understand, Isabel. Try to imagine what it is like to be a black person, choking inside with rage and frustration, bitterness, and then to discover that one of your own kind is a traitor, has betrayed you to those responsible for the suffering and misery of your family, of your people. What would you do? Remember there is no magistrate or court you can drag him to and demand that he be tried for that crime. There is no justice for black people in this country other than what we make for ourselves. When you judge us for what happened in front of the school four days ago just remember that you carry a share of the responsibility for it. It is your laws that have made simple, decent black people so desperate that they turn into "mad mobs."

Isabel has been listening and watching intently. It looks as if she is going to say something but she stops herself.

Say it, Isabel.

ISABEL: No.

THAMI: This is your last chance. You once challenged me to be honest with you. I'm challenging you now.

ISABEL *(She faces him)*: Where were you when it happened Thami? *(Pause)* And if you were, did you try to stop them?

THAMI: Isn't there a third question Isabel? Was I one of the mob that killed him?

ISABEL: Yes. Forgive me, Thami—please forgive me!—but there is that question as well. Only once! Believe me, only once—late at night when I couldn't sleep. I couldn't believe it was there in my head, but I heard the words: "Was Thami one of the ones who did it?"

THAMI: If the police catch me, that's the question they will ask.

ISABEL: I'm asking you because . . . *(An open, helpless gesture)* I'm lost! I don't know what to think or feel anymore. Help me. Please. You're the only one who can. Nobody else seems to understand that I loved him.

This final confrontation is steady and unflinching on both sides.

THAMI: Yes, I was there. Yes, I did try to stop it. *(He gives Isabel the time to deal with this answer)* I knew how angry the people were. I went to warn him. If he had listened to me he would still be alive, but he wouldn't. It was almost as if he wanted it to happen. I think he hated himself very much for what he had done Isabel. He kept saying to me that it was all over. He was right. There was nothing left for him. That visit to the police station had finished everything. Nobody would have ever spoken to him again or let him teach their children.

ISABEL: Oh Thami, it is all so wrong! So stupid! That's what I can't take . . . the terrible stupidity of it. We needed him. All of us.

THAMI: I know.

ISABEL: Then why is he dead?

THAMI: You must stop asking these questions Isabel. You know the answers.

ISABEL: They don't make any sense Thami.

THAMI: I know what you are feeling. (*Pause*) I also loved him. Doesn't help much to say it now I know, but I did. Because he made me angry and impatient with his "old-fashioned" ideas, I didn't want to admit it. Even if I had, it wouldn't have stopped me from doing what I did, the boycott and everything, but I should have tried harder to make him understand why I was doing it. You were right to ask about that. Now . . . ? (*A helpless gesture*) You know the most terrible words in your language, Isabel? Too late.

ISABEL: *Ja.*

THAMI: I'll never forgive myself for not trying harder with him and letting him know . . . my true feelings for him. Right until the end I tried to deny it . . . to him, to myself.

ISABEL: I'm sorry. I . . .

THAMI: That's all right.

ISABEL: Are the police really looking for you?

THAMI: Yes. Some of my friends have already been detained. They're pulling in anybody they can get their hands on.

ISABEL: Where are you going? Cape Town?

THAMI: No. That's the first place they'll look. I've written to my parents telling them about everything. I'm heading north.

ISABEL: To where?

THAMI: Far Isabel. I'm leaving the country.

ISABEL: Does that mean what I think it does?

THAMI (*He nods*): I'm going to join the movement. I want to be a fighter. I've been thinking about it for a long time. Now I know it's the right thing to do. I don't want to end up being one of the mob that killed Mr. M—but that will happen to me if I stay here.

ISABEL: Oh, Thami.

THAMI: I know I'm doing the right thing. Believe me.

ISABEL: I'll try.

THAMI: And you?

ISABEL: I don't know what to do with myself Thami. All I know is that I'm frightened of losing him. He's only been dead four days and I think I'm already starting to forget what he looked like. But the worst thing is that there's nowhere for me to go and . . . you know . . . just be near him. That's so awful. I got my father to phone the police but they said there wasn't enough left of him to justify a grave. What there was has been disposed of in a "Christian manner." So where do I go? The burnt-out ruins of the school? I couldn't face that.

THAMI: Get your father or somebody to drive you to the top of the Wapadsberg Pass. It's on the road to Craddock.

ISABEL: I know it.

THAMI: It was a very special place to him. He told me that it was there where it all started, where he knew what he wanted to do with his life . . . being a teacher, being the Mr. M we knew. You'll be near him up there. I must go now.

ISABEL: Do you need any money?

THAMI: No. *Sala Kakuhle* Isabel. That's the Xhosa good-bye.

ISABEL: I know it. U'sispumla taught me how to say it. *Hamba Kakuhle* Thami.

Thami leaves.

SCENE 5

Isabel alone. She stands quietly, examining the silence. After a few seconds she nods her head slowly.

ISABEL: Yes! Thami was right Mr. M. He said I'd feel near you up here.

He's out there somewhere Mr. M . . . traveling north. He didn't say where exactly he was going, but I think we can guess, can't we.

I'm here for a very "old-fashioned" reason, so I know you'll approve. I've come to pay my last respects to Anela Myalatya. I know the old-fashioned way of doing that is to bring flowers, lay them on the grave, say a quiet prayer and then go back to your life. But that seemed sort of silly this time. You'll have enough flowers around here when the spring comes . . . which it will. So instead I've brought you something which I know will mean more to you than flowers or prayers ever could. A promise. I am going to make Anela Myalatya a promise.

You gave me a little lecture once about wasted lives . . . how much of it you'd seen, how much you hated it, how much you didn't want that to happen to Thami and me. I sort of understood what you meant at the time. Now, I most certainly do. Your death has seen to that.

My promise to you is that I am going to try as hard as I can, in every way that I can, to see that it doesn't happen to me. I am going to try my best to make my life useful in the way yours was. I want you to be proud of me. After all, I am one of your children you know. You did welcome me to your family.

(A pause) The future is still ours, Mr. M.

The actor leaves the stage.

END OF PLAY